MURDERS IN MANATAS

The Saga of Halvar the Hireling
Book 1

ROBERTA ROGOW

ZUMAYA OTHERWORLDS   AUSTIN TX

2013

MURDERS IN MANATAS

© 2013 by Roberta Rogow

ISBN 978-1-61271-217-8

Cover art and design © William Neagle

"Zumaya Otherworlds" and the griffon colophon are trademarks of Zumaya Publications LLC, Austin TX.

Look for us online at http://www.zumayapublications.com

Library of Congress Cataloging-in-Publication Data

Rogow, Roberta, 1942-
 Murders in Manatas : Book 1 of the Halvar Saga / Roberta Rogow.
     pages cm. — (The Halvar the Hireling Saga ; Book 1)
   ISBN 978-1-61271-217-8 (print/trade pbk. : alk. paper) — ISBN 978-1-61271-218-5 — ISBN 978-1-61271-219-2
 1. Alternative histories (Fiction) I. Title.
 PS3568.O492M87 2013
 813'.54—dc23
                              2013017048

TO MY FATHER

Stanley Winston, 1918-2012, my
severest critic, and biggest fan.

Acknowledgments

Halvar has had a long and tortuous road to publication. Among those who contributed, knowing or unknowing, to this point:

- Rachel Kadushin and Lynn Holdom, who were there at Halvar's birth many years ago when I worked out the background for this version of history.

- Harry Turtledove and Eric Flint, whose alternate history novels inspired me to write this one.

- Most of all, Elizabeth Burton, who took a chance on this very weird universe and made me rewrite it until it was worth publishing.

PART ONE

MURDER IN MANATAS

Chapter 1

HALVAR DIDN'T MEAN TO STEP ON THE CORPSE.

He was still unsteady on his feet after the six-week journey across the Stormy Ocean. Dhows might be able to weather the tropical monsoons of the Indian Ocean, but they were not made for the battering of the waves on the expanse of water between Al-Andalus and Nova Mundum.

Like his forebears who went a-Viking, Halvar was not one to give his dinner to the fishes, unlike the frater who'd shared his tiny cabin and spent the entire voyage calling on the Redeemer to end either the voyage or his life. Still, his feet were used to shifting decks; and now he was on solid ground, he tended to overbalance and stumble at odd moments.

He had landed on the island called Manatas some thirty hours before, and had been swept up in ceremonies befitting the Hireling of the Calif Don Felipe, ruler of Al-Andalus. He'd taken part in a welcome from Sultan Petrus and a parade through the tiny settlement of Manatas Town. There followed a feast that introduced him to the local delicacies of maiz and gobble-birds, with a spicy sauce made from red tomatl, all washed down with sweet cider.

He had met the Sachems of the Mahak and Algonkin tribes. He had been warily polite to the trading-masters from Bretain and Franchenland, who were just as wary of him. He had exchanged salaams with the Afrikans who had come from their

1

vast farms in the southern territories of Nova Mundum to sell kutton, rice and indigo to the Franchen and Bretains. After all, this was why everyone was on this island in the middle of the Great River—to trade at the Fall Feria, the great gathering of merchants overseen by Al-Andalus as the one nation that claimed neutrality in the incessant wars between the followers of the Redeemer and the Prophet.

After the feasting, Halvar had retired to the room assigned him in the Rabat, the stone pile that dominated the "toe" of the island shaped as it was like a man's leg cut off at the knees. He'd tried to settle his brain and his stomach, both of which had absorbed a great deal of strange stuff in a short amount of time.

He was tall, by the standards of Al-Andalus, with fair hair thinner than it had once been that started higher on his forehead than when he had first joined the Free Companies of Dane-March as a lad of seventeen, His face was weathered from ten years of fighting across the fields of Oropa, and browned from the last five years in Al-Andalus, with the jutting nose and gray-blue eyes common in the Dane-March. A fair mustache swept from his upper lip down to his chin, adding to his fierce expression.

He had on his common gear—baggy woolen breeches tucked into the tops of his walking-boots, linen shirt under leather jacket, and a round leather cap, decorated only with an embroidered band of heavy silk. No one needed to know that the supple outer layer was lined with a stiffer cap of boiled leather, as tough as iron, but much lighter on the head.

He could not sleep on the hard plank bed, and the walls of the tiny cell seemed to close in on him after the spaciousness of the sea. Instead, he walked through the predawn quiet of Manatas. The Broad Way that had been laid out on the ridge of rock that formed the "long bone" of the island took him past the Muskat and Madrassa buildings—the largest and finest, after the Rabat—and the houses of the merchants, barred and shuttered against beasts, both animal and human, that might seek to enter. He slipped through the gate of the newly built Manatas Town Wall without being challenged (and made a mental note to question whoever was supposed to be in charge of the guards) and proceeded along the path to the Feria.

The Feria was laid out in a rough square, a small, if temporary, village of flimsy wooden sheds and tents with sectors devoted to a particular sort of merchandise. By far the largest and most complete buildings were those of the kutton merchants, where bales were stacked in locked wooden sheds protected from the rain that might fall Kutton would be traded for furs from the North and West, and Al-Andalus would collect a payment on each exchange for providing the Feria and overseeing the honesty of both sides Such had been the custom in Oropa for the thousand years since the armies of the Prophet had swept across the Middle Sea, dividing those who followed Ilha from those north of the Alps who continued to worship Chesu the Redeemer and his Mother Mara..

Halvar frowned as he paced along the beaten-earth path in the growing light of the rising sun. The stalls of the metalworkers were each marked by a signboard with a symbol on it specifying which metal was being sold—iron, bronze, copper. He had his orders, but how was he to carry them out? He didn't know this place, didn't have his usual allies, didn't even understand half of what was being said to him. The Arabi spoken in Manatas had an odd twang to it, and the Nova Mundans had incorporated local words to describe things not found in Al-Andalus. Even the people here were strange, merchants and craftsmen carrying themselves with a pride that went beyond a warrior's swagger, ready to argue any point at any time.

Then, he stumbled over a rock in the path and knocked his toe against something under a bush beside the path. As he caught his balance, he glimpsed two legs clad in the fringed leather leggings worn by some of the Mahak. He squatted to take a closer look.

It was the body of a man, sprawled face down. Flies swarmed about the bloody dent in the back of his head, and more buzzed angrily when Halvar gingerly turned the body over to see the face.

He gasped. He had seen many horrible sights, but even he had to swallow hard when he saw the ruin of what had been the man's face. The bones had been mashed to a pulp, crushing the teeth into the cavity of the mouth and shattering the skull. Whoever had killed this man had been very strong, or very angry, or both.

3

Halvar stood and looked about him for assistance. He didn't know who this was, or why he was dead, but he knew one thing—the mysterious message to the Calif had been correct. Something nasty was happening in this supposedly peaceful settlement, and it was up to him to correct it. After all, he was the Calif's Hireling.

Murders in the Feria endangered the collection of funds. If Calif Don Felipe was to finance his wars with the taxes taken in at the Feria, it was Halvar's duty to see those funds made their way to Al-Andalus. The letter sent to Don Felipe had suggested they were, instead, being diverted to other purposes.

Halvar Danske, the farmer's son who had been made into a soldier, then a delver into the tangled thickets of court intrigue, decided it was necessary for him to restore order in Manatas.

Chapter 2

HALVAR LOOKED BACK ALONG THE PATH. THE NEARest stall bore the sign of the ironmonger—a large hammer. A man had stopped in front of it with a donkey and cart, ready to unload his wares for the day's trading.

"Hoy!" Halvar called

The man peered down the path at him.

"Come here!" Halvar gestured with his arm. "There's a dead man here!"

The man trotted down the path. Now Halvar could see he was almost as tall as himself but much wider through the middle, with a broad red face mostly covered with a chestnut-red mustache. He wore the tight-fitting, garishly patterned trews favored by Bretains, topped with a red wool smock.

"What's this about?" the vendor asked in Erse-accented Arabi.

"I just found a dead one on the path," Halvar explained. "Who is in charge here? I have to report this."

The ironmonger stared down at the body.

"The Feria's not part of Manatas Town, nor Green Village, but in between," he said. "We've never had this kind of trouble before. Might as well send for Tenente Gomez, he's the head of the Town Guard. He's dealt with killings on the waterfront."

"You do that," Halvar ordered. "And who are you?"

"I'm Cormack mac-Cormack, of West Caster." He waved in the direction of his stall, indicating where a large youth was now unloading the donkey cart. "That's my boy, Padraig. We sell the finest iron tools in the Feria," he added with a self-satisfied smirk.

"And I—" Halvar began.

Before Halvar could respond to this, Padraig joined them. The boy took one look at the body and yelped, "That's Leon!"

"Oh, we know all about you, Don Álvaro," Cormack said with a knowing wink. "The Calif's Hireling, come to make sure we all pay our wumpum for the privilege of trading at the Feria."

"How can you tell who it is?" Halvar asked the boy.

"Those are the leggings he wears, and that's his jacket." Padraig gulped. "Oh, Redeemer save us! He's dead!"

The cry of the muezzin echoed on the early morning air, summoning all who heard it to prayer. Both Bretains made the gesture of the Crux, went down on one knee, and spoke the words "Patri Nostro." Halvar bowed his head and gripped the amulet he wore under his shirt, the little brass object that could have been the Crux or Thor's Hammer. Beside the tents and booths of the Feria, Afrikans, Andalusians and those Locals who had accepted Ilha and his Prophet prostrated themselves.

As he murmured his standard prayer—"May the Redeemer and his Mother and the God Thor help me this day"—Halvar's eye was caught by something in the leaf-litter on the path. He picked up a small blue bead. As far as he could tell, it was not from anything worn by the man lying in front of him. He tucked the bead into the pocket sewn into his jacket. Whether the owner of this bead was a murderer or a witness was yet to be determined, but Halvar would make it his business to find out.

His religious duty done, he turned back to Cormack and his son.

"Get someone from the Town Guard," he ordered.

"I'm here!" announced Tenente Gomez, the commander of the Town Guard.

He was a burly man whose dark eyes were shadowed by heavy brows, his nose squashed flat in some long-ago brawl, mouth and chin covered by a thick black beard neatly trimmed in the round style that was no longer considered fashionable in Al-Andalus. He wore the long green woolen coat and black breeches of the Manatas Town Guard and a green tarboosh stiffened with a leather lining to absorb blows from those who would dare to attack a representative of the Law. He strutted down the path, the built-up heels of his riding boots kicking stray leaves out of his way.

"What's this about a body?"

"I found him like this," Halvar said. "This boy has identified him as Leon. Leon who?"

Gomez squatted by the body and peered at it.

"Leon di Vicenza. That's his coat, all right, but it's hard to tell for sure with his face smashed in like that."

Padraig gulped and retreated up the path, pausing to lose his breakfast in the bushes.

Halvar was made of sterner stuff. He joined Gomez beside the body, studying the wounds in the man's head.

"Something hard made this," he pronounced. "We'll have to look around for the weapon."

"We?" Gomez snarled. "What have you to do with this, Hireling? *I* am tenente of the Town Guard, I will take charge of this matter."

Halvar shook his head.

"Oh, no, Tenente. According to what I've been told, your Town Guard only serves the town. This murder took place on the Feria grounds, beyond the Manatas Town Wall. Don Felipe, may he reign long, put me in charge of the Feria. Therefore, I'll deal with this murder."

"What do you know about murder, Hireling?" Gomez argued. "The story we heard was that you were a soldier, out of luck and out of place, picked up after a tavern brawl to bodyguard the young prince. All you've done since the Wars is follow a boy around the Madrassa in Corduva."

Halvar regarded Gomez through half-closed eyes, taking in the man's resentment at being replaced by a mere servant.

"If you don't like me, that's your business," he said evenly. "But let me remind you, Tenente Gomez, the calif sent me here. One reason was to oversee the goods and the revenues due from the Feria to Al-Andalus. The other is that Don Felipe wanted to find out what became of his fellow student from the Madrassa in Corduva, one Leon di Vicenza. And you tell me this is he, and he is dead? Don Felipe will be very distressed to hear it."

7

Gomez sniffed in utter indifference to the calif's distress.

Halvar looked up and down the path, noting how far it was from the stalls of the Feria.

"What was he doing here, anyway?"

"Doing?" Gomez echoed. "Knowing Leon, probably some lover's tryst."

"At the Feria?Why not somewhere more suitable?"

Gomez looked over at Padraig, who was still white around the mouth, making the freckles on his pale skin stand out more clearly in the growing sunlight.

"Leon liked 'em young," he said with a knowing nod in the boy's direction.

"And what do you suppose his father would say about that?" Halvar murmured, with a glance at the glowering ironmonger.

"It goes against the Prophet's Word," Gomez stated. "The Redeemer's, likewise. Even the wretched Yehudit say it's against their Law."

"But it happens," Halvar said philosophically. He frowned as he looked at the body. "There's something wrong. He wasn't hit here. Not enough blood." Now that it was light, he could see a trail of beaten-down weeds and shrubbery leading to a small dip in the landscape. "He must have crawled up here. Look at that trail."

He followed the signs to a small spinney of slender birches.

"He was struck down here," he said, pointing to drying blood and the cloud of flies feasting on the spatters of tissue on the ground. He stalked around the little clearing. His eye was caught by something tangled in the branches of one of the shrubs. "What's this?"

It was a club something like a mace, with a carved wooden handle that had been bent around an iron ball, secured with leather straps. More flies buzzed angrily around it as Halvar plucked the club out of the shrubs, holding it carefully by the very end, noting the carved symbols picked out with red and black paint. Someone had taken a good deal of time to make this object more than just a weapon.

Gomez frowned at the club.

"This is not good, Hireling. That's a Mahak war club, and if the Mahak are involved in this murder, we are going to have to deal with the Sachem."

"I thought we had made peace with the Locals," Halvar said.

"So we have, but there are always difficulties, especially if they take strong drink. They can't deal with it, it makes them mad," Gomez explained.

"Why would a Mahak take a club to an Andalusian? Especially one like Leon?" Halvar wondered as they made their way back to the path.

"You'd have to ask them," Gomez said, with another grimace and an expressive shrug.

Young Padraig was standing next to the donkey cart, which had been emptied of ironware to hold the body. Some of the other metal-dealers came to lift the corpse into the makeshift hearse.

"What now, Hireling?" Gomez asked with a slight sneer.

"We take this body into Manatas and let someone look at it who knows his business," Halvar said. "And then we find out just what Leon di Vicenza was doing in the Feria after dark."

"He was waiting for someone," Padraig blurted out, with an agonized glance at his father. "I saw him just as we were leaving for our lodgings in Green Village. He waved to me as I was leaving with Father."

"When was this?" Halvar asked.

"Just after sundown prayers," Padraig said. "I...I knew him. He...we...that is..." His voice trailed off. "I was one of the Seekers of Truth," he said finally. "There were four of us—me and Benyamin and Selim and Otter Tail. Leon was our teacher. He knew all about the stars, and the Old Roumi, and the Old Greco."

Cormack turned on his son.

"I thought I told you to stay away from that lot! Unbelievers! Heretics! Yehudit and Locals, all mixed up together, just like Leon's clothes. Local leggings, Andalusian jacket, and his face shaved like the fraters'!"

"But that was what Leon was telling us," Padraig protested. "He said that this was Nova Mundum, that we must turn outward, away from the old ways of Oropa, and become something totally new."

"Hmh!" Cormack grunted. "And look what it got him. Take that...Leon...into Manatas to the Rabat. Then come right back with that cart, do you hear? And if I hear any more about those Seekers of Truth, I'll see to it that you don't sit down for a week. You're not too big to beat, boy."

9

Padraig took his place at the donkey's head. Halvar recognized his expression of mingled fear and determination. *This lad wants to know how the world works,* he thought. *Leon di Vicenza, you would start a rival to Parigi or Corduva or Oxencross here in Nova Mundum? And see what it gets you!*

He caught sight of the green-and-yellow tabard of the Official Newscrier.

"Hoy! You!" he called out. The newscrier trotted over to him. "Get this message out—the body of Leon di Vicenza has been found in the Feria. Anyone with information about his death should bring it to Don Álvaro Dánico at the Rabat in Manatas Town."

The newscrier began declaiming the message as Halvar, Gomez, Padraig and the late Leon went through the gates of the town wall and down the Broad Way to the Rabat.

Chapter 3

THE DONKEY CART WITH ITS GRIM BURDEN GATHERED followers as it went as the newscrier's summons brought a crowd of chattering folk from the side streets and plazas. The town had been laid out in the same fashion as those of Al-Andalus, a style that had been established centuries before when the Old Roumi had first settled the farthest reaches of Oropa. On either side of the Broad Way, brick houses formed square blocks facing an inner courtyard, where a well or fountain had been sunk to provide water for the inhabitants.

Halvar noted the variety of people who stopped their work to watch—tall Afrikans in their striped kutton robes; Locals in a mixture of deerskin and woolen cloth; Andalusians in colorful shirts and baggy breeches; Franchen in wide-brimmed hats and tight-fitting coats; Bretains in their checked and striped trews and smocks. There were few women in the crowd, mostly Locals in deerskin skirts and kutton smock tops decorated with beads or Afrikans wrapped in wildly patterned draperies topped with extravagantly folded turbans. It was too early in the day for the Andalusian women to be out; and they would be well-hidden, some in full burka, some only with the hijab, fulfilling the Prophet's dicta on modesty.

The procession stopped as the Grand Mullah emerged from the Muskat. Mullah Abadul was as tall as Halvar, made even taller by his turban, which topped a long ascetic face that seemed to be all burning black eyes, jutting nose, and long gray beard.

"What is this?" he demanded.

"Leon di Vicenza," Gomez explained. "He's dead."

"He has met the end of all evildoers!" the mullah pronounced. "Shaitan has claimed his own!"

"He had some help," Halvar said. "Leon was murdered."

"And the one who did it will reside in Paradise!" Mullah Abadul announced. "This is what happens to those who question the Word of the Prophet and dispute the teachings of the fathers!"

Padraig burst out, "That's not so! Leon was a natural philosopher; he studied the workings of our world. Just because he didn't study all those musty old books—"

"You tell 'em!" A stocky young man whose round face was framed with the beginnings of a black beard on his cheeks and chin and two twisted curls in front of each ear, dressed in the black coat and fur-trimmed hat of the Askenat Yehudit, pushed to the front of the crowd and joined Padraig, arms folded, staring defiantly at the Mullah.

"Benyamin ibn Mendel," Gomez snarled. "Another of Leon's 'Seekers of Truth.'"

"Seekers?" Halvar echoed. He turned to the young Yehuda. "You're one of Leon's students."

It was a statement, not a question.

Benyamin stood his ground.

"Leon di Vicenza was a great man," he announced reverently, with a glance at the donkey cart. "Whoever killed him robbed the world of a mind that comes only once a century, if that. He observed Nature, and drew conclusions from what he saw not what someone else wrote years ago. He could draw images of what he saw—"

"Images!" roared Mullah Abadul. "Is it not forbidden, by both the Prophet's words and your own Yehudit Law, to make an image of any living thing?"

"Only to worship such images," Benyamin countered.

"And besides," Padraig added, "the images Leon made were like life itself!"

"Life itself!" The mullah was completely outraged. "Evil images! One does not create Life. Only Illia may do that!"

12

"Ilha didn't smash this man's head in," Halvar pointed out. "Sir, I ask that you permit us to continue on our sad mission so that we may take this body to the Rabat, where the sultan may be consulted as to how we shall proceed. Whatever else he was, Leon di Vicenza was of Al-Andalus, and as such, his killer must be found so that his death may be properly avenged. Padraig, go on!"

Mullah Abadul had to step aside to let the cart and its followers proceed to the gates of the fortress, where the Broad Way stopped.

"Go back to your shops and houses," Gomez ordered the crowd. "News will be cried when we know more."

They dispersed, muttering and mumbling. The cart continued through the gates and into the courtyard of the Rabat, where Padraig brought the donkey to a halt.

The high walls of the Rabat cut off the winds from the bay. A straggling set of wooden sheds had been built against the walls, whose roofs provided access to battlements where cannons had been placed, facing into the narrow gap between the Long Island and the Round Island.

Benyamin and Padraig approached Halvar.

"We want to help find out who did this," Benyamin said. "Leon was our teacher, but more than that, he was our friend."

"Oh?" Halvar put a world of meaning into that one syllable.

Padraig's freckles nearly disappeared into the blush on his face, while Benyamin sputtered, "No, no, nothing like that, he was more friendly to Otter Tail, but we understood that they were, um, special to each other. My father would never have allowed Leon into our shop if he thought...um, what I mean is..."

"It's all right, lad, I get your drift. Who is this Otter Tail?" Halvar asked, grinning under his mustache.

"Otter Tail is the Mahak apprenticed to Malik the Smith," Padraig explained. "Malik and Leon knew each other in Al-Andalus, I think, and they worked together. Leon would think of devices, and Malik would try to make them."

"They didn't always work," Benyamin admitted.

"Where is this Otter Tail now?" Halvar asked.

Padraig and Benyamin looked at each other and shrugged.

"At the forge, I suppose," Padraig said.

Halvar thought he might have added something else, but instead the Bretain youth shut his mouth over whatever words might have inadvertently popped out.

"If you see him, tell him I want to talk to him," he told the boys.

Gomez growled, "Enough of this schoolboy's chatter! You, Bretain, get back to your father in the Feria, and you, Yehudit, get back to your shop. These are men's affairs, no business of yours."

Halvar was kinder.

"Thank you for your help," he told them. "I may want to talk to you again."

"You'll find me at the Feria, or at our lodgings in Green Village," Padraig told him."We have rooms with the Widow Nic-Kinnock."

"My father is Mendel the Bookseller," Benyamin said. "We have a stand in the Souk, behind the Madrassa on the west side of the Broad Way."

"I'll find it," Halvar promised.

"The sultan is waiting," Gomez prodded him.

"One more thing to do," Halvar said. "Where's the doctor? I want this body examined before we bury it."

"Examined? Do you mean taken apart?" Gomez gasped. "Forbidden!"

"Not cut," Halvar assured him. "But without a face, who is to say that this is, indeed, Leon di Vicenza?"

"He's wearing Leon's coat and leggings," Padraig pointed out.

"A coat and leggings may be put on and off," Halvar persisted. "But there are other ways of marking a body."

A slender dark-skinned man in a long Afrikan tunic and round knitted hat emerged from one of the wooden sheds.

"Hah!" Gomez hailed him. "Dr. Moise! We have a client for you. That is, he would be, except he is already dead."

"So I hear," the Afrikan said. "What do you want me to do about him? I cannot cure him."

"I want him examined," Halvar said. "His face has been bashed in, but there are other ways of identifying a man."

"You doubt that this is Leon?" Gomez asked.

"I doubt everything until it's been proved true or false."

14

"Well, you'll have to take that up with the sultan," Gomez said. "Follow me, Hireling. Doctor, I wish you the joy of Leon."

Halvar tugged at his mustache to hide a grimace. He was not looking forward to this interview. Sultan Petrus was known for his explosive temper; what he'd say when he found out one of his own people had been murdered would not be pleasant.

Chapter 4

HALVAR AND GOMEZ CROSSED THE STONE-PAVED courtyard to the central of the three towers in the fortress that loomed over the rocky tip of Manatas Island. They mounted the winding stair to the second story where Sultan Petrus had his private quarters, which consisted of one large room that filled most of the tower. A second, smaller stair led to the third floor and the Harem, the sequestered domain of Lady Ayesha and her maids.

An Afrikan with a gold ring dangling from his left ear stopped them at the door to the sultan's rooms.

"Be careful," he warned them. "The leg is bad today."

Gomez grimaced. "Let's just hope the sultan isn't too ad-dled with hemp to listen to us."

"Hemp?" Halvar's eyebrows rose. "That's almost as bad as poppy juice."

"He uses it when the pain gets too much," Gomez explained. "But don't think less of him for that. Old Silver-Leg was a great fighter."

In his time, Halvar amended.

Sultan Petrus, Governor of Manatas Town by order of the Calif of Al-Andalus, was a full-bodied man, once muscular, now running to fat, whose watery dark eyes looked at the world over his grizzled beard. He sat in a chair of the Oropan mode rather than reclining on the pillows of a divan in the style of

16

Al-Andalus, draped in blue and green silk robes with a blue silk turban secured by a large turquoise pin. His silver-mounted ivory peg-leg rested on a small footstool in front of him,

The table beside him held charts and maps of the Nova Mundum coastline as well as a bowl of odd orange fruits and a tall brass pot with a spout for the serving of mokka. Halvar's midsection suddenly recalled that he had not eaten since the night before.

The sultan glared at them from under heavy dark brows. His round face flushed darker, and his very beard seemed to exude energy.

"What's this about Leon di Vicenza being found dead in the Feria?" he snapped before they could give the customary "Salaam aleikum."

"I found a body in the Feria wearing Leon's coat," Halvar said cautiously.

"But you don't think it's him?" Sultan Petrus drove straight to the heart of the matter.

"It might be, it might not be," Halvar said. "Leon di Vicenza had enemies. He also had a nasty sense of humor. He might think it a good joke to pretend to be dead for a while."

Sultan Petrus frowned. "Gomez, that's what you and your men are here for. To keep order." He glared fiercely at the guardsman, who seemed to shrink under that gaze.

Gomez cleared his throat.

"I keep out the riffraff," he said in a respectful tone. "What happens on the waterfront or in the Feria—"

"Is no concern of mine," Sultan Petrus said with a wave of his hand. "When one sailor stabs another in a brawl over women or dice, that's for the Town Guard to sort out. When someone like Leon, my own son's tutor, is found outside the town wall with his head bashed in, that's something else. I want his killer found, and found quickly."

"And I will put all my men on it," Gomez promised.

"I welcome your help," Halvar said evenly, "but let me remind you, Excellent Sultan, I am in charge of the Feria, and since this death occurred on the Feria grounds, it is up to me to find the killer."

Sultan Petrus regarded Halvar with half-closed eyes, taking in the long face, plain clothing, and businesslike dagger with the lump of amber in the hilt, worn where another man might have carried a sword.

"I know you," he said at last. "You were in the Free Company that made the final assault on Pisa. You were the one who dragged the old man out of the fighting and took a piece of lead in the arm doing it. That was very brave, and very stupid. You could have been killed yourself."

"We got cut to shreds when they brought up the muskets. You don't send pikemen against guns." Halvar's face twisted in a spasm of grief then resumed his usual placid expression. "The old man—that was Old Olaf, my sergeant, the finest man I ever knew, and the wisest. I got him out of the line, but he died before the surgeons could get the lead out of him. It was like seeing my father killed, and for what? The Pisans stayed where they were, Al-Andalus had to withdraw, and that Episcopous Innocente in Rouma, the one who started it all, claimed it was a sign that the Redeemer wanted all of Oropa for himself, free from the Prophet and Islim.

"And so the wars go on and on, and the Franchen and Bretains have made a truce and are aiming their guns together at Al-Andalus. But we're not here to talk politics, Honored Sultan. I'm here because the Calif Don Felipe, may he live long and reign well, received a communication from his old schoolmate Leon," Halvar said. "He won't be happy to find out that Leon's dead. I'll have to have a very good explanation for him."

"A communication?" Sultan Petrus echoed.

"A letter. It got into the packet of receipts from last year's Fall Feria. It took a while before it came to Don Felipe's attention, but when it did, he was not pleased. Certain charges have been made, and I am to investigate them."

"Charges? Against whom?" Sultan Petrus shifted testily in his chair.

"I cannot say at this time. My orders were to find Leon di Vicenza and verify his accusations. If Leon is dead, it is possible it is because of what he was about to tell me."

"Mmmph," Sultan Petrus grunted. "Very well. Tenente, you will assist Don Álvaro in every way possible. He is the Calif's Hireling and must be respected as such." There was a note of warning in that last statement.

"As you will, Honored Sultan." Gomez bowed and salaamed, but Halvar could sense the resentment lurking under the apparent acquiescence.

"So, Don Álvaro," Sultan Petrus continued. "Just how will you go about following these orders of yours?"

"I will need to question everyone who had any dealings with Leon. Beginning with your son Selim. I recall that he came here with you as Selim's tutor. Is that still true?"

"He taught Selim mathematics and history until about a year ago, at the time of the last Fall Feria. I had to let him go. He was making himself too obnoxious to Mullah Abadul, and there were questions about the, um, propriety of his being with my son when he was notorious elsewhere, especially at the Mermaid Taberna on the waterfront and the Gardens of Paradise in Green Village."

"Is that the settlement outside the walls?" Halvar queried. "Why don't those people stay here, safely in Manatas Town?"

"In any other place, it would be the foreigners' quarter," Gomez explained. "Here, we keep them out of the town altogether. They can consort with each other and stay away from good Believers. And keep their filthy goods there, too," he added piously

Halvar grinned under his mustache.

"Meaning that those things forbidden by the Prophet are for sale there," he said. "Alcohol, hemp, and swine's flesh."

"And other flesh, too," Gomez added with a smirk. "Leon spent a good deal of time there. If I didn't know better, I'd say he was bewitched by that Yehudit siren Dani Glick."

Halvar's grin faded.

"Dani Glick?" he echoed. "A Yehudit woman? With red hair?"

"You know her?" the sultan asked.

"I knew someone of that name…many years ago."

"Well, you might want to renew the friendship," Gomez said snidely. "If anyone can tell you what Leon was doing outside the walls after dark, it is she. For all we know, he was meeting her!"

"I'll ask her when I see her," Halvar said evenly. "Now, Honored Sultan, I would like to speak with your son. And then I want to see where Leon was living. You can tell a good deal about a man by the things he owns."

"I can have Selim called," Sultan Petrus said. "But he is of an age where he comes and goes as he pleases. Young people will do that, you know." He gave an indulgent smile. "He may not even be in the Rabat."

"While my men look for him, we can have something to break the night-fast," Gomez decided. "I can smell the mokka brewing."

"One thing more," Sultan Petrus said as Halvar and Gomez turned to leave. "Don Álvaro, you may be the Calif's Hireling, but I am sultan here in Manatas. You will report your findings to me. I will decide what to do about them."

"As you say," Halvar said, with a bow. To himself, he added, *If what Leon has to say is true, you may not be sultan for much longer, Petrus Silver-leg. How far would you go to silence him?*

Chapter 5

"WELL, HIRELING," GOMEZ SAID AS THEY MADE THEIR way back to the courtyard "Where do we start this investigation of yours?"

"With food," Halvar decided. "And Selim. Where do you usually break the night-fast?"

"At my lodgings, just outside the Rabat," Gomez growled. "But I was out early. There's a sutler's shed just by the Rabat gate. We can get mokka and maiz-cakes there."

They were interrupted by a startlingly handsome young guardsman whose generous height was intensified by his green tarboosh.

"Salaam aleikum, Tenente. What are the orders for the day?"

Gomez glanced at Halvar, then said, "I will be assisting the Calif's Hireling while he looks into this matter of Leon's death, Ruiz. You can run the new men through their drill, then take the morning squad to the Souk. We've got too many new people in for the Feria. Keep your eyes open for itching fingers."

The guardsman salaamed and went off to maintain law and order. Gomez led Halvar to the place near the gate where an enterprising Local woman had set up a brazier next to a small table and stools. They sat down and were offered earthenware cups of black liquid and a wooden plate that held several flat yellow cakes smeared with greenish paste.

Halvar frowned at the food. He sipped cautiously at the mokka and grimaced at its bitterness.

"What's in that?" he demanded.

Gomez smirked at Halvar's discomfort.

"They enhance the mokka with a local plant called chicory," he explained. "The cakes are maiz, and the green stuff on top is a mash of their broad beans, sort of like hummus. Try it."

Halvar took a cautious bite and decided the grilled maizcake was tolerable. The chicory-laced mokka, on the other hand, was clearly an acquired taste he didn't care to acquire.

"So," he said after he had finished two of the yellow cakes. "Where are your men? I want to find Selim. Then we look at the dead man."

"Even if the dead man's not Leon di Vicenza?" Gomez drank his bitter brew with gusto.

"If he is, then that's that. If not, how'd he get Leon's coat and leggings? And why? And where's Leon, if this isn't he?"

"Good questions, which I can't answer." Gomez beckoned to one of the guards standing at the gate. "Lovis, have you seen young Selim this morning?"

The guard shook his head.

"I thought he rode out last night, but I haven't seen him."

"Keep your eyes open, and send him to me as soon as he gets back to the Rabat," Gomez ordered before Halvar could object.

His eye was caught by a woman who emerged from the entrance to Sultan Petrus's quarters.

"That is Eva Hakim, Leon's sister," Gomez told him. "She's a Sister of Fatima, attending Lady Ayesha. I'd better let her know about Leon. She shouldn't have to hear the news from a stranger." He used a softer tone than he had all morning.

Halvar's eyebrows rose as Gomez approached the woman, who had on the brown robes and green hijab of those who devoted their lives to caring for the sick and injured. Eva Hakim was as tall as Gomez but much slimmer, with smooth olive skin, dark brows, and a nose that some might find too large for the rest of her face.

She ignored the tenente's fawning greeting and turned to Halvar.

"Is it true? Was my brother found murdered?"

22

"There's some question about it." Halvar said. "As his sister, you would be the most likely to know if the man is your brother or not. Can you…will you look at him?"

Two deep lines creased between her finely arched brows.

"It would be difficult," she admitted. "My brother and I were not as close as I would have liked. He had turned away from the Prophet's teachings. He was a scoffer, what they call a natural philosopher."

"So I've heard," Halvar said. "Eva Hakim, when was the last time you saw your brother?"

Eva Hakim shook her head.

"It was only a day or two ago, just before your ship came into the harbor. I had business on the waterfront—the Sisters of Fatima have a small booth there where we treat those waterfront women who care to come to us. Usually, it's because they've been beaten badly by their men or are about to give birth and need a midwife."

Gomez snorted disdainfully.

"More halflings," he grumbled."Afrikans and Locals, and another crop of bastard children running loose."

Halvar ignored him.

"How did Leon seem to you then?" he asked.

Eva Hakim shrugged.

"Much as always. He was either up in the clouds or down in the mire. He was with his Local paramour, the boy from the forge."

"Otter Tail," Halvar said.

Eva sighed. "His mother Nokomis stays with us at the House of the Green Crescent, to teach us the ways of the Locals, their herbs and some of their more useful practices. I was not happy to know that Leon had met Otter Tail at the forge."

"What about the lad's mother?" Halvar asked "What did she think of this, um, friendship?"

"That is not something we discuss," Eva Hakim said primly. "Nokomis is considered a very wise woman among her people, and as such, she has a certain status. She comes to us of her own will, and we are grateful for her knowledge.

"As for her son, he is her youngest. He comes to her for advice and comfort when he is troubled." She paused, then said, "I saw them together yesterday, when we were gathered to watch your entrance into Manatas Town. Otter Tail showed her his latest creation, a club he had made at the forge."

"We found a Mahak war club at the scene of the killing," Halvar said thoughtfully.

Gomez interrupted this digression.

"And when you saw Leon, how did he seem to you?"

"We parted in anger," Eva said. "We had heard that the calif's dhow had been spotted making its way up the coast. Leon was very full of himself, puffed up with pride, telling everyone the calif was sending his Hireling specifically because he, Leon di Vicenza, had reported on how the funds from the Feria were being misused, and how the sultan would be arrested for taking money that was supposed to go to Al-Andalus and using it to build the Manatas Town Wall.

"He told me he was going to get off this island, that he and Otter Tail were going into Mahak Country, away from all Oropans. I pleaded with him to change his ways, that his life was displeasing to Ilha and against the teachings of the Prophet, praise be unto him. He laughed, said that the Prophet, praise be unto him, was a moldy old fraud, and that he would do as he liked in Nova Mundum."

Eva Hakim stopped to take a deep breath and compose herself.

"I left him then. I did not wish to speak to him. I could not! To revile the Prophet's teachings!" She began to weep silently. "I thought he would put such thoughts aside once he got away from the freethinkers and scoffers at Corduba, but he only got worse the longer he stayed here in Nova Mundum."

"There seems to be something strange in the air here," Halvar said. "It leads people to do things they would not have considered back in Al-Andalus. Eva Hakim, will you come with us and identify this body?"

"One moment." She turned to another woman, a small, round Local with a face as brown and wrinkled as a walnut, also dressed in the brown robes of a Sister of Fatima. Long gray braids all that were visible of her hair, held in place with a leather band instead of hidden under a hijab. "Nokomis, Lady Ayesha is having her first pains. Send Sister Vera to her."

The older woman nodded and padded across the courtyard and out the gates.

Eva Hakim took a deep breath, as if to compose herself before an ordeal.

"I am ready now," she said. "I will see this body, and I pray to Ilha, the All-Merciful, praise be unto Him, that it is not my brother. I would hate to think that we parted for the last time in life in anger."

Together, Gomez, Halvar and Eva Hakim marched towards the grim task that awaited them at Dr. Moise's surgery.

Chapter 6

DR. MOISE'S DOMAIN WAS A TWO-ROOM SHACK BUILT against the stone wall of the Rabat. One room served as an office, where a scrawny Afrikan man sat at a low table, ink and paper before him, ready to take notes and keep records of the cases brought to the attention of the sultan's medical adviser. The other was the treatment room, sparsely furnished with a long table and a standing cupboard, shelves full of bottles in which Dr. Moise kept his potions and herbal preparations. A case of gleaming knives sat on a small table next to the long one, on which reposed the body in question.

Dr. Moise lit the oil lamp that hung from the ceiling over the examination table.

"I wish you did not have to do this," he said apologetically to Eva Hakim. "This is no place for a woman."

Halvar and Gomez crowded in behind her. They avoided looking at the dead man's ruined face.

"I am a doctor," Eva reminded them.

"Of women's complaints," Dr. Moise corrected her.

"True, but I have attended the anatomies at the Madrassa in Corduva," she countered. "I am not one to be shocked at the sight of male bodies."

"But this is your brother," Dr. Moise said.

"The Hireling thinks it's not," Gomez sneered.

"If anyone can identify this man, it's his sister," Halvar retorted. He turned to the brown-robed woman. "Eva Hakim, can you state positively that is the body of your brother, Leon di Vicenza?"

Eva closed her eyes, as if bidding herself to have courage. Then she gazed at the body.

"That is most definitely my brother's coat," she stated. "He was so proud of it when he got it, paid for with money he won at dice from young Don Felipe, who had not yet become calif. He had it made by the finest tailor in Corduva. Red damask silk, embroidered and padded. And the things on his legs—he just got them, from that Local person."

"Otter Tail," Gomez furnished the name.

"If you say so," Eva said dismissively. "I did not approve of their...friendship. It was unseemly. It went against the words of the Prophet, may his name be blessed, and the Will of Ilha the All-Merciful, may his name be praised."

Halvar frowned at the leggings.

"What are they for?" he muttered. "They don't have a bottom."

"The Mahak don't wear anything on their legs unless it's freezing cold," Gomez explained. "It's a point of honor not to show how the weather makes you feel. They never learned to make proper trousers, just these leg-wrappings they hang from their breechclout belts with leather straps when the cold gets to be more than a man can stand.

"And it does, Don Álvaro, when the wind comes off the Great River and tears right across this island. You'd wish you were nice and warm in Muscovy!"

"You said these leggings are held in place by straps?"

Dr. Moise and Gomez peered down at the leather-clad legs.

"These aren't attached to the belt," Gomez observed.

"Which leads me to believe they were put on after he was struck down," Halvar concluded. "Eva Hakim, you say these are your brother's clothes, but is it he who is wearing them?"

She looked away. "But if not he—who?"

"That's not what I'm asking now," Halvar repeated. "Can you state positively that this is your brother, Leon di Vicenza? Look again, please."

Eva closed her eyes for a moment once more then examined the dead man's hands.

"This is wrong," she declared. "My brother was a writer and a painter, he did not do hard labor. This person's hands show scars and calluses from using digging tools."

Dr. Moise opened the coat to show a rough linen shirt underneath. Halvar lifted it to reveal a nearly hairless torso.

"I don't know who this is," he declared, "but I can tell you who it isn't. It isn't Leon di Vicenza. Leon had a scar, right about here." He pointed to a spot just above the fourth rib under the man's left breast.

"And how do you know that?" Gomez challenged.

"Because I was the one who put it there," Halvar snapped. He fought the urge to spew and made himself look at the mashed remains of the man's face. "But this is interesting." He pointed to a dark bruise on the temple. "Doctor, would you say this was done before or after the man died?"

Dr. Moise frowned at the round mark.

"Blood ceases to flow after death," he recited. "This mark was made either just before or just after the man died. I could not say precisely which, but very close to the moment of death."

"What made it, do you think?"

The Afrikan peered closely at the mark.

"Something with a half-circle shape, flat. Not a stick, but something like it."

Halvar's frown deepened. "His chin," he muttered. He pointed to what there was left of it.

"What about it?" Gomez asked, dismissively.

"No beard," Halvar said. "No sign of any in the wound, either. And his hair on the back of his head cut very short, as if shaved."

"It was my brother's affectation to be beardless," Eva Hakim said. "He took a razor to his face every other day. But that is not his hair. He wore that long, tied back with a ribbon."

"Oh, yes, long hair like a girl and clean-shaved cheeks like a boy," Gomez snorted. "And him thirty, if he was a day!"

"Not quite thirty," Eva corrected him. "But, yes, he had been a very pretty boy."

"Every man wants to show that he can grow a beard," Gomez stated.

"Not the Locals," Dr. Moise said. "They do not grow beards."

"Why not?" Halvar wanted to know.

"Such is the Will of Ilha the All-Merciful, may his name be praised," Eva said piously. "But in a way, it is just as well. The Local women find Oropans unpleasant because of their facial hair. If they did not, we would have far more difficulty with halflings than we already do. As it is, there are always those unfortunate girls who are taken by force, and some women who degrade themselves to stay alive."

"So," Gomez brought the irrelevant discussion to a halt. "What do we do now, Hireling? If this isn't Leon—"

"For now, Tenente, I think we will keep that information to ourselves. As far as the rest of Manatas knows, Leon di Vicenza is dead."

Gomez opened his mouth to protest.

"But..." Then he shut it with an audible click of his teeth.

"I must make preparations for my brother's funeral," Eva Hakim said. "It would seem odd if I did not."

"Even though you disapproved of his, um, way of life?" Halvar said.

"He was my brother," Eva replied with simple dignity. "And whoever this is, I would not wish such a death on anyone."

Halvar nodded and turned to the doctor.

"Dr. Moise, I will leave you to finish this sorry task. I want to know exactly what kind of weapon made these wounds. If it wasn't the war-club, what was it? And what made the mark on his temple? I will take Eva Hakim outside so that I may continue my investigation."

"*Your* investigation?" Gomez snarled. "It's not Leon, so it's not your concern any more. Leave this matter to me."

"There are questions that need to be answered," Halvar said as he led Eva Hakim into the office. "A man might take off his coat, but there aren't too many reasons for a man to take off his trousers, especially not in the middle of the Feria at night."

Gomez glanced at Eva Hakim.

"Um, there's always the call of nature," he suggested delicately.

"You don't take off your coat to do that," Halvar said. "And there's the blow that took off his face. That wasn't made by a round ball at the end of a stick. Someone used something large, with a lot of force behind it, to do that."

Dr. Moise joined the trio in the courtyard.

"Eva Hakim, I am sorry you had to see such a sight, but glad, too, that it is not your brother," he said. "I do not know Leon very well. We were at the Madrassa in Corduva at the same time, but he went his own way, which was not mine."

Eva Hakim smiled ruefully.

"You do not have to be so polite, Dr. Moise. My brother was a disgrace at Madrassa. He made himself so obnoxious he was asked to leave and if Sultan Petrus had not offered him the post of tutor to Selim, I do not know what would have become of Leon without me to guide him."

"I thought Sultan Petrus took him on as a favor to the Old One, the Calif Carolus," Halvar said.

"Sultan Petrus's young wife Ayesha wished to have a competent physician with her when she came to Nova Mundum. I wished to establish a House of Fatima here in Manatas. Our two desires were met when I was appointed to accompany her here.

"At the same time, I was able to secure a place for Leon to tutor the sultan's youngest child in mathematics and languages. The child did not wish to remain with Lady Maryam in Al-Andalus, and Sultan Petrus gave in to Selim's pleadings to see Nova Mundum."

"How is Lady Ayesha getting on? Very near her time, isn't she?" Dr. Moise asked with professional interest. "I see you've brought in old Nokomis, the Mahak herb-woman."

"Yes, I have," Eva Hakim replied. "I am not so hidebound that I will not accept information from someone who has greater experience than I. Lady Ayesha has been confined to her bed in the Harem until she delivers. She wants a son, of course, but I am sure the sultan will be happy with another daughter so long as the lady survives. You know how he dotes on her."

"Mph! Old man's darling," muttered Gomez.

Halvar interrupted the professional discussion.

"Eva Hakim, can you tell us anything else that may untangle this problem?"

Gomez was blunter.

"Like, where you think Leon is now?"

Eva Hakim looked blankly from the tall Dane to the short Andalusian.

"I cannot tell you," she said. "If he is not lounging in those rooms of his over the Mermaid Taberna he might be with that she-Shaitan Dani Glick at the Gardens of Paradise. What will you do when you find him?"

"Ask him why he changed coats with a fellow with farmer's hands," Halvar said. "And what he's been doing since he did it."

"I do not know why he would have changed coats, or what he has been doing," Eva Hakim said. "I have my own matters to attend to. May Ilha, the All-Merciful, may his name be praised, guide you, Don Álvaro. You seem to be a man of honor, no matter where your prayers take you."

With that, she headed for the gate to join the Local herbwoman, leaving Halvar and Gomez with Dr. Moise.

"What about that young sprout Selim?" Gomez asked as he watched her gracefully cross the courtyard and exit the gate.

"He can wait," Halvar decided. "I want to see those rooms of Leon's first. Then I'll talk to those Seekers of Truth and find out whether they're a pack of fools or serious scholars led astray by a fellow with a flashy coat and a charming smile."

Chapter 7

"DO YOU KNOW THIS MERMAID TABERNA?" HALVAR inquired.

Gomez frowned. "Oh, I know it, all right. It's the tallest building on the waterfront, the one where most of the foreign traders meet, when they're not at the Feria."

"There are rooms to let there?"

"There were. Leon took all of them for himself," Gomez grumbled resentfully. "There was trouble about that, too, Not that it's any of *your* business, Hireling. I manage the waterfront, me and my men. It's the Town Guard's duty to keep the peace here in Manatas Town, and by the Beard of the Prophet, we do it! No thievery in the Souk, and the whores do business on the waterfront, nowhere else.

"Ah, yes," Halvar said, with a sympathetic sigh. "Waterfronts are always troublesome. Sailors get drunk, whores and thieves prey on them—it's the same all the world over, whether in Al-Andalus, Franchenland or Bretain."

"Thieves? We make sure they pay the price for their crimes," Gomez said as he strutted down the Broad Way and turned into a side street. " Sharia is clear on this. Once caught, lose a finger; twice caught, lose a hand. Not that there's all that much stealing goes on here. No point to it. No one to sell to but other thieves! Ha!"

"And the whores?"

Gomez smirked knowingly.

"Mostly Afrikans, bought by the whoremasters to serve the sailors. A few Andalusians, a few Oropans."

"No Local women?"

"They're no good," Gomez kicked at a stray dog that poked its head out from a rubbish heap. "Get out, you hound!"

The dog ran to its pack, yelping.

"Where are we going?" Halvar asked as they threaded their way along the alleys between the wooden warehouses.

"East Channel. That's where the shipping is. The big ships anchor in the bay, and the barges take cargo and passengers the rest of the way. Smaller boats can dock right on the wharf."

"Why not use the Great River? It's big enough for a dozen ships, one next to the other, with room to spare for a barge or two." Halvar followed Gomez through yet another reeking alley to a broad space that had been cleared so the goods that kept Manatas thriving could be offloaded from the barges. Barrels of tabak, bales of kutton, and wooden crates that held everything from beaver hides to smoked gobbler were stacked on wooden walkways that jutted out into the channel.

"The Great River is too swift," Gomez explained. "You might say, it's too great! An ocean-dhow can actually sail up it right into the Mahak country."

"And do they?" Halvar wondered.

"Mph," Gomez grunted. "One of the Bretain ships made it through the bay and up the Great River. The men on it didn't come back. The Mahak are very cautious as to who comes into their territory."

"I traveled with a Kristo Frater," Halvar remarked. "He was certain he would be welcomed by the Mahak, to tell them the Good News of the Redeemer."

"Ha!" Gomez laughed without mirth. "Maybe the Mahak women will listen to him, because of their respect for the Redeemer's Mother Mara. The Mahak men prefer the words of the Prophet, may his name be blessed, if they are willing to be taken away from their pagan spirits and forest demons. It's the Algonkin who are the most willing to adopt the ways of Oropa. Aha! There's the Mermaid. That's where Leon held forth every night, fomenting rebellion and riot."

Halvar breathed in the odors of saltwater, fish, and rotting vegetation, familiar to anyone who had been near ports anywhere in Oropa. Overhead, gulls wheeled and turned, diving into the water to snatch fish and scraps tossed in by the vendors who hawked their wares to the passersby. He could see the outline of the Long Island across the river to the east. Northward were three small islands, with ferry lines strung from wooden towers, one from the island to Manatas, the other to the Long Island, so that goods and passengers could get from one side of the East Channel to the other.

"This way."

The Mermaid Taberna was a two-story edifice built in the Franchen style, with the upper story jutting over the first and a pitched roof over all. Above the door, on an iron bracket, swung the image of a woman, very buxom from the top of her head to her waist. Below the waist, a fishy tail waved in the wind.

"Welcome, Tenente Gomez, to my establishment." The landlord was a Franchen, short and wiry of build with close-set eyes over a sharp nose, a thin-lipped mouth that twisted into a wry smile, and a small tuft of a beard on his chin. His eyes widened as he recognized Halvar.

"Don Álvaro! An honor, to be sure!" He bowed low, pulling off his broad-brimmed hat in respect. "How may I be of service to the Hireling of the Calif, may he have a long and prosperous reign?"

He ushered them into a large room with a stone fireplace at one end, where an Afrikan boy turned a spit on which several fowls were roasting. Their fat dripped into the fire, sending forth aromas that reminded Halvar that three maiz-cakes were not enough to keep a large man satisfied. Several wooden tables sat in front of the long benches that lined the walls, leaving an open space in the middle of the room. A door at the far end implied more beyond, the sounds and smells that emerged indicating a kitchen and someone hard at work within it.

"We're here to see the rooms used by Leon di Vicenza," Gomez said before Halvar could acknowledge the innkeeper's greeting.

"Leon di Vicenza is not here," the innkeeper said.

"We know that. He's dead," Gomez stated bluntly.

The innkeeper gasped.

"What! But...he can't be! He owes me two months rent!"

"What's this about Leon being dead?"

34

The innkeeper's wife, or so Halvar assumed her to be, emerged from the kitchen, a woman both taller and broader than her husband. She also wore Franchen dress—long blue-and-white striped linen skirt and white linen shirt, covered with a long apron stained with the spatters of many meals. An embroidered silk kerchief had been folded into the opening of the shirt for modesty's sake, but it did not quite cover her bounteous bosom. Gray-brown curls straggled out from a lace cap that had not been white for a very long time.

Her broad face was convulsed with fury.

"I told you, Jacques, get rid of him! Didn't I say that he was a troublemaker? Didn't I tell you he wouldn't be worth the custom he brought?"

"Yes, my dear," Jacques said. "My wife, gentlemen. Lizette, some dignity, if you please!"

Lizette recognized Gomez and bobbed a perfunctory curtsey.

Halvar took over the questioning.

"When did you last see Leon di Vicenza?"

Jacques tugged at his little beard in thought. Lizette's heavy brows nearly met over her bulbous nose as she, too, pondered the events of the previous three or four days.

"He was here when we got word the calif's dhow had been spotted," she said at last. "I remember, because he was boasting about what great chums he and Don Felipe were, back when they were students in Corduva at the Madrassa, and how he saved Don Felipe's life in some street brawl."

"He took the knife thrust that was meant for Don Felipe," Halvar agreed. "I was there. I was the one who got the knife away from the assassin, and I was the one who sewed Leon up. So, that much of the story is true. Whatever else he said, that was probably Leon's embellishment. He was good at it."

"He *mentioned* that he knew the Hireling," Jacques added to the tale. "But he wasn't too polite about you, Don Álvaro."

"No, he wouldn't be," Halvar said with a wry smile. "So, this was maybe three days ago? What did he do then?"

"There was a lot of custom," Jacques said apologetically. "I don't know when he left, or with whom."

"Was the Mahak with him?" Gomez asked.

"The one from the forge?" Lizette sneered. "We don't have Locals in here as a general rule, but Leon insisted we make the exception for his catamite."

"Which you did," Halvar observed.

"We built him the outside stair," Lizette said defiantly. "No need for our Oropans to know that a Mahak was upstairs."

"So, Leon could come and go as he pleased, without your knowing," Halvar summed up.

"He could," Jacques admitted. "But I can't say whether he did or didn't. I only know that I haven't seen him. He could have come in without my knowing since the dhow arrived. I can't say for sure."

"Show us the rooms," Gomez demanded.

Chapter 8

JACQUES LED THEM UP A SET OF RICKETY WOODEN stairs at the back of the room.

"When we built this place, Lizette and me, we thought to live here ourselves, but it's not a good thing to live over the shop. We've got another house, in the square behind us, and Lizette thought we could rent these rooms to sea captains who were here for the Feria."

"But Leon came along instead," Halvar finished for him.

"Well, it was after last year's Autumn Feria, and the rooms were empty," Jacques said. "And he was willing to pay more than any captain, and he'd be here permanent, not one time and gone. So, I thought it a good idea, and he painted us a fine sign. Did you see it?"

"We certainly did," Halvar grinned. "Very lifelike."

"He even got Malik the Smith to make the bracket to hold it so all could see," Jacques said proudly. "Everyone in Manatas comes to the Mermaid Taberna."

"If only to listen to Leon spout his nonsense," Gomez grumbled. "Don Álvaro, I've been called down here at least once a week to break up one brawl or another."

"I keep a clean house!" Jacques protested. "But these so-called natural philosophers are worse than sailors when it comes to arguments, and that's a fact. At least sailors fight over things you can understand—women, and gambling debts. When those

37

Seekers of Truth start their debates about whether the sun and moon go about the Earth or the other way around, or which is greater, the Redeemer or the Prophet...?" He shrugged.

"Sounds more like a madrassa than a taberna," Halvar observed.

"The fights were enough to get my men out," Gomez countered. "At least, if they'd stayed near the madrassa, the mullah would have been able to bring his own men to keep them in line. As it was, I couldn't do anything but scold them, what with young Selim in the middle of it all. Sultan Petrus would have had my arse in a sling if anything happened to his darling child."

"Here are the rooms." Jacques opened the door. "There are two, and we put a little roof over the outside stair landing so that visitors could wipe the mud off their shoes before they came inside."

"You put in a glass window," Halvar said, peering through it at the scene below and the river beyond.

"Leon paid for it," Jacques explained. "He said he needed light for his work."

"Work!" Gomez snorted. "Look at this!"

He stood in front of a small table with a triangular stand propped up on it; several little jars were lined up on one side and some quill pens shaved to points of varying sizes on the other. The stand held a board on which Leon had affixed a sheet of paper on which he had sketched a woman, in scanty draperies that covered only her breasts and crotch, lying on some sort of couch. Sitting next to her was a young man, bare to the waist with his hair in the distinctive shaved head and scalplock of Mahak warriors. Behind them loomed a gigantic, muscular Afrikan with a disapproving expression on his scarred face.

The faces were extraordinarily lifelike, even without colors. Halvar recognized one of them at once, although it had been more than fifteen years since he had seen her riding on her father's cart northwards as he had marched to the south.

"Dani Glick," he murmured. "What are you doing in Manatas?"

"Oh, that's Dani Glick, all right." Gomez was at Halvar's elbow. "The other two are Otter Tail and Malik the Smith. Very good likenesses, they are, indeed."

38

"I can see why Mullah Abadul is so angry at him," Halvar said. "This is truly extraordinary. I've seen something like this in Franchenland, where they're starting to make images of the Redeemer and his Mother Mara for the chapels. But this…this isn't Mother Mara, that's for sure!"

Jacques joined them in staring at the drawing.

"It's supposed to be a representation of one of the Old Roumi legends," he explained. "Leon told us the story in one of those debates. Their goddess of love was married off to the gods' blacksmith as a punishment for her pride in her beauty. She took a young lover to spite her husband."

"What a thing to paint!" Gomez exploded in righteous wrath. "And to use real people's faces in it, too!"

Halvar picked up one of the jars of colored ink, sniffed it, and touched it with the tip of a finger.

"Well, well, look at that!" He stepped over to the shelves attached to the wall opposite the window where Leon kept his library. "A reader, was Leon," He raised his eyebrows as he opened first one and then another. "He's got all sorts here— printed Arabi books, and this one's in Ivrit, and this one's in Ogham, from Bretain, and I think this one's in the Muscovy tongue. I don't read any of those, but I know the letters when I see them," he added before Gomez could remark on his scholarship.

"Books!" Gomez sneered. "Images! What does any of this have to do with that dead man in the Feria?"

"I don't know yet," Halvar said. "Is this all the rooms there are?"

Jacques stepped over to the inner door, which was separated from the sitting room by a curtain.

"This is the bedroom."

Halvar scanned the room from the doorway. It was sparsely furnished with a large, well-strung bed, a washstand with a jug and slop-bowl, and a small stand near the bed with an oil lamp on it, ready for use.

"His clothes are still here," Halvar said, noting a jacket hanging on a peg on the far wall.

"He keeps his under-linen in a chest," Jacques said.

"He's not the only one uses this room." Gomez pointed to the other garment hanging beside the jacket, a deerskin shirt in the Local style."

39

"We already know about Otter Tail," Halvar said. He surveyed the room again then sniffed and wrinkled his nose. "He used scent."

"Made it himself," Jacques said. "Testing different plants, making up different colors for his paints. He sold the scents, and the images, too, when he wasn't arguing with customers."

"Which explains how he lived once the sultan ejected him from the Rabat," Halvar murmured to himself. "But it doesn't explain what he's been doing since I got here." He turned back to Gomez. "Tenente, I think we're finished here. Landlord Jacques, thank you for your assistance."

"Oh, it is always my pleasure to help Tenente Gomez, as well he knows," Jacques said, with another low bow. "And the Calif's Hireling as well. If you wish a good meal, and perhaps some food from Oropa—good wheaten bread and wine—you will always find a welcome at the Mermaid Taberna. You don't have to go all the way to Green Village to find good food, good talk, and good wine. We have it right here in Manatas Town."

"And what will I find at the Gardens of Paradise in Green Village?" Halvar wondered aloud as he went back down the stairs.

"Trouble!" Gomez stated.

"Is that all?" Halvar said with a wry grin. "Then perhaps I'd better go there on my own, Tenente. In the meantime, I want you to find anyone who might have seen Leon between the time he left this taberna and the time we found someone in the Feria wearing his coat."

He and Gomez emerged from the taberna in time to hear the muezzin calling for midday prayers. Gomez obediently fell to his knees, while Halvar clutched his amulet.

That done, Gomez eyed him as if trying to fathom what this stranger would do next.

"Malik the Smith's busy at the forge," he noted. "He and Leon worked together. If anyone can tell you where Leon might be, it would be Malik."

"More than that," Halvar said, "that's where the Mahak Otter Tail is supposed to be working. Very well, Tenente, we'll have a chat with Malik."

Chapter 9

THE MERMAID TABERNA STOOD AT THE SOUTHERN end of the brick-paved street that fronted the waterfront. The forge was at the northern end, a brick building set back from the wooden warehouses, surrounded by a stone wall.

"We don't want the fire in the forge to get loose," Gomez explained as he opened the iron gate. "We'd use more brick, but the brickmakers up-the-hills can't keep up with the demand." He waved in a northerly direction.

"Brickworks take water, and wood," Halvar agreed.

"Well, we've plenty of both on the Great River side of Mana-tas Island," Gomez stated. He kicked at some leaves that had drifted down from the trees on the other side of the wall. "Hoy! Malik the Smith!"

The huge Afrikan answered from the inner reaches of the forge, where he was hammering at what looked like a wheel rim while one scrawny Afrikan youth plied the bellows to keep the fire going and another held the work in place with iron tongs. Both boys wore the gold earrings that marked them as slaves, and woolen breeches and heavy leather shoes as protection against the sparks of the forge.

"What is it?" Malik did not look up from his work. He gave one last whack at the wheel rim, grabbed the tongs from his assistant, and plunged the iron hoop into a waiting trough of water. Clouds of steam streamed up, and the two apprentices cringed away from the heat.

Malik regarded the two men with irritation but greeted them politely.

"Salaam aleikum, Tenente Gomez. What brings you here?" He interrupted his greeting to scold his apprentices, who had dropped the tongs on the stone floor of the forge. "Idiots!" he shouted at them. "That's no way to treat good iron tools!" He turned back to Gomez and eyed the second visitor.

"This is Don Álvaro, the Calif's Hireling."

Malik nodded briefly then shouted to his apprentices, "Bank the coals, don't let the fire go out. Then get something to eat, and put strength into those arms of yours." He glared at his two visitors. "I need someone with more sinew around here. Where is Otter Tail, boys?"

"H–haven't seen him," quavered the first apprentice.

"Went off with Leon yesterday," the second offered.

"Leon di Vicenza?" Gomez asked eagerly.

"Leon the Loony!" the first boy sneered.

"Leon the Letch," the other added. "Otter Tail and he went off somewheres."

"Leon's body was found this morning in the Feria." Gomez glowered at the two boys. "Someone took a hammer to him last night."

They gasped in horror.

"We didn't do it!" the first boy exclaimed.

"We was home, in the barracks," the second added. "You can ask anyone! Battu and me, we work the forge, and then we get taken to barracks, right, Baas?"

Malik nodded. "They take them away every night," he confirmed. "Is it true? That Leon is dead?" He shook his head in disbelief. "It doesn't seem right. He was too clever, too cunning, to be murdered."

"You and he were friends," Halvar said.

"We worked together," Malik corrected him. "That doesn't make us friends."

"You don't seem to feel much sorrow at his death."

The smith turned to face his accuser. He was taller than Halvar, with massive arms and chest barely covered by a thin linen shirt. A heavy leather apron protected him from flying

42

sparks, and his woolen breeches were tied up below his knees, showing mended stockings and broad leather shoes. Malik's people had been of the darkest Afrikans, those of broad faces and broad noses, and he bore the scars of their rituals on his chest and cheeks, rituals they continued to practice even though they gave lip service to the Ilha and his Prophet.

"Leon and I grew up together," he said. "We were both with the troops that followed Sultan Petrus to Italia. Difference was, I was the son of a prisoner, he was the son of the sultan's second wife's apothecary. I am a slave, the property of Sultan Petrus." He tapped the gold ring in his left ear. "I do as I am ordered. I was big, and I could learn, and I was set to learn the forge."

"Which explains what you're doing here," Halvar finished the tale.

Malik carefully put the tongs up on a hook set into the brick wall of the forge, alongside the hammers, rasps, and other tools of his trade.

"I came here with Sultan Petrus. I suppose you might say I am one of the lucky ones. I have a little house here at the forge. I may leave the forge to walk about Manatas Town during the daytime, and I even have a Local woman who stays with me when she pleases." His expression darkened. "But I cannot leave this island, not with this." Again he tapped the ring. "I am locked in every night. I can't tear this out myself, and anyone who does will be treated as a thief. All the payment I receive goes to the sultan, not to me."

"And where does Leon fit into all this?" Halvar asked, ignoring Gomez's irritation at his roundabout questioning.

"We hadn't seen each other since he went to Madrassa," Malik explained. "You might say we were thrown together by Fate. He had ideas but couldn't make them real. I can make things, but I can't imagine them."

"So, he came to you with ideas for devices, and you tried to make them work," Halvar summed it up.

Malik nodded. "Most of the things he thought up were impractical, impossible to make. A flying machine? A device to turn a wheel with a rod connected to a pumping-engine?"

Halvar gave that some thought.

"It could be done," he concluded. "I don't know what it would be used for, but I suppose it could be done."

43

"He had another idea—a small stove that would sit in the middle of a room instead of the huge ovens they use in Al-Andalus to heat a house in the winter," Malik said. "That might have been useful."

"Might have been?" Halvar caught the implications.

"He had drawn the plans but hadn't any idea how to put the thing together," Malik scoffed.

"But you could have," Halvar said.

"If I'd had the plans, yes, I could have built it."

Gomez interrupted the conversation.

"Never mind what you could have done," he growled. "When did you last see Leon?"

Malik frowned. "It must have been the day before the calif's dhow was sighted. He wanted to speak to Otter Tail."

"So do we," Gomez rapped out. "Where is he?"

"I wish I knew!" Malik said with an expressive grimace. "I haven't seen him since he walked out of here yesterday afternoon. He was supposed to be here this morning to pick up his tools and finish his work before he left for his own country."

"I thought the Mahak wanted nothing to do with Andalusian ways," Gomez said.

"I've seen plenty of Locals about," Halvar pointed out.

"They're from the Algonkin clans," Malik explained. "They were farmers before Oropans came, and they gave tribute to the Mahak for protection against the Huron in the north. No one wants to fight the Huron. Only the Mahak are willing to go against them, so the Mahak have taken on the task of protecting the other tribes. The Algonkin provide the food, the Mahak the protection."

"Even as in Oropa," Halvar murmured to himself. Louder, he said, "I hear that Leon and this young Mahak were, ah, friendly."

Malik snorted

"Be honest, Don Álvaro. Leon was besotted with Otter Tail. Well, he's a well-set-up lad, and as far as I could tell, he was amenable, but he had an eye for the girls as well as for the likes of Leon."

"What did Leon think of that?"

Malik shrugged. "That I cannot tell you. We didn't talk about Otter Tail. We talked about the work we were doing, what I was making and how he thought it would work."

"Any ideas of your own as to who might have struck him down?" Gomez regarded the Afrikan speculatively.

"Only half of Manatas Town, and maybe another half of Green Village" Malik snorted again.

"Not you, though," Gomez said.

"Every night the gates to the forge are locked," Malik pointed out. "How could I get to the Feria to hit Leon on the head?"

"How, indeed?" Halvar muttered.

"If you want to find out more about Leon, better you should ask at the Gardens of Paradise," Malik said. "He was there when he wasn't bothering me."

"That sounds like a very good idea," Halvar said. "I shall do that."

"If you want me, you know where to find me."

A plump young Local woman appeared at the door with a basket hung on one arm and a baby in a carrying-board strapped on her back.

"Ah, Shining Star—my woman," he explained. "She brings me my midday meal. With your permission, Tenente, Don Álvaro, I will eat it. I wish you luck in finding out who killed Leon, and I wish the killer joy in his accomplishment." He strolled out into the yard, leaving Gomez and Halvar facing each other across the anvil.

"So much for the smith," Halvar said at last. "Well, Tenente, that's that. If I want more answers, I suppose I'll have to get them at the Gardens of Paradise."

"I have to meet my sergeants at the Rabat and get the morning reports," Gomez said importantly. "And I have to make my rounds through the Souk, just to let anyone with sticky fingers know that someone's watching them. You'll have to get to the Gardens of Paradise by yourself, Hireling. As you said, my duty stops at the Manatas Town Wall. After that, you're on your own."

"Tenente, I think I can go from Manatas Town to Green Village by myself," Halvar said. "What I need from you is a list of everyone who might have been insulted or affronted by Leon di Vicenza."

"It will be a very long list," Gomez promised him. "And it will do no good at all."

"That's for me to decide. Just point me in the direction of Green Village."

"North, then west," Gomez told him. "Take a donkey cart and save yourself the shoe leather. It's one white wumpum, and don't let some thieving driver try to chouse you out of any more. You changed your coin for wumpum, didn't you?"

Halvar drew a string of beads out of the inner pocket of his jacket.

"How does it work? One purple shell is the same as ten white ones? Why don't they just use the same copper and silver as we do at home?"

"There's not enough metal coin here in Nova Mundum for ordinary folks. The Locals were using the wumpum before we got here, so it was just as easy for us to do the same.

"Most food and drink goes for one white. Five white is a day's pay for a Local, two purples for an Andalusian, and nothing for an Afrikan slave. Hireling, you take care in Green Village. I wouldn't want word to get back to the calif that his man was so careless as to be taken prisoner by the very man he was chasing."

With that final gibe, Gomez turned his back on Halvar and strutted off, back to the Rabat and his troop of guards. Halvar watched him with narrowed eyes. Then he looked northwards, shading his eyes against the glare of the midday sun.

"Leon di Vicenza," he murmured, "what have you been up to?"

Chapter 10

HALVAR STRODE OVER TO WHERE THE DONKEY-MEN
stood with their carts along the opposite side of the road from
the forge. In Al-Andalus, he would have been surrounded by
them, each one shouting out the fine qualities of his animal
and the beauties and cleanliness of his cart. Here, order pre-
vailed.

The driver of the first cart in the line beckoned.

"Where to, honored sir?" he asked as Halvar got into the cart,
carefully balancing his weight so as not to tip into the dust and
debris of the road.

"I want to go to the Gardens of Paradise in Green Village."

The driver frowned, then shrugged.

"I can take you as far as the Town Wall," he stated. "Once we
get there, you'll be on your own. No Manatas donkeys beyond
the wall. That's the rule, and I'm not the one to change it."

"I see." Halvar handed over one of the white beads from
his string. "What do I do after I pass the wall?"

"Walk, or take another cart. Outside, that's Local country,
and they make the rules. If you don't like 'em, they've got their
own ways of making sure you obey 'em." The driver gave an
eloquent twist of his lips and a jerk of his head.

The donkey plodded along as his driver chattered.

"New to Manatas, are you? It's a fine place, a fine place! Plenty
of work for those who want it."

"Not many beggars about," Halvar noted.

"Ha!" The donkey driver snorted. "Not with Sultan Petrus about, there aren't. Rules, rules, rules, that's Sultan Petrus's way, and he's got that dog Gomez and his Greencoats to enforce 'em. Anyone caught begging away from the Muskat gets set to building the wall or picking the streets clear of garbage. All middens must be cleaned once a month, all latrines twice a year. No one is to throw offal into the street.

"Rules, and more rules! Am I supposed to sweep after the beast? What are the Scavengers for?" He swatted the donkey gently with his long switch, and the animal responded with a loud "Hee-yaw" and a swish of its tail.

"A fine wall," Halvar commented as it came into view.

"Good enough to keep out the bears and wolves," the donkey driver agreed. "But the aragouns and opossoms and sekonks don't care about walls. They go and come as they will. Those are animals, small critters, they feed on the scraps left in the streets. Sultan Petrus is fighting a losing battle trying to get rid of them.

"Better he should think about getting rid of the Bretains and Franchen in Green Village. Here we are, honored sir. One white, as you were told. Although," he added as Halvar started to put the beads back into their hiding-place, "some kindly folk will add a little more, for courtesy's sake."

Halvar grinned to himself and slid one more white bead off the string.

"That's for the information," he said.

He eyed the new wall and decided that, as a means of defense, it was barely adequate. It stood about six feet high, made of large stones set into the same mixture of lime and sand that had been invented by the Old Roumi and was still used extensively in Al-Andalus. The main gate stood open, and one of Gomez's Town Guards lounged beside a small shack, obviously bored, while a motley procession of Locals and Oropans, Afrikans and Andalusians passed back and forth.

"You could march a troop through here, and no one the wiser," Halvar muttered. He joined the parade, swinging past the bored guard without being stopped. "Feria or Village?" he asked himself.

The Feria lay just ahead; he decided to retrace the path from where he had found the body. Perhaps one of the other merchants had seen Leon the night before.

He passed the tally booth, where the calif's tallymen sat at their table, one box full of metal coins, one full of white and purple wumpum beads, carefully doling out the correct sums and noting all of it down for the calif's taxmen to sort out later. He walked between stalls holding stacks of beaver pelts and furs of animals he could not identify, although one heap of small skins looked very much like the minks and martens he had seen in Oropa.

The odors of cooking meats assailed his nostrils, and Halvar remembered he'd not had anything all day but those few maiz-cakes and bean paste. Outside Manatas Town, sausages of swine's flesh were not forbidden. Halvar grinned at an Afrikan woman who had set up a stand with a small brazier, over which she grilled not only sausages but some small fish and the ever-present maiz-cakes.

"Come-a-here, Baas!" she called out, waving one fleshy arm. "Fine, fine food! One white wumpum for a sausage, one white for a drink!"

"What do you have to drink, Mamam?" Halvar asked, as he juggled the sausage folded into a thin maiz-cake.

"Fine sweet cider, Baas. Not nasty firewater, oh, no."

The Afrikan woman handed him a small cup made from folded birch-bark. Halvar sipped and raised his eyebrows appreciatively.

"Not bad, Mamam," he conceded.

Having satisfied hunger and thirst, he continued through the Feria, back to the scene of the crime. Cormack mac-Cormack was watching for him.

"Hireling!" he called out. "Don Álvaro! Hoy!"

"Salaam aleikum," Halvar greeted him.

"A goodly day to you, too. You told me to tell you if I remembered anything about yesterday, and especially when I'd seen Leon di Vicenza."

"And have you remembered?"

"Not me, but the lad," Cormack said, shoving Padraig forward. "Tell him, boy! And pray that the Redeemer will forgive you for abetting in sin!"

49

Padraig stumbled out of the shed, his freckles nearly invisible in the flush that spread across his cheeks.

"It's about Leon," he stammered, staring at the ground.

"You wanted to know what Leon was doing here?" Cormack told Halvar as he glared at his son.

"I...I let him use our stall," Padraig barely whispered. "When he wanted to meet Otter Tail."

"And you left the door unbarred!" his father roared. "And now there's a hammer missing!"

Halvar frowned. "What sort of a hammer?"

"A big 'un," the ironmonger told him. "A sledge. The sort of thing you need when you're ramming earth for a road or setting pegs for a tent."

"Not an easy thing to carry about."

"Not easy to steal, for sure," Cormack agreed. "We usually leave it here in the shed, and bar the door when we leave, and put on a stout lock. Only, that son of mine, that Seeker of Truth, left the lock unlatched so his mentor, that fornicator, could have a meeting in private with the Mahak! Now the hammer's missing, and Leon's face was bashed in, and it's no great stretch to think that my hammer's what did it." He stopped for lack of breath.

"You are sure it was here last night?"

"It was set all the ways in the back of the stall," Padraig said with a glance at his father. "Well out of reach of anyone who might think to just grab it from the door. We take the small things back to our lodgings, the knives and nails and such thieves sometimes steal to sell in the Souk, where no one questions where the goods come from, but a hammer that size? We're the only ones even think to have such a thing, and we don't sell but one or two a year. Mostly to Locals, who use them when they set up their camps."

"Never mind who buys them," Halvar snapped. "When did you see it last?"

"When we left last night," Padraig said.

"And when did you find out that it was missing?"

"I went to the back of the stall when I got back," Padraig said with another look at his father. "That is, after I got back from taking Leon's body to the Rabat. Father wanted me to take the inventory, to see if all was well, and that's when I saw the sledge was missing. I nearly didn't—the picks and spades had been moved so the space for the sledge was filled up. Then I saw that it wasn't there, and I thought...I mean, that awful..." He gulped hard.

"Don't think about that, lad," Halvar said gruffly. "This answers one of my questions about what we found this morning."

"Only one?" Cormack asked with a wry grin.

"I don't think you're the one took the sledge to Leon, if that's in your mind," Halvar assured him. "No matter what he did or didn't do with the lad. If it makes you easier in your mind, I think the worst Leon di Vicenza did with his students was to make them ask questions that have no good answers."

"Oh, that's a comfort, to be sure," Cormack said with another wry grin at his son, who blushed even more furiously.

"Who knew that Leon was in the habit of using this stall for his, um, meetings?" Halvar asked.

Padraig shrugged. "I did, and Otter Tail. It was just something Leon asked of me, when people got nasty about having Otter Tail at the Mermaid Taberna, and I didn't see anything wrong with it. There's no bed or anything..." He stopped in confusion.

Halvar tugged at his mustache to hide a smile at the boy's embarrassment.

"I don't think they did anything more than talk," he assured Padraig. "Now, mac-Cormack, how do I get to the Gardens of Paradise?"

"Just follow this path," Cormack explained. "It leads straight to the middle of Green Village. Then look for the biggest house in the village, surrounded by an iron fence. Just beware, Don Álvaro. There are serpents in Paradise, and some of them look very fine indeed."

"I'll be on my guard. Take care, young Padraig, and thank you for this information."

Halvar set out again towards the Gardens of Paradise and whatever pleasures awaited him there.

Chapter 11

THE DIRT PATH THROUGH THE FERIA WOUND AROUND
a stand of trees and broadened into a road paved with stone
slabs. The afternoon sun threw shadows across the road, making the trees seem taller and darker than they actually were. A
few bushes were already showing signs of approaching winter,
their leaves turning bright orange and yellow, their branches
heavy with red fruit.

Halvar stopped to listen to the sounds of the woods around
him—rustling and chirping of small animals and birds going
about their business and the incongruous clank-clank of the
chapel bell in the distance marking the hours instead of the
muezzin's piercing call. If nothing else, this reminded him he
had left Andalusian territory and was now in lands where Chesu
the Redeemer and Mother Mara the Comforter were worshi-
ped instead of Ilha and his Prophet.

He strode onwards along the road past a few wooden houses
built in the Oropan style, with pitched roofs and high chimneys
to carry away the smoke of the hearth fires within. A plank
bridge crossed over a stream where a group of women in long,
striped skirts, gaily colored shirts, and white caps stopped to
stare at the newcomer before going back to their work slap-
ping clothing in and out of the water.

The sound of the bell that was the signal for the women to
drop to their knees, make the sign of the Crux, and recite the

Old Roumi words came from a chapel somewhere north of the stream. Halvar stopped long enough to recite his usual formula then went on his way, trying to avoid the geese strutting along the road. The birds seemed to assume that all would give way before them and pecked viciously at the dogs that yapped at them from behind the wooden fences that surrounded the houses of Green Village.

The houses were arranged around a central common grazing ground, a grassy patch where tethered donkeys and loose sheep fed while the geese gabbled around them. Some of the houses had shops on the ground floor, visible through open windows whose shutters dropped down to make a counter for the merchandise offered for sale. Halvar sniffed the yeasty odor of baking bread and felt that here, at least, was a touch of home. He might have been back in his old village in the Dane-March.

One building towered over the others, set apart in an enclave surrounded by a fence of iron bars rammed into the earth. Behind the fence, Halvar could see the trees and shrubs of a formal garden, with small tables and chairs set out in what would be a shady resting place in the heat of summer. Now, with the onset of autumn, leaves drifted down from the shading oaks and elms, and most of the sweet-smelling flowers of summer had been replaced by the harsher, hardier, more garish ones that would give way, at last, to snow.

There was an elaborate gate in the fence, guarded by a robust man with a bristling beard, clad in the woolen plaid trews and red coat favored by Bretains. His flattened nose was the result of too many fistfights rather than an inheritance from an Afrikan ancestor.

"Hoy! Is this the Gardens of Paradise?" Halvar called out in Arabi.

"What else would it be?" the guard replied, also in Arabi but with a heavy Erse accent.

"I wish to speak to the owner. Take me to Dani Glick!"

"And who might you be?" The guard eyed him, assessing the plain dress and finding it wanting.

"Halvar Danske, also known as Don Álvaro, the Calif's Hireling." The answer came, not from Halvar, but from the woman who had appeared behind the guard. "Don't worry, Donal, I'll

53

take care of our visitor. Come into the Gardens of Paradise, Halvar, but be wary of serpents."

"Dani Glick." Halvar nodded in greeting.

When he had seen her last, she had been sixteen to his seventeen, a girl with a round face and gray-green eyes, red hair and budding breasts whose mocking laughter had spurred the young Dane to take insane risks.

The hair, seen through a filmy silk scarf, was still red, but Halvar suspected the color might have been enhanced by an infusion of henna. The breasts had ripened and were supported by a leather bodice, laced over a linen shirt in the Franchen style although her skirt was of Bretain plaid wool. Gold bracelets jangled on her wrists and gold chains hung around her neck. Her broad mouth still twisted in a mocking grin, and her voice was still musical, but there was a rough edge that had not been there when Halvar had last spoken to her.

"Shall I say 'salaam aleikum' or "God be with ye?'" Dani asked with a twitch of her lips and a lift of one eyebrow, reverting to the Danic Havar had not heard in many years.

"As you like," he said in his native tongue. "I see you've done well for yourself."

"Come into Paradise and find out."

Halvar followed Dani through the garden and into the house. It had been constructed in the Bretain manner, three stories tall with clapboard siding and shuttered glass windows. A small vestibule separated the main room from the outside elements. A young woman in a plaid woolen dress was stationed there within a small closet, where she stood guard over a rack, doling out tokens to those who wished to leave their coats and cloaks there.

"No weapons here," Dani explained as she nodded to the girl. "You leave the swords at the doo."

"And the knives?" Halvar's hand dropped to the hilt of his serviceable dagger with a lump of amber in the hilt, in the leather sheath that never left his side.

"Only for eating," Dani said, with one of her mocking smiles. "No longer than a hand's length."

"No fighting, then?" Halvar was dubious. He'd never been in any tavern where there had not been at least one brawl per night.

54

"Anyone who gets angry or upset can take their nastiness outside," Dani said firmly. "Donal and his men deal with anyone who doesn't."

Halvar looked around as they passed into the main room of the Gardens of Paradise and felt a wave of nostalgia. The room was filled with square-built tables and chairs of Oropan design rather than the low tables and cushions used in Al-Andalus and the other lands of the Middle Sea. The floor was of planks, sanded and polished, with none of the lush carpeting preferred by those who revered the Prophet. The walls were painted, covered with images, mostly of the local vegetation but some of recognizable people. At least one image made Halvar's eyebrows rise—the same young Mahak he had seen in the sketch in Leon's rooms.

"Leon di Vicenza did these," he stated.

"You've seen his work?" Dani caught the implication. "You've been to his rooms."

"On business only. You must have heard the news. A man was found dead in the Feria this morning. He was wearing Leon's coat and leggings."

"But you don't think it's him," Dani finished for him.

"I know it's not."

"Then why come here?"

"Because everywhere I go, people tell me to stay away from Dani Glick and the Gardens of Paradise," Halvar said.

"So, being Halvar Danske, you simply had to come and find out what the wicked houri was doing so far from home." Dani gave him another mocking smile. "I could ask you the same question, Halvar. How does a simple Dane find himself on the other side of the Storm Sea chasing phantoms?"

"I'm here because I was told to go here," he said bluntly. "What happened to you, Dani Glick? You were supposed to be married off to some trader."

"And so I was."

Chapter 12

SHE FOUND A SEAT AT A TABLE NEAR THE SIDE WALL, under the image of a Local peering out from behind a tree, and beckoned to one of the young men who lounged on the opposite side of the room, where a long table had been set up with jars of uskebagh, bottles of wine, jugs of ale, and platters of small, salty fish and slivers of sausage.

"May I offer you refreshment, Don Álvaro?"

"What do you have? Other than maiz-cake, that is? I've had enough of that today to last me forever."

Dani shrugged, setting her breasts jiggling at the top of her tight bodice.

"Wheat doesn't grow well here," she explained, "but barley does, and the Bretains brew a reasonably drinkable beer from it. And we've got something really unusual, from the Afrikan lands far to the south—batatas!"

"What are those?" Halvar asked. He'd become wary of the strange foods of Nova Mundum, which did evil things to his digestive processes.

"Some kind of root," Dani explained. "They have to be cooked very well, in oil or boiled, but they are very good. I think you will like them. Will you drink ale? Uskebagh? Burnt-wine? All are here at the Gardens of Paradise."

"Not for me, Dani Glick. I will take cider and keep my wits about me," Halvar demurred.

"As you wish, Don Álvaro."

"And you can forget that Don Álvaro business, Dani Glick I'm still Halvar Danske, and I am here to find out what you know about Leon di Vicenza."

"Still the country boy," Dani retorted. "No finesse, just plow ahead. Well, Halvar Danske, all I know about Leon di Vicenza is that he was a pretty boy who never quite got over it. He was clever, he could make images, he had a million ideas, and he never finished anything he started.

"Do you see those paintings on the walls?" She waved her hands about. "He was supposed to do all four walls. He stopped in the middle of the third one because he'd been distracted by the question of why the Great River goes both to and from the sea. That made him start thinking about why the tides rise and fall. And that got him into a vast argument with some of my best customers, the merchants and the captains who ride the tides and the waves and have their own ideas about how they work."

"And you don't like fights."

"I told him to take himself and his debating society back to Manatas Town and that scummy Mermaid Taberna, with its lousy beds and that blowsy Franchen frump in the kitchens who can't boil an egg without burning it," Dani said resentfully. Clearly there was a rivalry between the two establishments, but Halvar didn't see that this had anything to do with Leon and his presumed murder.

"When did you see him last?" he asked.

She rubbed her nose in thought.

"It must have been the night before your dhow arrived," she said at last. "We'd gotten word through the Algonkin runners that a dhow with the calif's sign on the sails had been spotted coming north from the Afrikan settlements, and that it would be here within the day. Leon came down the stairs from his rooms—"

"His rooms?" Halvar interrupted. "He had rooms at the Mermaid. What did he need rooms here for?"

"He used the top attics as a workshop for his image-making and devices," Dani explained. She went on, "He came down the stairs—he said he had always known his dear friend Don Felipe would not desert him, and he got as much attention as that deserved, which was none at all. He'd been telling anyone who'd listen about his friendship with the young calif ever since we got world from Al-Andalus of old Don Carolus's passing from this world to the next."

Halvar digested this with a swig of the cider in his earthenware tankard.

"What did he do then?"

"He left," Dani said. "That was the last I saw of him. Around the noon hour today, comes the word that a body's been found in the Feria, and it's Leon's."

"And what did you think of that?" Halvar persisted.

"That it was a stupid end for such a clever man," ahw snapped. "I thought he must have been set upon by someone he'd angered beyond endurance, and I can't tell you who, because it could have been one of my customers, and I don't want to put any of them at risk. It could have been done at the orders of Mullah Abadul, although that old fart doesn't usually work that way. He just bellows and waves his hands and makes a lot of noise."

"And his reign ends at the Manatas Town Wall," Halvar noted. "Green Village is Oropan, not Andalusian."

"There's an agreement with the Locals," Dani explained. "We may make our town here, just as the Mahak do. They have a settlement across the beaver pond, what we call up-the-hills. Of course, they don't expect us to stay put, any more than the Mahak do."

"Why not? I thought they had towns much like ours, only with long bark houses," Halvar repeated what he had been told by the sailors on the dhow.

"They stay in one place until the shaman tells them it's time to move on. The earth and the water are going bad, says the shaman, and off they go—pack up the longhouse or undo the wigwam and move to a spot about twenty miles away and set up all over again. One day, they'll insist that we move. Until then, Green Village is ours, and here we stay, whatever happens between Oropa and Al-Andalus across the ocean." She ended with a defiant snarl.

"I'd think as a Yehudit you'd stay out of the wars between the Redeemer and the Prophet." Halvar took another swig of cider. It had an odd tang to it, and he decided he liked it.

58

"Yehudit are in the middle whether we like it or not," Dani said with another expressive shrug. "Here in Nova Mundum, Yehudit can't be neutral. We must back either one side or another—Al-Andalus or Franchenland, Mahak or Huron.

"Mauritz, my late husband, found this out the hard way. He tried to sell to both the Mahak and the Huron. The Huron didn't like his selling his goods to the Mahak. They made this very plain."

She stared into space, seeing something that Halvar hoped never to see himself.

"It took him three days to die. They were going to do the same to me, but there was one warrior who wanted to see if the red on my head could be inherited. I spent a winter with them, while he found out."

"You managed to escape," Halvar said.

"The warrior's first wife decided I wasn't going to make a good second wife, and I wasn't going to give them a redheaded baby to play with," Dani said briefly. "I was allowed to leave, with a day's supply of food and a deerskin cape and shoes.

"I suppose Adonai was looking after me, because I met up with some of the fraters who were sent to preach the Good News to the Locals. They got me back to Bretain territory, where I met up with Donal and his brothers who were on their way to set up a tavern in Green Village. And that's my story, Halvar Danske.

"Now, if you please, I have a business to run. If you like, you may stay and enjoy the hospitality of the Gardens of Paradise." Dani beckoned to the nearest server. "Give Don Álvaro the best we have to offer. Let him know that he is always welcome in Paradise."

Chapter 13

HALVAR STRETCHED HIS LONG LEGS AS DANI GLICK left him alone at his table. A slender young woman appeared with a tray of dishes and another jug of the cider. He accepted both and leaned back against the wall to observe the clientele of the Gardens of Paradise.

This seemed to consist partly of the Oropan merchants who came twice a year to the Feria to do business with the Locals as well as each other, and partly of the full-time inhabitants of Green Village, the craftsmen and artisans whose work would be taken back to Oropa. There were a few Afrikans, but they sat at one or two tables apart from the rest and spoke only to one another.

For all the complaints of Gomez and Sultan Petrus, Halvar could make out no Andalusian dress in the crowd. He heard the accents of Erse as spoken in Franchenland and Bretain as well as Arabi, the language used everywhere south of the Alps. He tried to separate the various conversations, but all seemed to blur into one continuous noise as the merchants and crafts-men straggled in, in twos and threes, as the autumn twilight deepened into night.

One dish followed another, and Halvar's mug was never allowed to empty. His nose was tickled by the fumes of hemp sticks at the adjacent tables, mingled with the smoke of tabak leaves from the pipes used by the resident Oropans. There was something he was supposed to do, but he couldn't quite remember what it was. The intense activity of the last three days had left him drained.

The Gardens of Paradise provided more than mere food and drink. Attractive young men and women circulated among the tables, joking with the customers as they served them. Halvar noted a young woman leading one of the visiting merchants up the stairs to the private rooms on the second floor and a young man followed her with another customer.

A band of musicians plucked, tootled and pounded instruments, adding to the din. A storyteller in a mad mixture of plaid coat and striped trousers topped with a red fez recited one of the old tales of the Wise Fools of Gotham, with side references to current events that had most of the room rocking with laughter. Halvar missed most of the local jokes, but he had to grin when the storyteller added the character of "The King's Man" to the tale of how the Fools escaped the clutches of the king's taxman by pretending to be insane.

The storyteller was succeeded by a dancer, who writhed and wriggled, shedding her draperies as she slid between the tables until she was barely covered by a thin silken veil. This she refused to part with as she exited with a wave of her hand.

By this time, Halvar had eaten his way through two fowls and a platter of cooked vegetables and drunk three more jugs of cider. His nose felt stuffed with the odors of hemp and tabak; his ears throbbed with the drumbeats that accompanied the next entertainer, a singer of long and lugubrious ballads.

I don't belong here, he thought. It was time for him to leave.

He lurched up, unsteady on his feet. Immediately, the young woman who had kept his jug filled was at his side.

"Are you not pleased with the Gardens of Paradise, Don Álvaro?" she inquired solicitously.

"Gotta go home," Halvar muttered, and staggered for the door to the anteroom.

A young man caught him as he was about to fall through the door into the gardens outside.

"We will send for a donkey cart," he assured Halvar.

"I can walk," Halvar declared grandly.

"I can summon a donkey cart quite soon," the doorman insisted. Behind him, Halvar thought he heard the jingling of Dani Glick's many bracelets.

"I will walk through the Feria!"

Halvar strode out the door, back into the garden that surrounded the tavern.

The sun had set, and the moon had not risen. The garden was dark, lit by oil lamps strung between the trees that cast shadows on the path as they swung in the freshening wind that came off the Great River. Halvar's midsection spasmed, and he bent over to relieve himself of the food and drink he had so happily ingested.

He caught the movement of the shadow over his head as he spewed up fowl, cider and vegetables. The blow that should have landed squarely on his head fell instead on his left shoulder.

His arm went numb. He staggered across the path into a patch of shrubbery, mentally cursing himself for being fooled into thinking he was safe in this Paradise. His hand went to the knife at his belt, and he swung around to stab his attacker; but another blow fell across his back. Pain lanced his kidneys as he pivoted to face this second enemy. His feet slid on the slick leaves that littered the path, and he skidded across it and landed in another bush, this one filled with dead flowers and thorns.

A third person joined the fight, hauling Halvar out of the bushes and tossing him onto the path, stamping on the middle of his back and grinding his face into the gravel.

Halvar suddenly remembered Old Sergeant Olaf's warning: "Laddie, someday you will go into a tavern where a pretty girl will give you a free drink and a meal, but, laddie, do not take this drink, because that pretty girl will pick your pockets clean and send her brothers to finish you off."

Old Sergeant Olaf, I should have listened to you more closely, Halvar thought. He tried to clear his mind of the haze of alcohol and hemp long enough to take stock of his assailants so he might recognize them if he should ever meet them again.

Three men—two with cudgels, one giving orders. A woman, too, he added, hearing the tinkle of bracelets and smelling a whiff of perfume. He lay with eyes closed as they debated what to do with him.

"I told you I would deal with him," the woman said.

Dani Glick. Still scheming, still thinks she can play me like a puppet.

"He's getting too close," said one of the men in thick Erse-accents.

Donal, Halvar decided. *But what am I getting close to?*

"What are we going to do about him?" A third voice, some-where between the two in tone, with the drawl affected by the students at the Madrassa in Corduva.

Leon, you're here, and alive.

"Leave him to me."

Halvar heard the tap-tap of wooden heels on the gravel.

I've heard that one before, too, he thought just before something hit him in the side of the head, and he fell into a dark, whirling pit of pain and nausea.

Chapter 14

HE WOKE IN A BARE CELL WITH SUNLIGHT STREAMING in through a barred window. His jacket had been removed, and he lay on a plank bed, in his breeches and shirt, under a blanket woven from strips of cast-off cloth. He tried to sit up, but his head whirled, and he fell back, groaning.

He tried to remember what had happened to him after he had been attacked. He recalled the fight, and three men and a woman talking about him. Someone, somehow, had gotten him here, wherever here was.

Once more he groaned and tried to sit up. The Local woman Nokomis poked her head into the room.

"You're awake," she told him, unnecessarily. "I'll have Eva Hakim in to look at you." She sniffed her opinion of his behavior. "Drinking fiery-water and smelling of hemp! Is that how you do the calif's work? Pah!" She gave another snort of disgust as Halvar inched his way upwards.

Nokomis returned with Eva Hakim, who looked him over with scorn.

"Where am I?" Halvar croaked through dry lips. "And where are my clothes? My belt and my jacket? My cap?"

"You are in the House of the Green Crescent," Eva Hakim informed him. "We do not usually admit men, but in an emergency, one may be treated in our anterooms. I have sent for Dr. Moise to come and see you. You don't seem to be suffering from anything worse than overindulgence in cider and hemp, but there are a few bruises that may need tending."

"How…?" Halvar started to ask.

Eva Hakim lifted his shirt to look over his bruises.

"The donkey driver who brought you here said you had been set upon by thieves in the Feria. They must have thought you were carrying metal coin, since they didn't take your wumpum strings, but your jacket was sliced to shreds. Some merchants sew their gold and silver into their clothing to keep it safe."

"It wasn't thieves did this," Halvar stated. "Thor's Hammer! Old Sergeant Olaf was right. The worst thing a soldier can do is let himself be lured into a tavern by some pretty girl."

"You went to see that she-Shaitan, Dani Glick," Eva Hakim said. "What did it get you, besides a sore head and bruises?"

Halvar would have grinned, but the effort made his head hurt.

"I've a good idea as to where your brother is hiding," he said. "And there's something very nasty going on in Green Village, but what it is—that I cannot tell you. Not yet, anyway."

Eva Hakim stood aside as Nokomis ushered in Dr. Moise. The slender Afrikan looked over Halvar's bruises and pronounced him fit to be moved.

"That's odd," Dr. Moise muttered as he examined the round bruise on Halvar's temple. "I've see something like this before."

"Someone kicked me in the head," Halvar told him. "I was whacked by a cudgel, I think, and then, while I was pretending to be unconscious, someone made sure that I was."

"Thorough of them," Dr. Moise commented while his long fingers probed the wound on Halvar's head. "Your skull must be uncommonly thick, Don Álvaro. I find some bruising, but the skin is not broken."

"I had the inside of my cap lined with boiled leather," Halvar explained. "Works as well as mail. Now, if I can have my clothes, I will get on with finding out who killed that stranger in the Feria."

"You are going nowhere, Don Álvaro, until I am certain the blow on your head has not addled your brains," Dr. Moise insisted.

A cry of female indignation announced that another man had invaded the House of the Green Crescent. Tenente Gomez added his bulk to the crowd that filled the tiny room.

"Eva Hakim sent word to the Rabat that you'd been brought here," he said. "I brought your spare jacket, seeing that the one you were wearing got cut up in the fight. And while you were whoring and drinking at the Gardens of Paradise, there was another murder done."

He turned to Nokomis.

"Old Mother, I am sorry to be the one to tell you, but we found the body of your son Otter Tail early this morning in the scavenger's pit. He's been murdered, killed some time last night."

"What!" Halvar tried to sit up but fell back onto the bed, his head still pounding from the combination of blows and overindulgence.

Nokomis let out a shriek of anguish.

"How could this happen! He was supposed to be safe here in Manatas! The sultan gave his promise!"

"How did it come about that Otter Tail was here in Manatas anyway?" Halvar asked. "I was told that although the Algonkin have accepted the Prophet and are welcome in town, the Mahak keep themselves apart from both Andalusians and Orpoans."

"Otter Tail was not made to be a warrior," Nokomis admitted. "So my brother the Sachem thought he might become one of those who make the weapons for warriors. Otter Tail was a good, amenable boy. He did what was asked of him.

"We had many plans for him. He was to return to Mahak country to marry a girl of the Cayugas. It would be a good thing, to have the Mahak united with the Cayugas against the Huron."

"What about Leon? What is the law among the Mahak concerning men loving other men?"

Nokomis shrugged. "Such things happen between young men, warriors, and it means nothing. Otter Tail would do what his mother's brother asked of him. He told me when we last met that he had told Leon about the Cayuga girl and given him a gift, a war club he made at the forge, as a farewell present."

"The club we found in the Feria," Halvar mused.

"Otter Tail wasn't killed with a club." Gomez glared at Halvar. "Can you tell me where you were last night?"

66

"I was at the Gardens of Paradise, as you well know," Halvar snapped back. "And these marks on my back and head show that I was set upon as soon as I left the place. Where's my belt? And my knife? And my cap?"

He fumbled about in the bedcovers.

"Your knife? A dagger, with a lump of amber in the handle?" Gomez's eyes glinted with malice.

"It was given to me by my father," Halvar said. "There isn't another like it in the world."

"Then tell me, Don Álvaro, Calif's Hireling, how did it get into Otter Tail's chest?" Gomez cried out, triumphantly.

"I don't know. I only know that I didn't put it there, any more than I think that Leon di Vicenza would stab his lover. Whoever did this did it for one reason—to silence Otter Tail.

"Eva Hakim, Dr. Moise, I cannot take my ease here while I am accused falsely of murdering the one person I wanted to keep alive. Give me my jacket and my belt and my boots and my cap! Now!"

Eva Hakim frowned at him.

"Are you totally mad, Don Álvaro? You cannot possibly go out now. You must allow your body to heal."

Dr. Moise sighed. "It is of no use, Eva Hakim. This man is a soldier, one of those who refuse to admit that they hurt. Give him his boots, or he will go to the back of the house and find them himself."

"Here, then." Eva Hakim pulled the boots out of a basket in a corner. "And here is your belt, and that cap you are so fond of with the leather lining. And the sheath for your knife, since you insist on it."

Dr. Moise said. "Again, Don Álvaro, I warn you—"

"Dr. Moise, Eva Hakim, I thank you for your care, but I have work to do, and I can't stop now." He turned to Nokomis. "Old Mother, I will find the one who killed your son, you have my word on this."

He turned back to Gomez.

"Now, Tenente," he said grimly, "take me to Otter Tail's body. I am not a murderer, and I will not be taken to the Rabat by you or anyone else until I can prove it."

"Prove to me that you are the Calif's Hireling, then!" Gomez sneered. "How do we know that you are not some impostor? Where is your fatwa, your seal, your orders?"

"I will show them to you when I am ready, Tenente," Halvar said. He stood up, shaky but determined. "Are you ready to follow the calif's orders?"

"I obey Sultan Petrus," Gomez growled.

"And he obeys the calif," Halvar reminded him. "So, Tenente, let us get down to business and find ourselves a murderer."

Dr. Moise followed them out into the street.

"Don Álvaro," the Afrikan said. "A moment, before you go looking for more trouble. You asked me to examine the body that was brought in yesterday. I can now tell you that, whoever he was, this man was most definitely not either Islim or Yehudit. I could not mention such things in front of Eva Hakim, of course," he added, a reddish tint creeping into his dark face.

"Oho," Halvar said. "That narrows the search considerably."

"Of course," Gomez scoffed. "Now all you have to do is question every Oropan in Manatas to find out who is missing."

"If someone known in Manatas were missing, you'd have heard about it by now," Halvar pointed out. "It's not that large of a place. I think our mysterious corpse is that of a newcomer, an Oropan, not Andalusian or Afrikan. I think I should go back to Green Village."

"And let that houri Dani Glick have another go at you?" Gomez snorted scornfully. "Better you should stay at the Rabat and let your head heal before you go traipsing about on Manatas Island on your own again."

"No time for that," Halvar said, settling his leather cap back on his head and shrugging experimentally. "Show me this scavengers' pit, Tenente. Dr. Moise, thank you for your time, but I heal fast. I'll rest when I'm dead."

"That may be sooner than you think," Gomez muttered as he strode off, his heels tapping the bricks of the street that crossed Manatas Island.

Chapter 15

THE MORNING WAS WELL ADVANCED, A CLEAR AUTUMN day with only a few small clouds to mar the blue of the sky. Halvar blinked at the strong sunlight and winced as it penetrated his eyeballs, but he would not give in to his pain.

Gomez pointed the way across the island to the scavengers' pit, a stretch of gravel and sand at the western end of the Wall.

"This was Sultan Petrus's idea," he explained. "Before he got here, folks just threw their trash out into the street for the wild dogs to pick up.

"Then the sultan got Achmet the Beggar to keep order among the beggars and thieves and set them to collecting the rubbish, the odds and ends of foodstuffs householders throw out—and the night-soil from the chamber pots, that gets collected, too. Animal corpses, donkey dung, nothing is to remain on the streets of Manatas longer than a day." Gomez strutted with pride.

"There's been no plague in Manatas Town since the sultan came," he bragged, "and he says it's because he believes with the Prophet, may his name be blessed, that dead things bring evil upon the place that harbors them. All the dead are buried outside the Manatas Wall."

"What does Mullah Abadul have to say to that?" Halvar wondered.

"Oh, he agreed to a burial ground—one part for the True Believers, one for the Kristos. The Yehudit have their own place near the Great River."

The stench of the pit could be smelled long before it was seen.

"What happens to all this stuff?" Halvar wondered.

"The Scavengers sell the dung to the farmers up-the-hills to fertilize their fields. Locals prefer to put a fish in their maiz plots, but donkey dung works just as well. The rest of it gets picked through, just in case there's something worth selling."

Halvar dismissed the economy of garbage in Manatas with a wave

"Where was Otter Tail found? Who found him? When was he found?"

A burly Andalusian dressed in a stained and tattered caftan and shabby turban, his face disfigured by smallpox scars, sidled up to Gomez, salaaming ostentatiously.

"Tenente Gomez, Salaam aleikum. May Ilha, the All-Merciful, his name be praised, bless your work," he said between bows.

"This is Achmet, the Emir of the Scavengers," Gomez introduced him, with a wry grimace. "He's in charge here. Achmet, this is Don Álvaro, the Calif's Hireling. He wants to know all about this Local you found here."

Halvar's nose quivered under his mustache at the odor of garbage and offal that clung to the garments the scavenger had rescued from the rubbish-heap.

"First, show me where it was found," he ordered.

"It still lies there," Achmet said with an apologetic glance towards Gomez. "One of my boys found him early this morning when we came with the night-soil. We take it to the offal-pit, not to be mixed with the other stuff, the stuff we sift through," he added. "Sometimes we find good stuff in that, and the sultan in his mercy allows us to sell it, so that we can buy food and not depend on the good will of the Faithful, even though the Prophet, may his name be blessed, says all the Faithful should give alms to the poor."

"Which pit was Otter Tail lying in?" Halvar asked as Achmet led him to the site, a cleared space between the end of the wall and the rushing river. A fire smoldered between a hole in the ground that reeked of human and animal waste and a pile of twigs, leaves, and bits and pieces of human debris—broken pottery, scraps of cloth, wood shavings and leather snippets.

"He wasn't exactly inside the pit," Achmet explained. "He was between the dung-pit and the brushpile."

70

"Why is he still there?" Gomez blustered. "I told Nahum to take him back to the Mahak."

"The Mahak have come to see him for themselves," Achmet said.

"So they have," Gomez muttered.

Three Local men in breechclouts and macassins stood over the body of Otter Tail. None of them seemed to mind the chilly breeze that blew off the Great River and had Halvar wishing he still wore his heavy leather jacket.

"What cheer?" Gomez greeted them. "There's your friend, you can take him back with you and leave the rest to me."

"What rest?" The leader of the group, a tall Mahak whose status was indicated by a breastplate of animal bones decorated with dyed porcupine quills glared at him.

"The knife belongs to this man," Gomez announced, indicating Halvar. "He admits that he doesn't know what he did last night."

"I know what I did," Halvar rebutted him. "I got drunk and was set upon. I didn't kill anyone, and I had no reason to kill young Otter Tail. In fact, I wanted to talk to him, to find out what he knew about Leon di Vicenza." Halvar peered down at the body. "What's more, I don't think this is the knife that killed him." He pointed to the wound. "This was done after he was dead. Turn the body over, and let me take a closer look."

The Mahak jerked his chin at the other two, who obeyed silently.

Halvar let out a long sigh.

"See for yourself, Mahak. Here's a stab in the back, deep enough to reach the heart. It was done with a blade much longer and wider than my dagger. I didn't do this, and only a fool, or someone with a grudge against me, would insist that I did."

He stared pointedly at Gomez, who flushed with anger under his bristling black beard. Then he frowned down at Otter Tail's body.

"Is this exactly how you found him?" he demanded. "Where are his shoes?""

Achmet yelled at the crew behind him.

"Rachev! Osman! You thieves! Give back the macassins!"

Two of the scavengers were thrust forward by the others. One had only three fingers on his right hand, the other had no left hand at all.

71

"They weren't doing him any good," the taller one, Rachev, whined.

"We can get at least three white for them at the souk," Osman added.

"Where are they? Show me!" Halvar ordered.

Rachev reached under his ragged shirt and brought out a well-worn pair of macassins, the soft leather shoes worn by the Locals.

"Very nice beading on them," Halvar commented. "But one of the beads is missing."

"Enough!" the Mahak warrior declared. "We will take Otter Tail back to our village, and you, Calif's Man, you will explain yourself to my sachem."

"Gladly!" Halvar agreed. "There are a few questions I have to ask, and it may be that you and your sachem can answer them."

"And what am I supposed to tell Sultan Petrus?" Gomez wanted to know. "He ordered us to keep him informed."

"Inform him that whoever killed the man in the Feria killed Otter Tail. Then tell him that I want to speak to that son of his as soon as I have returned from the Mahak camp," Halvar declared.

"*If* you return," Gomez muttered as Halvar followed the three Mahak around the Wall and onto a faint trail that led to the interior of Manatas Island.

Chapter 16

THE TRAIL FOLLOWED THE COURSE OF A SMALL STREAM, skirting a pond where a family of beavers was stocking their larder for the coming winter. The largest male slapped his tail onto the water at the approach of humans, and Halvar chuckled as he watched the animals upend and dive for cover.

"I see these beavers have escaped the traps," he commented. "I thought this island was hunted out."

"They are our clan-animals," the young Mahak said curtly, as if that explained everything.

The path led up a hill to a clearing where a palisade of logs had been set up, with an opening at the western end. A gate of woven branches stood open, and a Mahak stood guard, armed with a war club of the same sort Halvar had found near the body in the Feria.

"We have Otter Tail's body," Halvar's guide said. "And we have the one whose knife was found with it."

"We will make him pay!" The guard fairly gloated. "The knives are ready, the fire is hot!"

"Not yet," Halvar warned him. "I want to speak to the sachem—now! I didn't do this, and I can prove it."

"How? By swearing some oath?" The young Mahak spat his contempt for Oropan or Andalusian veracity.

"No," Halvar said. "By looking at Otter Tail and seeing what he has to say for himself."

"The dead do not speak," the Mahak said with a sneer.

"Oh, but they do, to those who are willing to listen," Halvar countered. "Take me to the sachem, and let him decide."

The Mahak jerked his chin at the ones who were carrying Otter Tail.

"Take him to the women," he ordered. "I will bring this one to the sachem. He will not escape!"

They pushed Halvar forward, past rows of longhouses to what would have been called the central square or plaza in Al-Andalus. Instead of a fountain or Old Roumi statue, there was a fire laid out in a pit lined with stones; two Local men sat next to it on stumps, while three women stood behind them.

The entire Mahak population had come out to mourn the fallen youth and to execute his killer. They made their feelings all too clear, shouting and waving hatchets and war clubs. Halvar could not understand the words, but the intention was obvious.

He strode confidently through the barrage of hatred with steady steps, keeping his eyes on the sachem and his counselors. He had met the Mahak Sachem, Grey Goose Feather, briefly during the ceremonies when he had landed in Manatas Town, but this was the first time he was able to assess the man on whose goodwill the entire enterprise called Feria depended.

Halvar judged him to be as old as Sultan Petrus but much more fit, his wiry body visible since he wore only breechclout and legging. This left his torso bare except for a ceremonial breastplate of animal bones and porcupine quills similar to the one worn by Halvar's Mahak guard. He did not have the warrior's standing hair-roach and scalplock but had wound a length of patterned cloth around his head into a turban, decorated with the feathers of a wild goose, his totem-animal.

"Salaam aleikum, Noble Sachem," Halvar greeted him in Arabi. "I regret to tell you of the death of Otter Tail, one of your young men."

"He was my sister's son," Gray Goose Feather stated. His expression remained stern. "I am told you were the one who killed him."

"That is an error," Halvar said carefully, not wanting to call anyone present a liar to his face. "It is true that my knife was found on the body, but that is not what killed him, and I was not there when it was done."

"So you say!" sneered the young Mahak.

Halvar looked at the youth, then back at the sachem.

"Your firebrand over there tends to speak before he listens," he said. "If you will allow me to explain, I will tell you why I could not have done this evil thing."

"Heh!" one of the Mahak in the crowd chortled. "That's a good name for him! We will call him Firebrand, until he cools his hot head!"

There was a chorus of good-natured agreement from the other Mahak.

Gray Goose Feather ignored the interruption and jerked his chin at the escort, who shoved Halvar down to squat beside him.

"Why should I believe you?" the sachem asked.

"Don't believe me, believe your own eyes," Halvar retorted. "Look at Otter Tail. His body is stiff. He was not killed last night, he has been dead at least a day. I have been in sight of everyone in Manatas Town since yesterday morning, when I found the body of a man in the Feria." He pulled at his mustache and grinned sheepishly. "I'm too big to be lost in a crowd, especially here in a place where everyone is known and a newcomer will always be marked."

"You were seen in Green Village last night," Gray Goose Feather said with a knowing smile.

"I was. I have the headache to show that I took too much of what you call fiery-water, and the bruises to show that I was beaten for my foolishness," Halvar admitted ruefully. "But I did not kill anyone. I am not a Bear-shirt—"

"A what?"

Halvar had translated literally from his native Danic to Arabi, the only language the two of them had in common.

"In my country, there is a legend of warriors so fierce they run into battle wearing only a bearskin," Halvar explained. "I am not such a man. If I must kill, I do it under orders, or I do it with reason."

"When did Oropans or Andalusians need reasons to kill Mahak?" Firebrand shouted.

A chorus behind him muttered agreement.

Halvar willed himself to remain calm. Any sign of fear would be interpreted as weakness.

"I did not know Otter Tail, but I wanted to ask him questions about Leon di Vicenza," he said. "I heard he had become very friendly with Leon."

Gray Goose Feather grunted his opinion of that friendship.

"It was over," he stated firmly. "I told Otter Tail he would go back to our country as soon as the Feria was finished and marry the Cayuga girl before the snow fell. There would be a fine son for her brothers to rear by the next Fall Feria."

"When did you last see Otter Tail?" Halvar asked.

"What does it matter?" Firebrand interrupted again.

Gray Goose Feather had had enough.

"Be quiet!" he ordered. "Or go cool your hot blood in the Great River! This man speaks with good sense. Let him finish." He turned back to Halvar. "I am willing to listen, but be warned, I will not allow my sister's son's death to go unavenged!"

"I am of the same opinion," Halvar assured him. "And if you will allow me to examine Otter Tail, right here in front of all of you, I will prove I am not the one who killed him."

He stepped over to the litter where Otter Tail's body lay.

"Look at this wound in his chest." He pointed to where his dagger had been found. "There is no blood here. You are all hunters, you know that the blood stops flowing when the heart is pierced. This wound was made after Otter Tail was dead."

There was a mutter of agreement among the Mahak.

Halvar gently turned the body over.

"Here is the wound that killed him," he stated, pointing to the slash in the middle of the back. "This bled—you can see it, although the bleeding was mostly inside."

There was muttering among the Mahak,

Halvar continued. "I think Otter Tail was killed near where we found the man in Leon's coat then kept somewhere else and brought to the scavengers' pit later."

"Why?" Gray Goose Feather demanded.

Halvar tugged at his mustache as he thought aloud.

"Otter Tail was killed because he saw or heard something that made him dangerous to whoever did the first killing. That happened before I got to the Feria yesterday morning."

He turned Otter Tail over again. His eye was caught by a mark on the dead Mahak's face. He frowned in concentration, and his hand went up to his own forehead, where he touched a similar bruise. He looked at Gray-Goose Feather.

"Have I offered enough to prove my innocence, Noble Sachem?"

Gray Goose Feather frowned, mulling the evidence before him in his mind.

"If you did not do this, then who did?"

"That is what I am trying to find out," Halvar assured him. "I think last night's beating was a warning."

"Which you are not going to take," Gray Goose Feather said with a wry smile.

"I do not take orders from thieves and murderers," Halvar declared.

"You take orders from some sachem far away, across the great water," Firebrand sneered.

"I do," Halvar stated. "And those orders are to find Leon di Vicenza. If he is dead, I will find out who killed him, and why. If he is not dead, I will find out why his coat was on a stranger, and above all, I will find out who killed Otter Tail, who was simply in the wrong place at the wrong time."

"In this, you will get all our assistance," Grey Goose Feather announced. "You, Firebrand, you will go with Don Álvaro to the Square-house place. Stay with him and make sure he does not go on one of the big boats until he has found out who killed Otter Tail."

"And what will you do then?" Halvar asked, dreading the answer.

"Then we will deal with him, in our own way," Firebrand replied with a fierce grin.

Halvar struggled to his feet.

"Noble Sachem, I will name the murderer, but it will be up to Sultan Petrus to decide what to do about punishing him," he warned.

"Find him first, then worry about what to do with him," Gray Goose Feather ordered.

Halvar turned to his new companion.

"Come along, then, Firebrand. I hear your people are good hunters of deer and other large animals. I will show how my people hunt men."

Chapter 17

FIREBRAND LED HALVAR THROUGH THE MAHAK VIL-
lage into the wooded hills of Manatas, to a small clearing at the
top of the hill where the trail to Green Village wound down
into the trees past the beaver-pond.

"There," he said, pointing to the roofs of the houses that
could be seen through the trees. "There are the Square-houses,
where the Oropans live. Do you really think you will find the
killer of Otter Tail there?"

Halvar nodded. "Oh, he's there, I'm sure."

"Then I will come with you, and I will take him back with
us, and we will make him pay for it!" Firebrand hissed.

"Tell me about Otter Tail," Halvar said as they started down
the hill, fully aware that two more Mahak had followed them
from the longhouses, both armed with war clubs and sharp
steel knives bought from the Bretains at the Feria. "You must
have liked him very much, to be so hot to punish his killer."

"He was my clan-brother," Firebrand said. "He would follow me about when we were boys together, and I thought him
a pest, a nuisance. Like the otter's tail, wag-wagging behind,
without much real use. He'd step on twigs and startle the deer
when we were hunting, and he'd slip the traps and let the
animals loose. But that was clumsiness, not malice. He was not
like that. He only wanted to be friends with everyone. He'd do
whatever was asked of him, if only they would like him."

Halvar nodded again. "What did you think of his friendship with Leon di Vicenza?"

Firebrand snorted his indignation.

"That one! Always asking questions about things that needed no answers. Making pictures—images they call them—of our people. Even went so far as to learn some of our language, and all because he was besotted with Otter Tail."

"Not heard of among your people?"

Firebrand shrugged dismissively.

"Oh, there are stories about warriors who were more than friends, but only stories. No one takes them seriously. It is a man's business to take a wife and get sons and daughters upon her."

"So," Halvar summed up, "Otter Tail was willing to be Leon's playmate in Manatas, and he was just as willing to go home to his own people and marry the girl his uncle and mother told him to marry."

"What does it matter?" Firebrand snarled. "He's just as dead as if he'd stayed in Manatas and made iron tools for the Oropans and Andalusians."

Halvar seized on the thought.

"Whose idea *was* that? I'd heard that none of you Locals, Mahak or Algonkin, wanted anything to do with Oropan or Andalusian iron tools or pots, other than to buy them."

"Oh, we would make them ourselves if we could—those hard tools, the axes that cut better and keep their edges longer, and the cloth that does not stiffen like deerskin, and the firearms. Especially the guns! If we had those, we could clear those Huron out of their tents and out of our lands!"

"'But you don't have the skills or the materials to make them," Halvar finished for him.

"If Otter Tail had been allowed to live, we would have had them," Firebrand stated. "That was my uncle the sachem's plan. Otter Tail was no warrior, but he could learn from the Andalusians and Oropans, and then bring his knowledge back to us. Whoever killed him must have known this and wanted to deny us that knowledge."

"That is why you think he was killed?"

"Why else?"

"I think it was as *I* said. He was in the wrong place at the wrong time, and he saw something he was not supposed to see, someone in a place they were not supposed to be. He was killed before he could tell anyone what that was."

"How do you know this?" Firebrand demanded. "Do you have the shaman's gifts to talk to the dead?"

"The dead speak through what they leave behind," Halvar said, showing Firebrand the blue bead. "This was near the body we found yesterday in the Feria. It's the kind of bead your people use on their macassins

"It wasn't from the ones on the body, and the Oropans who use that trail wear brogans—the leather shoes with thick soles that tie around the ankles. Today I saw Otter Tail's macassins, and there's a bead missing from the design on one shoe." Halvar held up a hand, imitating the pose of the teacher at the Madrassa. "Conclusion: Otter Tail was at that place where the body was found."

Firebrand had followed the argument.

"So, if Otter Tail was there…"

"He either did the deed, or saw who did it," Halvar finished. "Everyone tells me how mild-mannered Otter Tail was, how he was never angry. Whoever did that murder was *very* angry, so that murder was not in Otter Tail's nature. Therefore, it would be very unlikely for him to have done it."

"So, what do you think happened, Don Álvaro?" one of the other Mahak, who had been listening to the conversation, put in.

"What I think is this," Halvar said. "I think that Otter Tail and Leon had a meeting near the ironmonger's stall. I think Otter Tail gave Leon the war club as a parting gift and explained that he was leaving. I think Leon had one of his temper fits, and they quarreled, and Otter Tail went away. Then someone else came along."

"Who?" Firebrand asked.

"I don't know yet," Halvar admitted. "But when we get to Green Village, I am going to find out, because that person is the one who was killed, and Otter Tail saw it because he went back to make it up with Leon before he left him for the Cayuga girl."

"That would be in his nature," Firebrand agreed. "Otter Tail hated to quarrel with anyone."

They moved along the narrow path, back through the afternoon shadows, past the beaver pond. Halvar heard the rustle of small animals scurrying to get out of the path of the huge ones who were marching through their territories, while insects whirred somewhere in the leaves above them. He smacked at a mosquito that landed on his arm just as the beaver in the pond smacked his tail as a warning to the others to hide.

Firebrand's hand went to the club that swung from his belt. Halvar smelled something all too familiar and shoved the young Mahak down as a pellet whizzed past where his head had been. It buried itself in a tree across the trail as a loud bang shocked the small creatures in the woods into flight.

"Thor's Hammer!" Halvar swore. "They've got guns! Pistoias, or muskets."

"Where are they?" Firebrand was back on his feet.

He got his answer as two men jumped out of the shrubbery, long knives at the ready, while a third somewhere behind them fumbled with something that smelled of burning kutton.

Chapter 18

HALVAR LET THE MAHAKS DEAL WITH THE SWORDSMEN and launched himself at the shooter, intent on retrieving the weapon before it could be loaded again. He crashed through dry leaves and branches towards the sounds of clicks and the smell of black powder, with which he had become familiar on the back streets of Corduva and Savilla in Al-Andalus. The shooter was trying to reload, but it would take at least a minute, maybe more.

In that minute, Halvar's long legs carried him through the underbrush to where a man in the long green coat and high-crowned tarboosh of the Manatas Town Guard was fumbling with a pistoia.

"I see you! Stop!"

He ran, hoping to get to the man before he could reload and fire again, but the shooter turned and ran down the path into the darkness. Halvar followed, stumbled over a root and collided with a fourth man who had been stationed to protect the first pistoiero.

Halvar grabbed his attacker by the ears and banged his head against the nearest tree. He could barely see, but he could still smell the smoldering cord every shooter had to carry to light the powder in the pan that would send the lead bullet to its mark. He tossed the watcher into the underbrush and headed down the trail after his first quarry.

At a bend in the trail, the shooter turned and fired once more then fled toward Green Village. Halvar felt the sting of the bullet in his shoulder and let out a cry of pain. Inwardly, he cursed all inventors, especially those who had devised gunpowder and all the weapons that used it.

Behind him the fight had ended with one Mahak clutching his arm, one leaning against a tree, and Firebrand standing over last of the attackers, a man in Bretain trews and red smock. With one swipe of his war club, the Mahak demonstrated just how effective a weapon it was before Halvar could stop him.

"I wanted to talk to that man!" he croaked, wincing at the pain in his shoulder. He didn't think the bullet had shattered the bone, but he was bleeding, and his arm was numb.

Firebrand grabbed a handful of moss from the nearest tree trunk and stanched the bleeding as best he could.

"Brother Beaver gave us warning," he said.

"Brother Beaver didn't smell that match," Halvar retorted. "That was me. Get me to Green Village. They should have someone there to get this lead out of my shoulder. You have to do it fast," he explained as Firebrand looked him over. "There's some kind of poison in those bullets. If they stay inside, they rot the flesh."

Firebrand looked grim.

"I do not go to Green Village," he stated.

"Well, laddie, someone has to get me there, and you're the closest. Your sachem told you to stick with me, and you obey your sachem the way I obey my calif. I just wish you had waited before you used that club on our friend there."

"No friend of mine," Firebrand spat out. "Using fire-sticks on the trail!"

"He didn't do this for his own pleasure," Halvar said. "He was under orders. I want to know who gave them. I've been waiting for someone to make a mistake, and they just made it."

"By shooting at you?"

"Pistoias are not so easily come by," Halvar said. "Expensive toys for Oropans, not common even in Al-Andalus. Get me back to Green Village, and I'll have another chat with my old friend Dani Glick. If she's not behind this, she knows who is."

Firebrand propped Halvar against a tree while he conferred with the other Mahaks. The one with the cut headed back to the

Mahak camp, while the other shouldered past Halvar and headed towards Green Village.

"I've sent word ahead of us," Firebrand told Halvar. "They should come with a cart for you."

"Help me walk," Halvar gritted out.

"You cannot—"

"Thor's Hammer, man, get me on my feet, and I'll move them!" Halvar staggered forward.

"You are as stubborn as a Mahak!" Firebrand grumbled.

He got Halvar's good arm around his neck, and they walked slowly down the hill towards Green Village. They were met halfway by one of the omnipresent donkey carts, driven by a Kristo frater in the brown robes of the Begging Order.

The frater tut-tutted as he lifted Halvar into the cart.

"You should not be walking about," he scolded.

"I didn't have much choice," Halvar retorted. "Do you have a good surgeon at your fratery? One who knows about wounds caused by firearms?"

"I will take you to Frater Iosip. He fought in the Oropan Wars," the frater assured him.

" I will stay with Don Álvaro," Firebrand stated.

"Afraid that I'll run away?" Halvar asked.

"Not with that wound," Firebrand said. "But I want to make sure one of those fraters comes to take the dead Oropan off the trail. He must go back to his own people. We do not want his spirit to stay here to do us harm."

The frater made the sign of the crux.

"I will send another cart for him," he assured Firebrand. "He must not be buried in unhallowed ground."

Halvar sank into a restless doze until he felt hands tugging at him. He opened his eyes to see the broad face and blue eyes of a man who must be Frater Iosip peering at him through glass lenses set into gold frames perched on a large red nose.

"So, this is the famous Halvar Danske, the Calif's Hireling," the frater said in Erse-accented Arabi.

"I wish I were not so famous," Halvar muttered. "It seems to draw too much unpleasant attention."

He hissed as Frater Iosip probed the wound in his shoulder.

"A good thing you came here," the frater said. "The ball penetrated the muscle but did not reach the bone."

"Can you get it out?" Halvar asked.

"Of course I can get it out." Frater Iosip said testily. "I'm not some Mahak witch-doctor to wave a rattle and call it medicine, nor an Andalusian who pretends that black powder doesn't exist. I've dug lead out of more men than I care to recall."

"When you do, don't toss it away. I want to keep it."

"As a memento of a close escape from the Hand of the Destroyer?"

"As a way of finding the one who shot me."

Frater Iosip had set a daunting collection of polished knives and probes on a table, next to a lit candle. He passed the knife through the candle-flame three times, murmuring a prayer in Erse, then made the sign of the Crux.

"That should keep the evil spirits away," he said with a satisfied nod. Then he turned back to Halvar. "Drink this," he ordered, pressing a small cup to Halvar's lips. "It's a potion of poppy juice and willow bark. It will dull the pain."

Halvar jerked his head away from the cup.

"Just do what you have to do and get that lead out of me before it poisons my whole arm. I've been through this before, Frater. I know how long that stuff can knock you out, and I cannot—"

"You cannot do anything until I get that bullet out," Frater Iosip observed. "And I do not want you bounding about while I do it. You, Mahak, make yourself useful. Hold him down until that poppy juice does its work."

With a practiced hand, he seized Halvar's jaw, forced his mouth open and poured the stuff in, making sure that it got swallowed. Halvar downed the drink, grimacing at its bitterness and coughing as it went down.

Within minutes, he was muzzily aware of more faces hovering over him, and voices coming from afar. Then there was a searing pain in his shoulder, and he fell into another dark pit of unconsciousness.

Chapter 19

HE WOKE UP ON A STRAW MATTRESS LAID ON A PLANK bed in a wood-paneled room. As his eyes cleared, he thought he saw two people peering down at him from a window in the wall.

Then he realized the faces were not real, but a startlingly lifelike painting of Chesu the Redeemer and his Mother Mara, standing on a cloud in the middle of a blue sky with golden rays surrounding their heads, set into a frame of gilded wood shaped to look like more clouds.

It took another minute before Halvar recognized the faces. *Did Don Felipe ever fancy himself the Redeemer?* he asked himself. As for Mother Mara, he hoped the formidable Queen-Mother Zulaika never found out that she had been used as a model for the Redeemer's mother

He heard the jingling of bracelets and tried to lift his head to see who was there.

"You're awake."

Dani Glick moved into his line of vision. She had discarded her houri's garb for a modest wool jacket; her red hair was neatly covered with a white lace cap of the kind worn by Yehudit wives. Her bosom was concealed by a white kerchief tucked into the front of her blouse, but she had kept the golden bangles and chains that were her fortune on her person. Her green eyes glittered with malicious enjoyment at Halvar's weakened state.

"Small thanks to you, I'm not dead," Halvar muttered through dry lips. "Can I have something to drink? Not that cider of yours, either," he added.

"Water, pure from the well," Dani assured him, holding the cup to his mouth as he struggled to sit up. "And don't try to move. You've got a nasty wound there."

"I was beaten up last night and shot this afternoon. Or is it night?"

"You've been asleep these twelve hours," Dani said. "It's just past dawn."

"Thor's Hammer!" Halvar swore. "Twelve hours? Anything can happen in twelve hours! I've got to get him." He shifted angrily on the bed.

"You are hardly in a state to get anyone or anything," Dani told him, holding him down with one hand. "Even a hero like you needs to let his body heal."

"Where is he?" Halvar gritted out, trying to sit up. He hissed at the stab of pain in his shoulder. "Where is that—"

"Frater Iosip is at his prayers," Dani said, deliberately misunderstanding him. "The Mahak lad went back to his village to tell his sachem what happened."

"That's not who I meant, and you know it," Halvar said. "Dani Glick, where is Leon di Vicenza?"

"I heard he was dead."

"You know he's alive," Halvar retorted. "I heard his voice the night you drugged me. That painting on the wall was done by none other."

Dani pouted. "What if it was?"

"You're giving aid and comfort to a dangerous criminal," he warned her.

"Nonsense!" She sniffed. "Leon's no criminal. At least, not a dangerous one," she amended. "Leon wouldn't hurt a fly."

"He's hurt at least one man that I know of," Halvar insisted. " Of course, that was back in Al-Andalus. You yourself said he's flighty. Just how long do you intend to keep him here?"

"As long as he cares to stay," Dani said defiantly.

"And then?"

She shrugged, setting her many chains and bracelets jingling.

"I suppose he will go his own way But until he does, he's going to be very useful to me."

"Making images?" Halvar jerked his chin at the painting
"Doing what I ask of him."

"With or without Otter Tail?" he taunted.

"Otter Tail doesn't matter anymore. Leon didn't kill him, that's all I know. He was so upset when he found out it was all that I could do to stop him from rushing back to Manatas Town to find the one who did it."

There was a rap at the door, and Frater Iosip stepped into the room, Firebrand behind him.

"Don Álvaro, may the Redeemer be praised, you are looking well," the frater greeted him. "How does the shoulder feel?"

Halvar moved it gingerly.

"It hurts," he acknowledged, "but I can sit up."

"Good." The frater checked the linen bandage that held a pad over the wound. "This is healing well, no redness, no pus. I have bound a small poultice made from the Holy Bread over the wound. Leave it be—the mold seems to help the healing. You will keep that arm."

"That's good to know," Halvar said dryly.

"You should attend the Holy Meal and give thanks to the Redeemer," Frater Iosip told him. "After all those years in Al-Andalus, you have a good deal to make up for. You must do this quickly, or risk the consequences in the next life. And for your information, Halvar Danske, we follow the Bretain Rite, not the Roumi. You will have to go to the waterfront chapel for the Roumi Rite." He sniffed, dismissive of the rival sect's theological errors. "They may risk eternal damnation in the next life, but you should not."

"I'm more interested in this life than the next one," Halvar told him. "As for which rite we use, the fraters come and go in the Dane-march so often that we take the Holy Meal from whoever wants to give it to us, and no questions asked about whether we say the words in Erse or Old Roumi.

"In Al-Andalus the students who come to study from Bretain and Franchenland and even Italia are allowed their own chapels, so long as they pay the *dhimmi* tax and do not bother the followers of the Prophet with their quarrels over what the Redeemer said or did not say. In fact, one of the fraters from the Italia chapel in Savila was on the boat with me. How is he? Has he recovered his stomach? He was heaving all the way across the Storm Seas."

Frater Iosip looked puzzled.

"Do you mean Frater Leonidas? He came to us two, no, three days ago, but he was not ill. In fact, he looked quite healthy and fit for someone who had been at sea two months."

Halvar heaved himself up.

"I want to see this Frater Leonidas," he insisted. "Get me out of this bed, Dani Glick, I will not be put off any longer! Get me my breeches and my jacket. And my cap."

"Breeches, boots, belt, cap—those you may have," Dani said. "But your jacket is gone, destroyed. That bullet tore a hole no tailor will ever mend. I'll see if any of my people have something that will fit a great lummox like you, but it won't be easy."

"I'll take what I can get," Halvar grumbled as the frater draped the shirt around him and contrived a sling to take the pressure off his shoulder.

One of Dani's personable young men appeared with a garment made of heavy wool. It was woven in the stripe-and-check pattern the Bretains used to indicate their clan loyalties but fashioned in the manner of the deerskins used by the Algonikin Locals. The sleeves and body were attached to a yoke decorated with fringes that fluttered distractingly when Halvar tried to put it on.

"This is the biggest we have," the server apologized.

"It will have to do until I can get back to Manatas and get a coat from Gomez. Maybe the Town Guards have something I can use." Halvar paused as a half-formed thought struck him then muttered, "Town Guard..."

He tried to clear the cobwebs out of his head. He had seen a green coat and high-crowned tarboosh very recently, but where? He tried to think, but his brain was still foggy from the potion. It would come to him, he knew. For now, he would go to the Holy Meal, and either the Redeemer or Thor would come to his aid as they always had.

Chapter 20

THE BELL CLANGED, CALLING THE REDEEMER'S FLOCK to their Holy Meal. Halvar swung his legs off the bed and heaved to his feet, willing himself to ignore the way the room swung crazily about him.

"Let us go and partake of the Redeemer's Holy Meal," he ordered. "Then I want to have a word with Frater Leonidas. I want to congratulate him on his quick recovery."

The chapel, a small cabin built in the Scanian fashion of rough logs notched together, was meagerly furnished—there were no seats, and the Holy Table was little more than a board set on two trestles. The fraters stood around the Holy Table with the rest of the worshipers behind them. The Holy Meal was served by the Abbas Mikhail, the leader of the fratery, a tall, gaunt man whose burning eyes reminded Halvar of those of Mullah Abadul.

It had been a very long time since Halvar had actually partaken of the Holy Meal, but he mumbled the correct responses, knelt at the correct times, and allowed a crumb of the Holy Bread to be placed on his tongue, as the frater had taught him back in the Dane-March when he was a lad. Once blessed by the abbas, he shuffled back toward the crowd of Oropans,

He stopped in front of one frater and stared at the man's feet. Then he yanked the hooded cowl away revealing a smooth-skinned face with piercing blue eyes and high cheekbones, a mobile mouth and classically straight nose—a face that some might even call beautiful.

"God be with ye, Leon," Halvar said. "Don Felipe will be very please to know that you're alive and well and ready to return to Al-Andalus."

Abbas Mkhail strode angrily through the crowd to confront Halvar in righteous wrath.

"What are you talking about? This is one of our fraters, just come from Al-Andalus," he insisted.

"He's from Al-Andalus, but he's no frater," Halvar retorted. "Look at his feet!" He pointed to the abbas's sandaled feet then Leon's. "Fraters wear open sandals in all weathers, even snow and wind. Back home in the Dane-March, I've seen fraters with blisters and chilblains. Maybe they'll put on a stocking against the cold, but their feet are hard as leather.

"This man's been wearing shoes—his feet aren't callused, and his nails are neatly clipped. I'm sorry to tell you this, Abbas, but there's a man on a table in the dead-house in Manatas Town with his face smashed whose feet and hands are those of someone used to hard toil, such as is done by the fraters on their farms and garden plots."

Abbas Mikhail turned from Halvar to Leon and back.

"I will go to Manatas Town," he decided. "I will see this dead man. If he is, indeed, one of us, he should not be buried in unholy ground."

"Do you really believe this man?" Leon asked, his eyes willing Abbas Mikail to deny Halvar any credibility. "He's the Calif's Hireling, a servant, some soldier picked up after a tavern brawl and set to watch over the calif's grandson as a reward for saving the lad's life."

"A brawl where you took a knife across the ribs," Halvar said. "And I sewed you up, because you didn't want your sister to know you'd been drinking and fighting again." He pointed at Leon's midsection. "Do you want to show these good people that I'm lying? That you're not Leon di Vicenza, philosopher and image-maker, companion to Don Felipe in Corduva, banished from Al-Andalus these five years?""

Leon looked around at the faces of the fraters and the villagers and smiled ruefully.

91

"I don't suppose I can deny it," he said at last. "I'm caught, right and proper. Now, Hireling, what do you want to do about it?"

"For one thing, I want to sit down," Halvar said. "Somewhere less public. We have a lot to talk about, Leon. I've been sent here to take you back to Al-Andalus. Don Felipe wants you home."

"Suppose I don't want to go?" Leon said. "I have taken the water, I'm Kristo now. My sister will be horrified, I'm sure, but I can't stay in Manatas Town, and I won't go back to Al-Andalus."

Halvar took a deep breath and regretted it as his head swam. Dani Glick materialized behind him with two of her ever-present young serving-men.

"You need to rest," she chided. "And you…" She turned to Leon. "…you need to get away from Manatas."

"Not until he's explained himself to me," Halvar insisted.

He was half-dragged, half-pushed back through Green Village to the back door of the Gardens of Paradise, through the kitchens, and into Dani Glick's private parlor and office—a small, square room simply furnished with a chest, table and Oropan reed-bottomed chairs. A shelf displayed a row of books in leather bindings; the table held ledgers, pens and inkpots, and a sheaf of coarse paper. A lantern hung from a beam in the ceiling, lighting the otherwise dark room whose only window showed a sliver of the outside gardens.

Dani shoved Halvar into one chair and Leon into the other and stood between them, arms folded, to referee the coming debate. The two men eyed each other, sizing each other up, probing for weaknesses.

Finally Leon burst out, "It took him long enough to get around to answering my letter."

"Don Felipe's been busy," Halvar said evenly. "When the Old One died, there was a good deal of trouble about Don Felipe's right to rule."

"A calif's grandson doesn't automatically take over," Leon agreed. "So I suppose he had to do a bit of fighting. His mother must have been delighted to help him."

Halvar tugged at his mustache.

"Lady Zulaika has always been active on her son's behalf," he said. "Once that was settled, Don Felipe had to deal with the Franchen across the mountains. You know they've made peace with the Bretains and are negotiating with the Afrikans to split Al-Andalus between them."

"I'd heard," Leon admitted. "We're not completely ignorant here at the end of the world."

"So you wrote your letter and put it in with the receipts for last year's Fall Feria," Halvar recapped.

"And it took a whole year before Don Felipe decided to do something about it, and then he sends you!" Leon exclaimed indignantly. "A Hireling!"

"Who better?" Halvar said with a wry twist of his lips. "I know you by sight, I go where I'm told, and I always finish what I've set out to do. I'll take you back to Al-Andalus, Leon. I thought that was what you wanted."

"I've changed my mind," Leon said pettishly. He leaned forward, tapping Halvar's knee with one finger. "Do you know what's beyond that river out there?"

"More land."

"Much, much, much more!" Leon stood up and began to pace. "Otter Tail told me about the country north of here, at the end of the Great River. There is a whole set of long lakes, like dammed-up beaver ponds, only much, much bigger, and there's a wall of water, and behind it, more lakes, like inland seas! Animals that have never been seen before—bears twice again as large as anything in Oropa, and cattle with huge horns, and wolves! And people who speak strange tongues that even the Mahak don't understand."

"The Afrikans ran into some of them," Halvar reminded him.

"A totally different people," Leon said, waving his hands. "And there's a tale of a place where the Nether World opens into ours, and there are huge fountains of boiling hot water spewing up out of the ground!

"I want to see them, Halvar Danske! I can't stay in this little place, with all these little people peck, peck, pecking at me!" His voice rose to a hysterical pitch. "And Otter Tail was going to help me get there!"

"Only someone killed Otter Tail." Halvar brought Leon out of his vision. "Killed him because of what he saw on the path in the Feria. What did he see, Leon? Was it you, taking the robe off the frater who had just come off the dhow and was heading here, to Green Village? You, using the war club he'd given you to knock the frater's brains out then putting your coat and leggings on him so we'd think you were dead and not search for you? You, slamming him with the sledgehammer you took from Padraig mac-Cormack's shed? That you knew would be there because you'd used that shed for your assignations with Otter Tail? Is that why you killed your own lover, Leon di Vicenza?"

Halvar rose to confront him. Dani Glick decided to take action, interposing herself between the two tall men.

"This is going to have to wait," she told them. "There's a party of armed men heading towards Green Village."

"Mahak?" Halvar asked, fearing Firebrand's vengeance upon the one who'd killed his cousin.

"Town Guard," Dani said. "Tenente Gomez has been very busy while you've been out of your senses, Halvar. He's decided you are the murderer of Otter Tail, and that you must be arrested and taken to the Rabat for trial and execution. To this end, my dear Danske, he's on his way with a squad of the Town Guard to take you there, dead or alive. Both of us know which one he'd prefer."

Leon caught Halvar by the arm.

"I never killed Otter Tail! You must believe me, Halvar!"

"I never thought you'd killed Otter Tail," Halvar said. "The one who killed the frater did that."

"And you know who that is?" Dani asked.

"Oh, I do," Halvar assured her. "I didn't until I saw Otter Tail's body, but now I'm sure."

Chapter 21

SHOUTING VOICES OUTSIDE DISTRACTED HIM.

"What's going on out there?"

A server hurried in.

"Fru Glick, the Bretain merchants are preparing for battle. Cormack mac-Cormack is leading them, he's got a musket."

"Thor's Hammer!" Halvar swore.

"And the Mahak have come from their village," the server continued.

"Get me up!" Halvar ordered. "This can't go on!"

"Just what can you do about it?" Dani asked sarcastically.

"I'll talk to them. No one wants a war in Manatas."

"No one wants it, but you may have it," Leon said as he and Dani propped Halvar up between them.

"Not if I can stop it," Halvar stated. "This is all because I found a body in the Feria. It's up to me to make an end to it."

By the time he got to the grassy Common three different squads of armed men were glaring at each other The fine weather that had held throughout the Feria had broken, and Green Village was now half-hidden in a dank fog that had come off the Great River, driven by a cold wind that seemed to pierce Halvar's borrowed shirt.

On the path from the Feria stood Gomez, flanked by young Ruiz and five more guardsmen in long green coats and tarbooshes, each armed with a heavy cudgel and a long dagger. Gomez had added a curved sword to his weaponry, and he swaggered forward, the heels of his boots digging into the damp earth of the path.

Across from Gomez and the Town Guard stood the Green Villagers—ten or twelve sturdy Oropans from Bretain and Scania holding edged tools that split logs and could just as easily split skulls. Cormack mac-Cormack stood at their head, proudly brandishing a large and elaborate musket; Padraig was next to him, staunchly holding a halberd with a well-sharpened blade.

Between the Oropans and the Andalusians were five young Mahak men stripped down to breechclouts and warpaint, their chests gleaming with condensation, war clubs at the ready. Firebrand greeted the new arrivals in Mahak then turned to Halvar.

"We are here to avenge my clan-brother. Show me his killer and be done with it!"

Halvar shook off his two supporters and strode to the middle of the Common where he could face all three leaders.

"First, let me say this. I am not here to support Manatas Town or Green Village against each other, nor do I want to start a war between Oropans and Mahak. I am here only as the Hireling of Calif Don Felipe. Any disputes between Green Village and Manatas Town or between Al-Andalus and Oropa, or between any of you and the Mahak will have to be settled by Sultan Petrus and the sachem. I am not here to supplant the sultan, or to take him away from Manatas, or to promote myself as ruler of Manatas. Is that understood?"

There was a general muttering as his words were translated for the benefit of those who did not speak Arabi.

"So, Hireling, why should we listen to you?" Gomez shouted. "You are a servant, nothing else, and we don't have to listen to servants. You killed the Mahak, and I am here to take you back to Manatas for trial and execution."

"I did not kill Otter Tail, Tenente Gomez." Halvar strolled around the Common to where Padraig stood clutching his halberd. "But I know who did."

He took the weapon from the young Bretain, casually leaning his weight on it so he would not betray just how much he needed the support.

"Who? And why?" Firebrand demanded.

"Why?" Halvar answered the last question first. "Because, as I told you, Otter Tail saw something he shouldn't have seen. Leon di Vicenza!" He lowered the halberd so its steel head pointed at the artist.

"You met with Otter Tail the night I arrived in Manatas, is that true?"

Leon pushed back the cowl of the hood so his face could be seen.

"I saw you when you got off the dhow, and I knew you were coming for me. I wanted to get away from this island, so I sent word to Otter Tail to meet me in the Feria, at the ironmonger's stall. I asked him to get me to Mahak country.

"He told me he we were finished, that he was going to marry a Cayuga girl. Then he gave me his parting gift, the war club he had made at the forge as a master piece to end his apprenticeship and show his skill.

"I was angry—very angry—but I took the club. I told Otter Tail he was a false friend, a traitor, that I never wanted to see him again. Then along came this frater, very weak from his voyage, looking for a chapel for the Roumi Rite to give thanks to the Redeemer. And I let Shaitan into my heart. Abbas Mikhail, may the Redeemer forgive me!

"I thought I would take his place. I told him the chapel was in Green Village, and I would take him there myself. No one from the Waterfront Chapel ever comes to Green Village, and I never went to the Green Village chapel, so they didn't know me by sight. Since this was a new frater, not known to anyone, I thought I could easily impersonate him.

"I took him up the path, I struck him down, but I swear to you all, by the Blood of the Redeemer shed for us, and by the Beard of the Prophet of Ilha, I did not mean for him to die."

"Still, you left him in the woods, away from the path," Halvar went on relentlessly.

"But he was breathing when I left him," Leon assured him. He turned to Abbas Mikhail. "I repent of my evil deeds. I gave in to the Evil Impulse, the Shaitan that lies within us all. I put my coat and leggings on the frater and took his robe and sandals, but he was alive when I did it." He knelt before the abbas, the very picture of a penitent. "I did not kill that man! I was so upset, I even threw the war club into the bushes."

Abbas Mikhail made the sign of the crux over his head.

"The Redeemer forgives all, but you must still answer for your deeds," he said. "You left our frater to be found by strangers and took his place. That was a falsehood. You have been among us for three days, eating our bread, taking part in the Holy Meal. You pretended to be Kristo—"

"Oh, I am," Leon protested. "I took the water in Al-Andalus, at the Madrassa in Corduva with the Franchen students from Parigi. My sister and I have quarreled over this. I believe in the Redeemer and his Mother Mara—"

Abbas Mikhail held a hand up for silence.

"You have repented of your sins, and the Redeemer will pardon you. However, for your soul, you will serve the Redeemer with us here at the fratery. You will do labor, and pray to the Redeemer and his Mother Mara, and we will protect you. Take your place among your fraters and rejoice in the mercy of the Redeemer."

Leon got to his feet and joined the fraters, head bowed, hands tucked into his sleeves. Halvar grinned wryly. Leon would be watched carefully for signs of backsliding. He had only exchanged one prison for another.

"So, Hireling, if Leon didn't kill that frater, and Otter Tail, who did?" Gomez challenged him.

Halvar started toward the Town Guards, using the pole of the halberd as a staff.

"Someone who followed Leon to the Feria. Someone who saw him strike the frater and take his robe. Someone who helped him dress the frater in his coat and leggings and then had the idea of smashing in the man's face, so that Leon would be counted as dead. That someone was you, Tenente Gomez."

"You accuse me? I had nothing to do with Leon di Vicenza when he was in Manatas. Ask anyone! He and I never met except while he was teaching young Selim at the Rabat. I have no authority outside Manatas Town, and no one's ever seen me in Green Village."

"For someone who never met Leon, you know a lot about him. You told me about his liaison with Otter Tail. You knew about the debates at the Mermaid Taberna. As for leaving Manatas, you were in the Feria when I found the frater's body," Halvar reminded him. "And I heard your voice while I was lying on the ground in the Gardens of Paradise. What's more, I was kicked in the head, Tenente, by your boots!"

Chapter 22

BY THIS TIME, HALVAR HAD EDGED AROUND THE COM-
mon until he was within reach of Gomez, with the villagers
behind him. He dropped the blade of the halberd again.

"Tenente Gomez, I accuse you of the murders of Frater
Leonidas and Otter Tail. What do you say to this?"

Tenente Gomez stepped back to avoid the point of the halberd.

"I say you have no proof," he blustered. "All this is lies and
conjecture. You have no witnesses, and Sharia is clear that there
must be witnesses."

"There is a witness," Halvar said. "Look at your feet, Tenente,
and look here!" He lifted his hair to show the round bruise on
his temple. "Then look at the bodies of Frater Leonidas and Otter Tail. They show the same mark. You wear boots with built-
up wooden heels, Tenente, and you kick with them. It is a bad
habit you have, to kick what displeases you. You kicked me
when I was lying on the ground in the Gardens of Paradise,
you kicked the head of the frater, and you kicked Otter Tail when
you killed him."

Halvar stepped forward, jabbing the halberd with each
step. Gomez backed down the path then turned and ran, his
boot-heels making dents in the mud. The guardsmen blocked
the way to give their leader time to escape. The Mahak screamed
in fury, while Donal and the Green Villagers moved between the

two factions, torn between their fear of the Mahak and their hatred of the Andalusians. No one wanted to be the first to start the fight that might turn into an all-out war.

Halvar ran after Gomez to get to him before Firebrand could use his war club. Gomez reached a fork in the path. One way went into the Feria; the other, little more than a track through the woods, headed west towards the Great River.

He heard footsteps behind him and turned to face Ruiz and Firebrand, each fiercely eager to find Gomez.

"I want that man!" Firebrand spat as he shouldered Ruiz out of his way.

"You will not get him, Mahak!"

Ruiz pivoted and raised his cudgel. Firebrand parried with his war club.

Halvar had had enough. He interposed the blade of the halberd between the combatants, forcing them apart.

"Stop this!" he roared. The fighters were shocked into obedience by the tone of his voice. "Where does this path go?" He pointed to the muddy track that led down to the Great River.

Ruiz straightened his tarboosh and stood to attention.

"It leads to the scavengers' pit. May I remind you, Don Álvaro, that Tenente Gomez is the head of the Manatas Town Guard and is protected by Sultan Petrus himself. You cannot allow these savages to take him!"

The Mahak grinned nastily.

"Tenente Gomez murdered my clan-brother in cold blood, and then tried to make it seem that Don Álvaro did it, which is a shameful thing. For this, he must answer to us, and to Sachem Gray Goose Feather. And we will have our revenge!"

"Catch him first!" Ruiz taunted him.

Firebrand pointed down the trail and shouted, "There! He has gone to the place where the sekonks go to eat!"

"The scavengers' pit."

Halvar followed Gomez down the trail towards the Great River, whose rushing waters could be heard over the rustling of the leaves in the rising wind. He could see the Town Wall ahead of him through the misty rain. The path underfoot was slippery and Halvar dug the pole into the ground to keep himself from falling.

He lengthened his stride, hoping to catch the fugitive before he could claim the protection of Sultan Petrus. He arrived at the malodorous midden to find Gomez, gasping for air, clutching the wall.

"Not as fit as you should be, Tenente," Halvar gritted out, knowing he was as breathless as the Andalusian.

"Fit enough to take you on, Hireling!" Gomez turned to face his enemy. "This is my place, Danske! I was born here, to the first woman to come to Manatas as a free soul, not a slave. My father was captain of his own ship. I am a faithful follower of Ilha the All-Merciful, may his name be praised, and his Prophet, may his name be blessed, and I will not allow you, or anyone else, to tell me what I can and cannot do in Manatas Town!"

"But you took that hammer to the frater *outside* Manatas Town," Halvar reminded him. "And you didn't do it to protect anyone but yourself. You knew Leon di Vicenza had sent word to Don Felipe that there was a massive fraud, that funds belonging to the calif were being diverted to build this Wall.

"How much of that money was going into your pockets, Tenente? How much does it mean to you, to have the merchants bow to you? How important is it that everyone respect Tenente Gomez, who is the true ruler of Manatas Town, no matter what Sultan Petrus may think?"

As he spoke, Halvar stepped closer to Gomez; the pointed end of the halberd was aimed at Gomez's chest. "You had some kind of agreement with Leon, Gomez. Was it to share in the money that you took from the Feria? But thieves fall out—you cheated him, and he betrayed you by sending that message to the calif. You hated him for that, as much as you needed him.

"You saw him strike down the frater, you helped him take the frater's robe and put his own coat and leggings on the unconscious man.

"Then you had the grand idea of smashing in the man's face so he would not be identified. If you were the first to find the body, you'd identify it as Leon, and he'd be counted as dead. Meanwhile, he'd be safe in Green Village."

"I said he was dead," Gomez insisted.

"You knew that body wasn't Leon's," Halvar repeated. "And you knew the face had been smashed with a hammer before I went back to the Feria and found out from the ironmonger that his sledge had been taken."

Again he stepped forward, jabbing with the point of the halberd's axe-blade. Gomez sidestepped and swung his sword to deflect the pole.

"And then there was that ambush on the trail back from the Mahak camp. Who knew I was going there? The Mahak, the scavengers—and you and your men, Gomez. No one else.

"The attacker was someone in the green coat and tall tarboosh of the Guards. Someone with a pistoia. Do you have a pistoia, Tenente? Perhaps one given to you by Sultan Petrus's predecessor, Sultan Minitos? He thought enough of you to recommend you to Sultan Petrus and confirm you as tenente. But he wouldn't name you *capitán*, would he? That honor goes only to those from Al-Andalus!"

"A pistoia?" Gomez seemed genuinely puzzled. For a moment, he dropped his guard, and Halvar jabbed at him with the blade of the halberd.

Gomez flinched away, raising his sword as he stepped backwards. His heels slid on the damp muck of the midden, and he slipped down toward the riverbank.

Halvar heard men shouting behind him. He lunged to pin Gomez down. Instead, he, too, slithered on the slimy mud. It was all he could do to remain upright.

Gomez scrambled to gain his footing. The Andalusian tried to dig his boot-heels into the riverbank, but the rushing waters had undercut the soft earth. With a yell of despair, he fell into the river and was carried away from the shore.

"I can't swim!" he howled.

Halvar tested the ground beside the river then extended the pole of the halberd to the south of the floundering man. To his surprise, Gomez was instead carried northwards, upstream, away from the bay and the ocean beyond.

Behind him, Firebrand and Ruiz watched as Gomez's head bobbed in the waves of the Great River.

"This is the River that Goes Both Ways," Firebrand said with great satisfaction as he watched Gomez struggling in the current. "If he lives, he will come to Mahak lands. We will be watching for him. He will not escape, one way or the other."

Halvar leaned on the pole of the halberd.

"Perhaps it's better this way," he decided. "An execution would be difficult. Hoy, you. Ruiz?"

"That is my name." The handsome guardsman stared at the river a few moments more then turned to Halvar.

"Well, laddie, it looks like you're going to be the new Tenente of the Guards, until Sultan Petrus can find someone better," Halvar told him. "Now, get me one of those donkey carts, and you, Firebrand, you're coming with me as a witness. We've got to report this all to Sultan Petrus."

"Why must I go with you?" The Mahak stepped back, away from the enclosing walls of Manatas Town.

"Because you're the only one I can trust to give a true account of what happened to Gomez," Halvar said, collapsing into the newly arrived donkey cart with a sigh of exhaustion. "There's going to be no end of trouble about that."

"Tenente Gomez was not liked," Firebrand agreed. "But what of you, Don Álvaro? What happens to you, who pushed him into the river?"

"I'm the Calif's Hireling," Halvar stated. "What happens to me is decided by the calif."

With that, the procession moved back toward the Rabat, where Sultan Petrus waited impatiently for news.

Chapter 23

NEWS OF THE FIGHT BETWEEN THE CALIF'S HIRELING and Tenente Gomez spread rapidly through the Souk thanks to the Scavengers, who had witnessed it from the safety of their hovels in the shadow of the wall. The town's newscriers proclaimed that the Calif's Hireling had tossed Tenente Gomez of the Town Guard into the Great River, having first accused him of the murders of Otter Tail the Mahak and an unnamed frater of the Roumi Rite.

The donkey cart bearing Halvar to the Rabat drew a crowd of bystanders—Andalusians and Oropans who were doing business in the Souk. The club-carrying guardsmen marched alongside to keep the crowd away, while the Mahak warriors paced behind. The procession was greeted at the gates of the Rabat by a newscrier with information of greater importance than the mere death of a Town Guard.

"By the grace of Ilha, the All-Merciful, may his name be praised, the wife of Sultan Petrus has been delivered of a fine daughter," the newscrier announced. "In his joy, Sultan Petrus has declared that all who wish to join him may come to the Rabat for sweet cakes and cider! May Ilha, the All-Merciful, may his name be praised, and his Prophet, may his name be blessed, look with kindness upon the child, who is to be named Zulaika, after the lady Ayesha's kinswoman, the mother of Calif Don Felipe, may he live long and reign well!"

The promise of free food was enough to divert the crowd. Halvar's squad of guardsmen had to struggle through the press of people, past the Afrikan servants bringing out boards and trestles to set out the cakes and cider, into the courtyard, where Dr. Moise and Eva Hakim waited for them.

Dr. Moise assisted Halvar out of the donkey cart, tut-tutting over his latest injuries.

"I see the Oropan frater has used the bread cure on that wound," he observed, poking at Frater Iosip's bandage and poultice. "I would not have put such a tight bandage on it, but the bread cure works. Sometimes," he added, sniffing at the moldy bread.

"I have to see the sultan," Halvar insisted. "Never mind that bandage!"

"You have to go to your room and rest," Eva Hakim told him.

"I have important news for the sultan!" Halvar thrust the two physicians aside. "I've found your brother Leon, Eva Hakim. I'm sorry to tell you this, but he's joined the Kristo Fraters."

She closed her eyes and shuddered then opened them again.

"It is as he said it would be," she said, at last. "He always questioned the will of Ilha, the All-Merciful, may his name be praised, and the Prophet, may his name be blessed. I hope he finds peace in the company of those unbelievers, but I do not think he will. They are closed to the Truth."

Halvar turned to Dr. Moise.

"Get me up those stairs," he ordered. "I've got to explain what happened to Tenente Gomez."

"According to Achmet the Scavenger, you pushed Tenente Gomez into the Great River," Dr. Moise said as he complied. Ruiz followed them.

"I didn't push him," Halvar protested. "He slid on the mud and fell in. I thought he'd be swept onto the rocks downstream, but the river carried him north, upstream! What kind of a river flows *away* from the sea?"

"The kind that is fed by the tides," Dr. Moise said. "And right now is not a good time to give the sultan bad news. He's beside himself with joy. A lovely child, and the lady Ayesha came through in fine shape—tired, of course, but well enough to nurse the child herself until a wet-nurse can be found to her satisfaction."

The Afrikan servant at the sultan's door admitted them. Sultan Petrus stood at the window of his tower room, looking out over the bay. He turned to face the trio before him, joy fading to anger as he looked Halvar over.

"What did you do to Gomez?" he demanded.

Again Halvar explained what had happened.

"It was Gomez killed Otter Tail," he concluded. "He tried to arrest *me* for it, but between the Green Villagers and the Mahak, he couldn't. He ran, we fought, he fell into the river, he's gone."

"And what am I supposed to do about Manatas?" Sultan Petrus asked.

Halvar pulled Ruiz forward.

"This fine fellow was Gomez's second," he said.

"Ruiz," the man introduced himself. "Born in Manatas, as Gomez was. Educated by the fraters at the waterfront chapel. I came into the Guards just before you arrived here, and served at the Rabat until Tenente Gomez learned that I can read and write Arabi. I have been his second for three years. I know all he did about the Town Guards."

"Hmph," Sultan Petrus grunted. "I suppose you'll do as well as any other. You're tenente, Ruiz, until I can find someone else, or until they send a *capitán* from Al-Andalus. Get downstairs and see to it there's no brawling when they serve the cakes and cider. I want all Manatas to rejoice with me that my lady Ayesha is well, and that my little Zulaika will grow to be a beautiful woman, fit to be married to our gracious calif."

Halvar blinked at this ambitious project. Ruiz salaamed and strode out, proudly ready to take over where Gomez had once ruled.

Dr. Moise glanced at Halvar then said, "Excellent Sultan, I congratulate you on the birth of your daughter. I have been consulting with Eva Hakim and the Local midwife Nokomis, and we agree the lady Ayesha should rest after her ordeal. May I be excused to attend her?"

"Go, go, and take care of my wife and the child," Sultan Petrus waved the doctor out He turned on Halvar, all traces of good will gone from his ruddy face. "Well, Hireling, you've had a busy three days," he snarled. "You were supposed to run the Feria. Instead, you've killed the one person who kept order in this place, you've got the Mahak Sachem out for blood, and my son Selim's missing. Now, what have you to say for yourself?"

Halvar took a deep breath then let it out slowly.

"I've been doing what I was sent to do," he said. "I was sent to find Leon di Vicenza, and I found him. I also found out who the dead man in the Feria was, and I found the one who killed him."

"Gomez," Sultan Petrus said glumly. "What made you fix on him?"

"He was in the Feria," Halvar said. "From the time I got here, I was told the Feria was like Green Village—a place outside Manatas Town. If that was so, what was he doing in the Feria so early in the morning? If all had gone as he supposed it would go, *he* would have found the body of the frater, declared it was Leon, and Leon would have been free to go wherever he chose.

"When I was attacked outside the Gardens of Paradise, I heard his voice, as well as that of Leon. I knew then the two of them were working together.

"The murder of Otter Tail was a bad mistake. The Mahak must have seen the two of them dressing the frater and didn't understand what he'd seen. When he came back to talk to Leon, he found Gomez instead and got stabbed for his trouble. I suppose Gomez hid the body in one of the scavengers' huts until he decided to blame me for the Mahak's death.

"That was his next mistake. The worst one was trying to kill me with the pistoia They're expensive, and don't work very well, even at close range.

"I'm sorry that your confidence was misplaced, Excellent Sultan, but Gomez was usurping your power. How long has it been since you called a Divan to settle arguments between the waterfront people and the merchants in the Souk? You should call another, and soon!"

"Gomez handled all of that," Sultan Petrus said testily. "Now, I suppose I'll have to trust this Ruiz to do it. I have more important things to worry about. Selim has gone off somewhere, and I want him back!"

"You didn't seem too worried three days ago," Halvar pointed out.

"That was three days ago. He's never gone off on his own for so long, and no one's seen or heard from him in that time. "

"Perhaps his nose is out of joint with the fuss over Lady Ayesha and the new baby."

"Selim knows better," Sultan Petrus snapped. "What are you going to do, Hireling, now that your mission has failed? You may have found Leon, but you can't take him back to Al-Andalus, not if he's stuck in that Kristo fratery in Green Village."

"The Feria has two more weeks to run," Halvar said, placidly. "There's time for me to persuade Leon to be on the dhow when it goes back to Al-Andalus."

"While you're doing it, you can find Selim," Sultan Petrus ordered. "You may be the Calif's Hireling, but you take your orders from me while you're here in Manatas. Find my son, Hireling. That's what you do, isn't it? Find things, take care of things?"

Halvar nodded slowly.

"They call me The Tracker back in Al-Andalus," he admitted. "It's what I was trained to do. I notice things that others don't. I find things for the calif, and if that is what the calif wants, I will do it. But remember, Sultan Petrus, in the end, it is the Calif Don Felipe to whom I owe my loyalty."

Sultan Petrus stumped over to the window that looked out over the bay.

"There is trouble in Al-Andalus," he admitted with a sigh. "I was not happy to be sent away but perhaps I can do something here in Manatas for Al-Andalus. And you, Hireling, what are you going to do?"

Halvar smiled under his mustache.

"Right now, Excellent Sultan, I think I am going to take a short rest. Then I will find out just why Leon di Vicenza was so anxious to be dead, and what he and Tenente Gomez were doing in Green Village."

"And when you do?" Sultan Petrus prodded him

"I will do what I always do," Halvar said. "I will follow my orders."

PART TWO

THE CORPSE IN THE CLAM BED

Chapter 1

HALVAR DANSKE DID NOT WANT TO DEAL WITH ANY more dead bodies.

He sat in the bathing pool in the *hammam* connected to the barracks of the Rabat while one Afrikan slave scraped the stubble off his chin and another added warm water to the rapidly cooling bath and gloomily contemplated the results of his first three days in Manatas.

He had been sent with one major task and one minor one, and he had failed at both. Officially, he had been sent by Don Felipe, Calif of Al-Andalus, to oversee the Feria, the twice-yearly trade meeting that was a principal source of revenue for Al-Andalus. His secret mission had been to find the artist and inventor Leon di Vicenza and bring him home. Don Felipe wished his genius to be harnessed for the good of the calif, to combat the enemies forcing their way across the northern mountains from Franchenland.

In pursuit of these goals, Halvar had been shot, sliced, drugged, whacked on the head and kicked; he had discovered who killed a Kristo frater, and why; and he had deposed and disposed of the petty tyrant who had almost taken over the governing of Manatas Town.

All to the good, he thought, *but I haven't got that slippery soul Leon di Vicenza, and as long as he stays at that Kristo fratery in Green*

Village, I won't. The Feria will go on whether I oversee it or not. And the wars go on back in Al-Andalus, and I'm not there!

He ground his teeth in impotent fury and stretched his legs as far as the pool would let him. It wasn't very far—the pool had been built to accommodate the short, stocky Andalusian soldiers who had been sent to keep order in Manatas. Tall Danes were uncommon here, and Halvar was tall, even for a Dane.

He let out an involuntary "Ow!" as he shifted position.

He had been ordered by three different medical practitioners to rest. Frater Iosip, the Kristo frater who had removed the lead pellet, had even gone so far as to dose him with a potion that left him unconscious for twelve hours. Dr. Moise, the Afrikan attached to the Andalusian military, had scolded him when he returned to the Rabat to report to Sultan Petrus on the morning's events.

Even Eva Hakim, the Sister of Fatima whose rightful field of expertise was midwifery and the care of women's complaints, had lectured him when she encountered him in the courtyard of the Rabat, informing him that he was a stubborn fool, and that any injury he had suffered to his internal parts would only be magnified if he persisted in running about indulging in male heroics.

Halvar ignored all of them. He had done what he felt necessary, and as a result, Gomez, the killer, had slid into the Great River and been swept away by the current that ran north, contrary to all reasonable rivers. That seemed to be normal here—everything was almost like Al-Andalus but twisted in some way, so that rivers ran away from the sea and women were allowed to own property and underlings could take over the reins of government from the sultan who had been sent by the calif to bring order out of the chaos that was Manatas.

A shadow fell over him; Halvar squinted up to see his two guardians. Ruiz, newly appointed tenente of the Town Guard to fill the place vacated by the unlamented Gomez, stood beside the pool with the Mahak called Firebrand next to him. The young Andalusian, who had excessively refined features and the small chin-beard now fashionable in Al-Andalus, wore the long green coat of his unit. He had added Gomez's badge to his green tarboosh to mark his new rank. He wore no sword, but a businesslike cudgel swung from his belt.

114

Firebrand was taller than Ruiz, with the copper-colored skin and distinctive narrowed eyes and jutting nose of his people. He had donned a sleeveless jacket trimmed with porcupine quills as a nod to Andalusian ideas of modesty, but his lower half was defiantly bare except for a breechclout and soft leather macassins to protect his feet from the brick-paved streets. He wore no head covering; his scalp had been shaved except for one strip of hair running from his forehead to the nape of his neck. His weapon of choice was a war club, thrust into the belt that held the breechclout in place.

"I do not wish to disturb you, Don Álvaro," Ruiz said, apologetically, "but there is a problem,"

"A problem?" Halvar echoed.

"A…a situation," Ruiz explained. "You are being called on once again."

"To do what?" Halvar thought he knew, but he wanted to hear it spoken.

"There is a body," Ruiz said.

"Whose?" Halvar tried to heave himself out of the pool and fell back. The two Afrikans grasped his hands, and between them he was hauled up, wrapped in a kutton cloth, and led off to be clothed.

"We do not know." Ruiz said as he and Firebrand followed Halvar into the dressing room. "Don Álvaro, we opened your sea trunk without your permission to get you clean underthings, but we could not find a coat or jacket, except for one decorated with silver embroidery, which I deemed not suitable for daily wear. I took the liberty of getting a coat from the Guards' storeroom, which will have to serve until you can have a new jacket made."

Halvar nodded ruefully—he had lost two jackets in as many days. At this rate, he would have to spend all his hard-won savings on tailors' bills!

He tied his kutton braies and hauled on his baggy woolen trousers, then slipped a linen shirt over his scarred torso, wincing as the fabric brushed the new bruises and cuts. The Afrikans helped him into a green wool coat that barely reached his knees instead of hanging halfway to his heels as it should. It was tight in the arms and across the shoulders, but it would do. At least he could keep his own hat, a padded item lined with boiled leather that had saved both his wits and his life on many occasions.

The Afrikan handed him his belt and sheath, plain leather with no decoration except for his dagger, a utilitarian blade embellished with a lump of amber set into the top of its silver hilt. It was the only thing of value he owned, and he patted it as he put the belt on as though to assure himself it would not be taken from him again.

Ruiz looked him over.

"The coat will tear if you exert yourself," he said. "But it is better than that Local-made *wamus* you were given in Green Village." He sneered at the garment, a shirt made of Bretain cloth woven in a multicolored pattern of stripes and squares. It was sewn in the Local fashion with the body and sleeves attached to a yoke, the whole thing decorated with fluttering strips of fringe.

"Oropans!" Firebrand sniffed. "We do not need to cover ourselves with these things against the cold."

"It's not the cold I'm worried about, it's the knives," Halvar muttered. Louder he said, "There must be someone in the Souk who sells used clothes. As long as there are no extra riders—fleas or lice—I'll be satisfied until I can have a new jacket made. Is there a tailor you can recommend?"

Ruiz coughed gently.

"May I remind you, Don Álvaro, that today is the Rest Day, when all who follow Islim will attend the mullah's sermon at the Muskat? And the following day is the Shabbat for the Yehudit, who are our chief sellers of clothing." He looked Halvar over then added, "You might try Manolo's pawnshop on the waterfront. Some of the sailors pawn or sell their clothes if they are unlucky at cards or dice."

"I'll think about it," Halvar said, moving his arms back and forth to get the blood flowing, feeling the fabric of the coat stretching dangerously taut across his broad back and chest. "Now, what's this body got to do with me? I thought bodies found in Manatas Town were your responsibility, Tenente Ruiz."

"This body was not found in Manatas Town," Firebrand told him. "It is in the clam beds, just the other side of the Wall. That is our country, and not any business of Andalusians or Oropans."

116

"Then why don't you deal with it?" Halvar wanted to know.

"We *are* dealing with it," Firebrand told him with a malicious grin. "Since you are so clever, my sachem has sent me to ask you to find out who killed this girl."

"What?" Halvar looked up from pulling on his boots. "A girl?"

"Yes, Don Álvaro, it is a girl they have found," Ruiz said.

"Not one of ours." Firebrand spoke confidently. "Not an Afrikan, either. This girl is most definitely Oropan or Andalusian, and that makes her your business, Don Álvaro, not ours. You must take her away before her spirit haunts the clam beds."

"Very well," Halvar grunted out. "Get Dr. Moise—"

"Oh, no, I don't think that would be wise," Ruiz demurred. "I have already asked Eva Hakim to accompany us. It is not fitting that a man should examine a girl."

"You're sure it is a girl?" Halvar asked.

"Oh, yes, most certainly." Firebrand said with another grin.

"She is, um, not clothed." Ruiz's olive-toned face took on a reddish tint.

Firebrand was not so prim.

"She is naked, Don Álvaro. That is how I know she is not Mahak or Afrikan. But who she is, and how she came to be in our clam beds is for you to find out."

"If the sachems think I can, then I surely will try," Halvar said. He settled his dagger more firmly in its sheath and shrugged to settle the bandage affixed by the Kristo frater earlier in the day.

Ruiz hovered at his side with a small pouch.

"You forgot this, Don Álvaro. Your wumpum, and some silver. You may need it."

Halvar tucked the pouch into his trousers pocket then turned to Firebrand.

"Let's go see this girl." *And then, maybe, I can get on with my own business, and get back to Al-Andalus before it's too late, and the Franchen have destroyed everything that was built since the Old Roumi left.*

Chapter 2

RUIZ HAD COMMANDEERED A DONKEY CART, FOR which Halvar was grateful. He had no wish to spend the afternoon tramping from one end of Manatas Town to the other, although it was not all that great a distance. He clambered up on the open cart, where Eva Hakim was already waiting with a small leather bag at her feet.

"Salaam aleikum, Eva Hakim. I'm sorry you have to be called away from Lady Ayesha's bedside for such an errand, but Tenente Ruiz thinks it's more proper that you examine this female body than Dr. Moise." He remembered his manners and asked, "How are the lady and the child? A girl, I heard. The sultan was pleased?"

"Lady Ayesha and her daughter are doing very well," Eva Hakim said. She was tall for a woman, with features that might have been more appropriate to a man's face—large nose, prominent eyebrows, and broad mouth. She wore the brown robes and green hijab of the Sisters of Fatima, the women who provided medical care for women and children. "As for Sultan Petrus, he regards the child as the gift of Ilha the All-Merciful, may his name be praised, in his old age. He already has sons. A daughter can be married into a high-ranking family, bringing honor and fortune to both."

Ruiz hopped into the cart, while the Mahak stood beside it.

"Salaam, Eva Hakim," Ruiz said, nodding respectfully to her. "I have news of your brother. I regret to tell you that he remains with the fraters in Green Village."

"Leon is stubborn," Eva Hakim said with a sigh. "But I do not think he will be happy under the Kristos' rules."

"He can always come back to Al-Andalus with me," Halvar reminded her. "Calif Don Felipe, may he reign long, is eager for his return."

"Don Felipe was just as eager for him to be gone," Eva Hakim retorted. "But Leon will do as he wishes. He always has, even as a child." She closed her lips over any further revelations and looked focused her attention on the streets of Manatas, where donkey carts jostled each other, and people of all sorts threaded their way through the traffic, each intent on his own business.

The cart jolted north along the Broad Way past the Muskat and the Madrassah to the Town Wall. The donkey plodded not much faster than a man could walk, but Halvar was just as happy to ride slowly as to walk quickly. Firebrand had to moderate his stride to accommodate their slow progress.

At the Wall, Halvar noted the Town Guards posted at the gate seemed to be more alert than on the previous day. Under Gomez's influence, there had been an atmosphere of slackness. Already things were different.

The donkey driver urged his beast along the path that flanked the ditch on the other side of the wall, while Halvar marveled at the landscape before him. He recognized maple and birch trees, whose leaves were still green, but here and there was a bush heavy with berries. Local women in deerskin skirts and Bretain-woven shirts moved among the bushes, carefully placing their harvest into reed baskets. A few of the low-lying shrubs had already started to turn, their leaves golden against the green of the surrounding grass.

At the end of the wall lay a stretch of muddy pebbles where a delegation stood waiting for them. Halvar recognized the Mahak sachem Grey Goose Feather and the Algonkin sachem Mahmoud, the first tall and lanky in Local leather garb, the second short and round in the loose cloth shirt and trousers favored by those who had accepted the Prophet. Between them was a short, wizened individual in a cape made of fox fur trimmed with the tails of minks who shook a turtle shell rattle filled with pebbles.

This must be the shaman, Halvar reasoned, chanting a prayer to avert evil spirits from the place. Mahmoud might have adopted Islim, but he was clearly taking no chances. Ilha came from far away; the ghost of this dead girl was here and had to be placated.

The donkey cart pulled up at the very end of the wall, where the muddy clam beds began.

"Stay here," Halvar ordered, as the donkey driver prepared to leave. "You'll have to take this…the girl with you."

Eva Hakim was handed down by Ruiz; Firebrand consulted his sachem. Halvar clambered out of the cart, wincing as the tight coat pressed against his many bruises, and greeted the Locals politely.

"What cheer, noble sachems? Why have you sent for me?"

"There is this woman, dead." Gray Goose Feather indicated the naked corpse half-hidden in the weeds. "She is not ours. We want her gone."

"We have come to take her away," Halvar assured him, indicating the donkey cart. "Who found her?"

Three women in colorful Oropan shirts and deerskin skirts stepped forward.

"These are the ones who found her," Firebrand said. He turned to the women. "Who speaks Arabi?"

"I speak a little," the tallest of the three said hesitantly. "I am Bean Blossom. I speak Arabi. I sell food to eating-places. I go to clam bed to get clams to sell to eating-places that make them into soup. I see her at the end of the wall, in the burnweed. I do not touch burnweed. I go to Sachem Mahmoud, and tell him, and he go to Sachem Gary Goose Feather of Mahak."

"And he sends Firebrand to get me," Halvar finished the chain of command. "Well, let's see this body of yours."

She lay with her back to them in a cluster of spiky shrubbery, facing the wall, her pale flesh covered with flies. Eva Hakim eyed the body. Before she approached it she put on a pair of thin leather gloves.

Halvar raised his eyebrows questioningly. Gloves were expensive luxuries, and these were of the finest kidskin.

"A precaution," she explained.

"This burnweed," Halvar asked. "What's wrong with it? Why is everyone afraid of it?"

"It is Manitou's punishment for laziness," Firebrand replied. "It springs up where the ground has been prepared for planting, but nothing has been planted. It will grow anywhere, even climbing trees. If you touch it, you get blisters that sting, and if you break the blisters it only gets worse. You can even get burned if your clothing touches the leaves.

"And the berries are deadly poison. The medicine women make a salve that takes away some of the sting, but only time will cure the blisters. Every Mahak and Algonkin child learns to stay away from burnweed."

"Even as we do in Manatas," Ruiz admitted. "Gomez used to send beggars and thieves out to pull it up, where it grows between the houses or in the streets, as a punishment. There are other plants here that can bite, but this burnweed is the worst of them. If you see a plant with three leaves, red this time of year, and white berries, stay far away from it, Don Álvaro."

"Good to know," Halvar said, peering at the body of the girl from a safe distance. "Eva Hakim, how long would you say she has been dead?"

The doctor stepped carefully around the weeds, holding her robe away from the poisonous leaves, to shoo the flies off the body.

"That would depend on the tides." She touched the girl's arm gently to check for rigidity.

"The water was up to the wall when day broke," said Bean Blossom. "I could not get past it to go to the docking-place for my canoe until after it went down. The sun was a hand high by then, and the people in Manatas Town were shouting for their praying-time."

"Midmorning prayers," Ruiz translated.

"About the time I was fighting Gomez at the other end of this wall," Halvar recalled. "And this poor girl was lying here all that time!"

One of the other Local women spoke up.

"We see her when bell rings for Holy Meal. We go to Holy Meal in Manatas Town, to pray to Mother Mara."

"Sun was high by then," Bean Blossom added. "Water half gone."

121

"So, she must have been put there around daybreak," Halvar reasoned. "High tide."

"It would have been dark," Ruiz agreed. "And this side of the wall would have been in shadow."

"So they didn't know they were putting her in burnweed," Firebrand said.

"Probably thought the tide would carry her away," Halvar concluded. "Only it didn't. Now all we have to do is find out who she is, and we'll be on our way to finding out who put her here. Eva Hakim, can you tell how she died?"

"She was strangled." She pointed to a thin line on the girl's neck. "A very thin cord must have been used. I have not seen such a thing before."

"I have," Halvar said, grimly. "It's a way of killing used by the thieves of Parigi, called a garrote. If one of them has made his way to Manatas, then the sooner he is caught the better. I dealt with them back in Al-Andalus when a gang tried to set up shop in Corduva. They're out for gold and silver, and nothing stops them. This poor girl must have been one of their doxies—"

"She was not," Eva Hakim stated. "I will have to make a more complete examination, but as far as I can tell, this girl is virgin. Whoever she is, she is not a waterfront doxy. Her hair has not been braided, she shows no signs of abuse. This is a gently reared girl, Oropan or Andalusian, and how she came here I cannot tell.

"She must be brought back to Manatas quickly, Don Álvaro, and her family, whoever they are, must be notified as soon as possible!"

"Tenente Ruiz, get back to Manatas," Halvar ordered. "Have the newscriers announce that this girl has been found. Then check with the Andalusian families and see if any have girls missing."

"There aren't that many such families in Manatas," Ruiz told him. "Most of the Andalusian soldiers leave their women behind when they come here and take Local or Afrikan women to wife. The ones who bring their families are wealthy merchants.

"And, with respect, Don Álvaro, we can't go into such a man's home looking for girls. It is not fitting!" He seemed more upset at the thought of intruding into the private lives of the wealthy than by the sight of the dead girl.

"I don't care if it's fitting, we have to find out who she is," Halvar fumed.

"Yes, Don Álvaro," Ruiz said with a grimace of distaste. "Get the girl up on the cart," he ordered the donkey driver.

Halvar stopped them as they carefully lifted the body from its poisonous bed.

"Wait, what's this?"

"Her hand is clenched tight," Eva Hakimm said. "Perhaps there is something in it. I will take her to the House of the Green Crescent for further examination. Salaam, Don Álvaro, and Ilha the All-Merciful, may his name be praised, and the Prophet, may his name be blessed, guide you in your investigations."

Ruiz joined her in the cart, and off they went, back to the town gate.

Firebrand turned to Halvar.

"So, Don Álvaro, you have your dead girl. What do you do next?"

"I find out who she is," Halvar decided. He grimaced in pain as he prepared to follow the donkey cart.

Chapter 3

"BEFORE YOU GO, DON ÁLVARO, THERE IS ONE MORE thing you must do for us." Gray Goose Feather stepped forward. "You were sent here to oversee the collection of the calif's share of the money and goods to be sent from the Feria, is that not so?"

"Yes, noble sachem, that was my commission from the calif."

It had been as good a reason as any for Don Felipe to send his personal Hireling all the way across the Sea of Storms. A letter had come into his hands accusing the Sultan Petrus of skimming the funds sent back home for the calif to pursue his war.

"Then there is something that you must see," Sachem Mahmoud said firmly. "There is something very bad happening in the Feria."

"More bodies?" Halvar asked.

"Worse!" Firebrand smirked. "Someone has learned how to change white wumpum to purple, and it is throwing the merchants into fits!"

The warrior seemed to think this was funny. Halvar knew better.

"Let me see this wumpum," he ordered.

The two sachems marched westward toward the collection of tents, huts and wooden warehouses that marked the Feria. The twice-a-year gathering of buyers and sellers was a source of income for the calif and the reason for the very existence of

Manatas Town. Afrikans brought bales of kutton and barrels of tabak from their vast farm-holdings in the south to meet with Bretain and Franchen merchants from the rocky shores and mountains of New Bretain and Kibbik. In those territories, many streams provided power for spinners and weavers to make the cloth so prized by Local women.

Here, also, the Locals could trade their pelts of beaver, wolf, fox and lynx for the iron tools they craved, as well as for luxury items like glass beads. From the Mechican savages to the far south and west came lumps of gold and silver, sometimes formed into weird images of their demonic deities, and medicinal plants that could be boiled into potions that allayed pain and stopped the shivering of ague.

The Feria was now in full motion, a constantly shifting population of long-robed Afrikans, Bretains in colorful woolen trews and smock-shirts, Franchen in striped breeches and embroidered coats, and the Locals, whose clan and tribe could be deduced by the beading on their sleeveless jackets or macassins and leggings, all extolling the virtues of their own wares and denigrating the quality of any others.

Afrikan or Local women added their shrill voices to the din, the Afrikans in colorful draperies with artfully tied cloth headdresses, the Local women in woolen smock-shirts and deerskin skirts, their hair shockingly visible, wound into braids held in place with leather headbands. There were no Andalusian women in sight; they preferred to remain behind the wall, shopping at the Souk, where they were concealed by their burkas and veils from the prying eyes of strangers.

Arabi was the principal language of trade in the Feria, but Halvar heard Erse and Franchen along with Munsi, the Local trade language spoken by both Mahak and Algonkin that took its words and grammar from the two different Local tongues.

The noise of the traders was pierced by the voices of the muezzins, announcing the mid-afternoon prayer. There was a sudden hush as those who gave their devotion to Ilha and the Prophet prostrated on the ground while those who followed Chesu the Redeemer merely knelt to recite their own Patri Nostro. Mahmoud followed the former group; Gray Goose Feather and Halvar remained standing.

Halvar bowed his head, clutched the amulet that hung around his neck, and whispered, "May the Redeemer and his Mother Mara and the God Thor help me for the rest of this day."

For his part, Gray Goose Feather said nothing. His glance flickered over the prostrate figure of his colleague, Mahmoud, but his expression did not change. He regarded both Kristo and Islim with the same impassive silence, judging them to be alien to him and, therefore, not worth the trouble to accept or deny.

Their religious duty done, the merchants resumed buying and selling, and Halvar followed the two sachems to the tally house, a small wooden hut in front of which the tallymen had set up their table. He had already met the supercilious chief tallyman, an Afrikan in the long shirt and loose trousers favored by the planters of southern Nova Mundum, at the ceremonial dinner following his arrival three days before, but he could not recall his name

The tallyman confronted Halvar.

"What are you going to do about this?"

He thrust a string of wumpum beads at the Dane. Halvar looked at the beads, purple cylinders half the length of his thumbnail strung on a twisted kutton cord.

"What is the matter with them?"

"They are false! Counterfeit!" The chief tallyman glared at him.

Halvar squinted at the beads. As far as he could tell, they looked like any other bits of shell.

The chief tallyman enlightened him.

"Look carefully, Don Álvaro. Here is a string of true wumpum." He produced another set of purple beads and a small glass lens, a sure sign here was someone who would not be fooled by false coin of any kind. "If you look through this glass, you will see that there are small lines, almost invisible, in the true wumpum, but the false wumpum is solidly colored."

Halvar squinted at the beads through the glass. Sure enough, there were tiny white lines on the true beads, made visible by the lens.

"Wumpum is made from the shell of a particular kind of clam," Sachem Mahmoud explained. "Each household is responsible for making a certain amount, and it is collected by our shamans, who count it carefully. We have learned from our

Andalusian and Oropan neighbors to do this," he added sanctimoniously, with a glance at his Mahak colleague.

"We used to trade goods for goods," Gray Goose Feather admitted. "But when our spring and fall trading became the Feria, it was easier to use wumpum to mark the value of the furs and tools so that no one would be cheated. Ten white wumpum are the equal of one purple. Ten purple are the equal of a small silver coin. Twenty purple, two strings, are the worth of a large silver coin with the calif's seal on it. So we mark the value of our goods."

The two sachems nodded firmly in agreement.

"And the calif gets his tax for keeping the Feria honest," the chief tallyman put in.

Sachem Mahmoud continued. "This color is very hard to copy. There is no plant that can make this particular purple, and while some earths can be ground to make pigments, they will not cling to the shell. This stuff has been made so that it cannot be easily scratched off. Only after a few days of being rubbed in someone's pocket does the white shell show through the purple paint."

"That's how we found out about the fraud. I was given some of this false wumpum as a part of my own tribute. I saw the white shell behind the purple paint."

"Whoever has put this false wumpum into the Feria must be using it to get goods at no cost to himself," Sachem Gray Goose Feather declared. "Why else?"

Halvar pulled at his mustache as he thought through the counterfeiter's probable plan.

"Maybe so. Or maybe someone is trying to get Andalusian coin," he decided. "Trading the false purple wumpum for silver." He rubbed the false wumpum, feeling the slickness of the paint. "Someone who knows colors and can make paint. I have a very good idea of who that someone is."

"He's in the fratery in Green Village," Firebrand reminded him, guessing whom he meant.

"I think it's time I had another chat with our mad artist," Halvar said. "Noble Sachems, good tally men, I have been sent here by the calif to oversee the Feria. This false wumpum is something I should deal with, and I shall. Salaam aleikum, and be assured, I will find out who is responsible for this. Falsifying currency is punishable by death, even if the currency is a bit of shell."

Torches were being set up to light the paths through the Feria, to be lit at sunset. Halvar turned towards the west side of the island where he could see the roof of the Gardens of Paradise just above the red and gold leaves.

"I will come with you, Don Álvaro," Firebrand stated. "Every time you go to that place, you get into some kind of trouble. Maybe this time you will come away without being beaten, drugged, sliced or chopped up."

Halvar grinned under his mustache.

"Maybe so, but I don't think you can protect me from the wiles of a certain redheaded houri. Dani Glick is more dangerous than a whole army of pikemen!"

They headed towards Green Village, and the serpents in the Gardens of Paradise.

Chapter 4

HALVAR AND FIREBRAND STRODE THROUGH THE FERIA, heading for the straggling set of huts, sheds and houses arranged around a common grazing-ground that made up Green Village. They were stopped at the stream that marked the boundary of the village by a Bretain hefting a large cudgel.

"You, Mahak!" He pointed at Firebrand. "You're not to come into Green Village."

Halvar intervened. "He's with me. You know me, I'm Don Álvaro, the Calif's Hireling."

"He's the one who started the fighting this morning," the Bretain countered. "He stays out of Green Village. You, Calif's Hireling, you come along with me."

Halvar was about to protest, but Firebrand stopped him.

"I do not argue with fools. Go on, Hireling. I will wait for you here."

Halvar knew he had to tread carefully. There was bad blood between the Green Villagers and the Mahak, no matter what Dani Glick told him. He didn't want to start another fight that might turn into a war.

Bad enough that his confrontation with Gomez was being thrashed over by knots of men, some in multicolored trews and smock-shirts of the Bretains, some in the loose shirts belted over full trousers favored by the Scanians. Every man carried a knife at his belt; every man wore some kind of head covering, whether it was the knitted cap on the Scanians, or the flat cap favored by the Bretains.

The women of Green Village had gathered apart from the men, adding their voices to the hum of talk that stopped as Halvar approached.

Cormack mac-Cormack, the ironmonger, was the self-proclaimed leader of the Feria merchants lodging in Green Village, stepped forward to confront him, his hulking redheaded son Padraig looming behind him protectively.

"What do you want here, Don Álvaro?" Cormack demanded, speaking Arabi with a strong Erse inflection. "Haven't you done enough damage for one day?"

Halvar grinned wryly.

"The damage was done on both sides," he admitted, using Erse. "Still, I think I got the better of the bargain. Gomez is no more."

"He might have been swept ashore on the other side of the river," Padraig said.

"If he was, he will have to deal with the Lenape and the Mahak," his father reprimanded him. "I wish him the joy of that! They are known to eat their captives, one bit at a time."

There was a collective grunt from the Green Villagers behind him.

Halvar ignored this bit of local lore.

"I have more important news," he stated. "While we were playing games at this end of the Wall, a young woman was found dead at the east end. She's very young, brown hair, slim build. I ask you, does this sound like any girl from one of your households?"

MacCormack's truculence faded into horror.

"A girl? Dead? How?"

"Strangled with a cord. And she was not Local nor Afrikan. So, I must ask again, are any girls missing here? Before I can find the one who killed her, I must know who she is... was," he corrected himself.

The crowd parted to let someone through. Dani Glick was still in her Yehudit garb—dark jacket fastened up to her neck with bone buttons, dark full skirt decently covering everything below the waist down to the ankles, white cap covering her auburn hair, the only splash of color in her somber attire. One would have taken her for a modest Yehudit matron were it not for the gold chains and bangles around her neck and wrists, and the slash of red across her wide mouth, and the kohl around her green eyes.

"What's this about a girl being dead?" she demanded.

"She was found by Local women at the east end of the Wall," Halvar repeated.

"No one in Green Village goes to the East Side of Manatas."

"Not even some lovesick girl?" Halvar hinted. "Girls have been known to take a fancy to a man their parents wouldn't have for a son-in-law." He looked pointedly at Dani, who grimaced, also remembering a long-ago tryst in the Dane-March and the subsequent furor.

MacCormack had taken a poll of his fellow Villagers.

"All our girls are accounted for," he announced. "And if any of them took a fancy to a Local lad, she wouldn't go that far from the village to meet him."

"I'd beat my Gretel bloody if she did," growled one of the Scanians. The rest nodded agreement.

Halvar looked beyond the men to the women.

"Women!" he shouted. "If you know of any girl who has not come home, or any who has been outside the Green Village markers, speak now!"

Dani added, "It's important! No harm will come if you speak up. Don Álvaro can be trusted to keep his word."

There was a murmur of female voices; then a stout dame in multicolored skirts spoke for the group.

"All our girls are either here or at the Feria with their mams, Fru Glick."

"Perhaps this discussion should be held in private," Dani suggested. She beckoned to Halvar. "Come into my parlor, Halvar Danske."

"As the spider said to the fly," Halvar murmured, but he followed her around the Common, through the iron fence that surrounded the plants that gave the Gardens of Paradise their name, and into the back entrance of the tallest building on Manatas Island, except for the Rabat.

"Now," Dani said when she had led him through the empty eating-room to the tiny cubicle that served as her private office. "What is this about a dead girl?"

131

She made herself comfortable in the wooden armchair that had been enhanced with a small embroidered cushion, set behind a small table covered with the detritus of business—ledgers, papers, pens and inkpots. Halvar had to prop himself against the nearest wall, his head almost brushing the low ceiling.

"She was strangled," he said. "From what I saw, with a garrote."

"Franchen," Dani muttered. "Bloody hellfire Franchen!"

"You don't like them," Halvar observed.

"No Yehudit does," Dani snarled. "They've gone over to that Rouma maniac who's decided all Oropa belongs to the Redeemer and anyone who doesn't agree should burn, not at the End of Days but here and now. Mauritz and I barely escaped Franchenland with our lives, and the Franchen in Kibbik were the ones who sent him into Huron lands to his death.

"The news from Al-Andalus is that those fanatics are coming through the passes of the mountains, and that they will take as much land as they can before winter comes. Your young calif has his work cut out for him, Halvar."

"I should be there!" He smacked the wall with his fist. "Instead, I'm here on the other side of the Storm Sea!"

"Looking for murderers," Dani added. "Well, Halvar, I can tell you right now that whoever this dead girl is, she is not from Green Village."

"What about your own, um, girls?"

"When was this girl killed?"

"Eva Hakim thinks sometime last night. The body was left in the clam beds at high tide."

Dani shook her head

"Then I can tell you right now, she's not one of mine. All my girls were working last night, and I keep a careful watch on them. As for going all the way across to the East Side? That's just not possible."

"It's a small island," Halvar observed. "It could be done."

"It could be, but it wouldn't. There's a line drawn between the Local Algonkin and Green Village. We stop at the Broad Way, they stop at the Trail. We meet in the middle at the Feria. But they keep to the East Side, we to the West. No Green Village girl would go that far, not for anyone or anything." She stopped then said, "Was the girl…harmed? Other than being strangled."

"If you mean raped, no, she wasn't," Halvar told her. "And that's odd, too. I've seen my share of killings in Al-Andalus and in Italia. I know there are some twisted souls who enjoy hurting women before they enter them. This girl wasn't harmed. Just killed."

"Just killed," Dani echoed. "Why?"

"That's why I have to find out who she was," Halvar said. "If she wasn't killed for sport, then she must have been killed because she saw or heard something the killer didn't want known. Until I know who she was, I won't know *where* she was or who she saw or heard." He slapped his leg in frustration then winced at the pain of moving his shoulder.

"You shouldn't do that," Dani chided him. "Have you seen the frater who bound up that hole in your shoulder?"

"I don't have the time," he protested. He thrust his hand into the pocket of his coat then remembered one more reason to consult his old friend. "One thing more." He took the string of wumpum out of his pocket and laid it before her. "Have you seen anything like this in your Gardens of Paradise?"

She glanced at the wumpum.

"Of course I have. It's being brought into the Gardens of Paradise all the time. The traders in the Feria take it for their goods. Then they exchange it here for silver coins to take back to West Caster or Bretain."

"Look again, Dani Glick. It's not purple; it's white, painted to look like purple. Are you sure you haven't seen this?"

Dani took the beads over to the window. She squinted as she examined them, rubbed them with her thumb, then held the string up so she could peer at the end of the string.

"Shaitan take whoever made this!" she exploded. "It's fake!"

"So it is."

"And you thought I was the one who made it?" Dani's cheeks took on a crimson blush that had nothing to do with cosmetics. "Are you mad? No Yehudit would meddle with currency. We know better. I've been giving out good silver coin for strings of…" She couldn't find an expletive low enough.

"The question is, who would be able to devise a paint that would fool even you?" Halvar asked, knowing the answer.

133

"Leon! I'd string him up by his balls if the Kristos hadn't done it already!" Dani swore.

"Then he's still in the fratery?"

"As far as I know," Dani said with a nasty grin. "Abbas Mikhail is keeping him close. You can find Leon di Vicenza right where you left him, Halvar Danske, and I wish you the joy of him.

"Take your false wumpum and get out! I'll have to go through every single bead that came through here over the last week. Do you know how long that will take? And then, to try to figure out who gave them—it's impossible! Go, Halvar, and find your murderer, and your forger. And when you do, give them to me, and I'll take care of them as they deserve!" Dani ran the false beads through her fingers again.

"While I'm at it, have you seen Selim? The sultan's son," Halvar added, in answer to Dani's blank look.

"Selim?" She looked up from her examination of the wumpum. "What has that stripling to do with the dead girl? Or the fake wumpum?"

"I'm not sure," Halvar said slowly. "But he disappeared from the Rabat two days ago, and he hasn't been seen since. I don't suppose you'd know anything about that?"

"I've never set eyes on the lad. Sultan Petrus keeps him safe behind the Manatas Wall. Ask Leon about Selim, Halvar. I have more important things to worry about than a moody youngster."

She bustled out of the office, muttering in the Askenat dialect that sounded so much like Danic.

Halvar grinned. Whatever schemes were being hatched in Green Village, he was certain forgery wasn't one of them.

Chapter 5

THE KRISTO FRATERY WAS ON THE NORTHERN EDGE
of Green Village, surrounded by a tall fence of logs rammed
into the ground upright to form a palisade. Behind the palisade
were the chapel where the Holy Meal was served, a long barn
to keep livestock and their fodder, and a low rambling building that served as sleeping, eating and working quarters for
the fraters, with the latrine and the wash-house behind them.
A small garden had been planted next to the palisade, where
the fraters grew vegetables for their meals and herbs for their
apothecary.

Halvar pulled the string next to the gate and heard the rattle of a door-clapper. He waited impatiently for nearly five
minutes before he heard the shuffle of sandals on the other
side of the fence. The weatherbeaten face of an old frater peered
through the gate.

"What is your business here?" the frater asked brusquely
in Erse. "We are at evening refectory."

"I have to speak with Frater Leonidas," Halvar said in the
same language, answering rudeness with rudeness.

"He is at table," the doorkeeper snapped out.

"That's too bad. He'll have to finish his meal later. I am on
a mission for the calif."

"The calif does not rule here," the doorkeeper said. "This is
the House of the Redeemer. I will ask Abbas Mikhail if he will

allow Frater Leonidas to speak with the Calif's Hireling." He shuffled off.

Halvar's stomach reminded him that the last food he had eaten was a thin gruel, served by Frater Iosip very early that morning and spiced with much tut-tutting and medical advice. The odors of cabbage and salt fish assailed his nose. The fraters of Green Village were no gourmets, if that is what they had to sustain themselves.

Halvar's meditation on Kristo dining habits was interrupted by the return of the doorkeeper with Abbas Mikhail looming up behind him. The leader of the fratery stood almost as tall as Halvar but was much thinner, gaunt from fasting and prayer, and had the light of a fanatic in his cold gray eyes. Behind the abbas Halvar barely recognized Leon di Vicenza.

The painter's long fair hair had been cropped, and a strip shaved from front to back to indicate humility. He wore the simplest of undyed wool robes, girded with a leather belt in place of the elaborately embroidered and padded jackets worn in Al-Andalus, and open sandals in place of the soft leather shoes favored by the Madrassa dandies. His cheeks had been scraped clean, leaving his face pink.

Leon shoved the doorkeeper out of the way when the frater opened the gate, hurtling towards Halvar, who stepped back to avoid a vigorous embrace that would only open the bruises and cuts sustained in the morning's battle.

"Halvar! My dear old friend! You must get me out of here!" Leon pleaded, ignoring Abbas Mikhail's glare.

"I thought you wanted to stay here, to be Kristo, to take the place of the man you killed," Halvar said evenly. "You've been here for three days, Leon. You knew what it was like."

"That was when they thought I was ill from the voyage. Then Abbas Mikhail explained exactly what I would be expected to do." Leon lowered his voice. "Halvar, they get up at dawn to pray! They eat only vegetables and fish! And this robe—I had to give up my nice, clean under-tunic and wear their linen shirt. It itches!"

Halvar tried hard not to smile at this list of grievances. He had already won the bet he had made with himself as to how long it would take the luxury-loving Leon to regret his choice.

"You can always come back to Manatas with me," he told him. "Don Felipe needs you in Al-Andalus. Of course, you'll have to face the Sultan's Divan and do punishment for what you did to the Kristo frater you hit with the Mahak's war club."

"But I didn't *kill* him," Leon pointed out. "Gomez did that. And he's gone, drowned in the river." He dismissed the former tenente of the Town Guards to Sheol with a wave, to the tender mercies of the river or the Mahak, whichever would claim him first.

"Perhaps," Halvar said. "It's possible he'll survive being swept off by the tides. He might even escape the fury of the Mahak." He turned to the leader of the fratery. "Abbas Milhail, may I have a private word with Frater Leonidas? It is a different matter, something of great importance, nothing to do with the death of Gomez or your frater."

Abbas Mikhail nodded gravely and led Halvar through the courtyard to the main building, and into a small, bare room that contained only a pair of stools

"This is our place of contemplation," he said. "You may speak here. But I shall be at the door listening."

Leon plumped down on one stool while Halvar carefully settled on the other.

"What's this about?" Leon asked peevishly. "If you can't get me out of here—"

"The only way I can do that is for you to confess to killing the frater so the sultan can hang you," Halvar reminded him. "Meanwhile, there's something I want you to see."

He took the string of purple wumpum out of his pocket and handed it to Leon. The painter held it close to his eyes, then to his nose, sniffing it with increased puzzlement.

"This is painted," he declared.

"It is, indeed," Halvar said. "And I've seen that color before. You have paints and inks in your room. One of them is just this color."

"I was trying to make new colors," Leon admitted. "This looks like one of them. Do you know anything about paint, Hireling?"

"No, I don't. That's why I came to you."

Leon took on the cadence and tone of a professor lecturing at the Madrassa.

"The most important thing that paint does is to cling to the surface of the object being painted. Dyes are made from some kind of plant stuff—leaves or stems or buds, even roots, can have substances in them that can sink into the fibers of the material, thus imbuing it with their colors.

"Paints are made from minerals ground down to make a powder, which must be done carefully because many of them can be nasty poisons if taken by mouth or if their dust is breathed in. Then the powder must be mixed with a binder so the grains will blend on the surface being colored."

"That explains why painters go mad," Halvar said with a grin. "They ingest those poisonous minerals."

Leon ignored the interruption.

"Listen to me, you ignorant Dane. What is important is the *binder*, the material that holds the bits that make up the pigment so they lie evenly on the wood or cloth being painted. Most painters use the white of an egg, although there are some in Bretain that use fat or oil, to give a jewel-like finish to the work.

"But some surfaces don't take a binder at all. You can lay paint on wood or cloth or even ivory, and it will soak in, but something like this shell—it's slick. You really can't paint on it, not with the usual paints or inks. I've tried with all kinds of things, just to see what would happen, but every time I tried to paint on the inside of the clam's shell, the paint flaked off. It wouldn't bind."

"Someone's found a way to do it," Halvar said.

"And he's used my seaweed ink to do it, too!" Leon fumed. "I made this color from the seaweed that collects on the mudflats where the clams are found. I think the clams get their color where the flesh of the clam joins the two halves of its shell when they eat this purple seaweed. The rest of the inner portion of the shell is white."

"Which explains why the purple has more value than the white." Halvar nodded, pleased by his grasp of the problem of values of wumpum. "There's less of it, so it's all the more valuable. So, Leon, what's this binder?" He sniffed at the string of beads again. "It smells like fish."

Leon picked at the purple wumpum with one fingernail.

"This paint doesn't cling permanently. It can be chipped off."

"Not until someone's already gotten ten times'-worth of goods for it than he would have otherwise," Halvar pointed out. "And it's making the sellers at the Feria distrust the tally men, who have been accepting this false wumpum. That leads to distrust of the leadership of Al-Andalus." He rocked back and forth on his stool. "And who, of all people on this island, had the paint, and the skill, and the dislike of Al-Andalus to concoct such a scheme?"

He stared pointedly at Leon. Leon stared back.

"You think *I…I* would do this? Are you mad? No, you really think I would paint white wumpum purple! Whatever for?"

"For a joke, maybe? To prove that you could?" Halvar regarded the painter with narrowed eyes. "You've done nastier things, back in Al-Andalus."

"But that was different!" Leon protested. "And I was much, much younger! I swear to you, by the Redeemer's Mother Mara and anyone else you like, this is not my doing!" He clutched Halvar's sleeve. "The business with the frater, well, that was impulsive, but this? This is something quite, quite different! Someone is using my paints, my skills, to disrupt the business of Manatas, but it isn't me!" His voice rose to a shriek. "And whatever this binder is, it's not anything that I made!"

Halvar nodded gravely.

"You know, I believe you. I shouldn't, but I do. You don't have it in you to sit and paint bead after bead, tiny little things, then string them up on cords just to play a joke on the sellers of the Feria. And you don't buy and sell things, so you wouldn't do it to get more goods for less wumpum."

"Thank you for that. I think. If it will help you find out who is doing this, you should go back to my rooms at the Mermaid Taberna. That's where I left my paints. My paints!" He clutched at Halvar's arm again. "You must get me my paints, and my books! Abbas Mikhail wants me to make images for the fraters, for their contemplation. Perhaps a picture of the Redeemer and his Followers having the first Holy Meal together. I must have my pens and inks!"

He scrabbled under his robes for something that wasn't there then realized he could not jot down whatever had suddenly occurred to him.

"I need my notebook! I have ideas. I must get them down on paper before they vanish. I left my leather-bound notebooks in my rooms at the Mermaid Taberna. Please get them for me, Halvar, my dear old friend?" He smiled winsomely.

"I can do that," Halvar agreed. He rose then sat again. "One more thing, Leon. Before you took leave of Manatas, did you happen to see young Selim ibn Petrus, the sultan's son? He's gone missing."

"Selim?" Leon was jarred out of his vision of the prospective painting. "I haven't seen the lad for days. I was, um, preoccupied

"With Otter Tail," Halvar said, with another nasty grin. Leon's obsession with the Mahak had led to the young man's death.

Leon nodded. "I was shocked to hear of his death. He didn't deserve it."

"He saw the you and Gomez together, and he saw Gomez kill the frater," Halvar said. "That was enough to destroy him. When did you last see Selim? Wasn't he one of those Seekers of Truth, the students who came to the Mermaid Taberna?"

"He was my first pupil. I wouldn't have come to Manatas at all if it wasn't for him. My sister persuaded the sultan to bring me along as Selim's tutor." He frowned in thought. "Now, let me see, when did I last see him? It might have been when we got word that your dhow had been spotted coming up the coast. That was a day or two before you landed at Manatas.

"Then there was all the ceremony and other foofaraw when you arrived, including that banquet, to which I was not invited." Leon's voice took on a pettish whine. "And after all I did for that ungrateful boy, Don Felipe, who is now calif, thanks to that conniving mother of his. Taking him under my wing at the Madrassah in Corduva, letting him attend classes he was not entitled to attend, letting him join our discussions—"

"We're talking about Selim, not Don Felipe," Halvar reminded him.

"Selim. Of course. Wasn't he at the banquet?"

Halvar pulled at his mustache.

"I don't recall seeing him there. And the next day, I was dragged all over the Feria, and then there was the business with the dead frater. Then Lady Ayesha decided to have her baby, and everyone at the Rabat was in turmoil. The boy seems to have left the Rabat some time between the banquet and the time Lady Ayesha went into labor."

"I heard she had a girl." Leon grinned. "I hope that satisfies the old goat, and he leaves the poor little thing alone."

"You are familiar with Lady Ayesha?"

"When we first came to Manatas, I was quite the favorite," Leon said airily. "Almost a eunuch, you might say. Being young Selim's tutor, I had the run of the Rabat, including the harem. Sultan Petrus knew his precious little girls were safe with me."

"What kind of lad is Selim?" Halvar asked. "Where would he go, if he didn't want to stay at the Rabat?"

"There's the bookstall at the Souk," Leon suggested. "The Seekers of Truth meet there when they don't come to the Mermaid Taberna. Of course, the lad might have gone directly to the Mermaid the night of the banquet."

"But you were already gone," Halvar objected.

"Likely I was." Leon tightened his grip on Halvar's sleeve. "Halvar, my dear old friend, you must go and get my paints and inks and my notebooks before that rascally innkeeper sells them off. He's just mean enough to do it, too. And after all I did for him—painting his sign, starting my debating society, bringing in custom from the Muskat and the Madrassah."

"By what I hear, that kind of custom wasn't the sort he wanted," Halvar said. "But you may have a point. I'll go back to that taberna and see what I can find out. And I'll get you your paints and inks."

"And my books," Leon reminded him. "Especially my notebooks. I need them." He looked around the bare walls. "This room will do very well for a librarium. Every fratery needs books," he called to Abbas Mikhail, who was standing in the doorway. He brushed past the abbas as he strode out, obsessed with his next project.

Abbas Mikhail escorted Halvar to the door of the fratery.

"We will care for Frater Leonidas," he promised. "His mind is clouded with strange thoughts, but he is touched by the Redeemer with a gift. Bring us his paints and inks. He will use them for the greater glory of the Redeemer and his Mother Mara."

"And his books? What about his notebooks?"

"They contain nothing but lies and delusions. We do not want them here. You may do with them what you will."

Halvar left the fratery and turned his steps back to Manatas Town as the long shadows of the autumn evening settled around him. Mullah Abadul would have burned the books, he

141

thought. Perhaps the Kristos were a little more enlightened—but not by much!

He was Halvar Danske—he would do what he came here to do. And even though Leon di Vicenza insisted on being a Kristo frater, he would find some way to detach him. Those were his orders, and he would obey them.

Chapter 6

BY THE TIME HALVAR MADE HIS WAY BACK TO THE
path from the Gardens of Paradise to the Feria, the autumn sun
was approaching the horizon, flooding the sky with brilliant
color. Torches had been lit along the trail so that the returning
merchants could find their way in the twilight.

The last rays of the setting sun sent long shadows across
the path as Halvar dodged vendors hauling overloaded hand-
carts as well as the ever-present donkey carts, all heading back
to the haven of Green Village, where food and friendship awaited
them.

Halvar left the stragglers behind him when the road from
Green Village turned from flat paving stones to a path through
the trees, worn to packed earth from many years of brogans,
boots and macassins. The light that filtered through the trees
got dimmer, and the first stars began to show. The huge harvest moon had not yet risen, and all was quiet, save for the
rustling of the small creatures of the Manatas woods.

Halvar strode along the path, considering what he should
do next. If the girl in the clam bed was not from Green Village,
then she had to have come from Manatas Town. That meant
she was either Andalusian or Yehudit. If she was Andalusian,
was she from a merchant family, or had she been with one of
the waterfront traders? Was she Yehudit? The Yehudit were
often mistaken for Andalusians.

He stopped and cocked his head to listen. There had been footsteps behind him, he was sure of it. Not Locals, who wore soft macassins so they could pass silently through the woods. These were the heavy brogans worn by the Bretains.

"I am getting very tired of this," he said in Danic-accented Erse. "What do you want with me? I have business in Manatas, and I have no time to play with you now." He turned to face whoever had decided to follow him from Green Village.

Two men surged out of the darkness, armed with stout clubs. One swung at Halvar's wounded shoulder, the other at his head. Halvar sidestepped the first and dodged the second, drawing his dagger as he did. He slashed at the first attacker, who jumped aside, letting the second get another whack at Halvar's injured shoulder. Halvar grunted at the pain of the blow but clenched his teeth as he tried to make out the positions of his attackers. He slashed out again and heard a satisfying howl of pain. At least one of his opponents was out of the fight.

Suddenly, a third man joined in, gripping Halvar tightly from behind. The remaining assailant drew a fist back, aiming for Halvar's head.

Halvar went limp, leaving a small gap between himself and the man behind him, then stretched his shoulders, a move that took the attacker off-guard. He heard an ominous ripping when the borrowed coat split at the seams as he tried to wrench himself out of the grip that held him and dodge the blow aimed for his chin.

"Yi-yi-yi!"

Half howl, half scream, the sound sent the attackers flying from the scene.

"Mahak!" screeched one of the attackers.

"Stay away from Green Village!" the third attacker flung at Halvar as they ran back along the path to the settlement.

Halvar felt his knees give out as Firebrand grabbed him by the elbows.

"What were you thinking, going into these woods alone?" the Mahak scolded.

"You took your own sweet time getting here," Halvar shot back. "What took you so long?"

"You didn't wait for me, did you. Besides, you were doing quite well for a wounded man. It wasn't until that one decided to jump on your back I thought I should take a hand."

"Well, thank you for that. You didn't happen to see their faces, did you?"

"It's too dark but they were large, and wore the loose shirts and flat hats of Bretains."

Halvar grimaced as he moved his shoulders to see how much damage had been done.

"They must have known about the bullet wound," he observed. "They knew just where to hit."

"You should not have left your bed. Even a Mahak knows when it is time to let himself heal." He turned Halvar around. "You've been cut. Your coat is torn."

"That's not a cut, that's what happens when the seam rips," Halvar said, twisting to examine his coat. "I'll have to find a tailor in Manatas Town to sew this up."

"Otter Tail used to go to the Souk—it is where the Andalusians and Yehudit get their clothing. I suppose you can find someone there to sew your coat together."

"The best tailors are Yehudit," Halvar said. "I hope there's one who's not so particular about his Shabbat he will turn away a customer who comes a little late."

By this time, they were through the Feria and had reached the Wall, where the Town Guardsmen were preparing to close the gates.

"Come to the Rabat tomorrow," Halvar told Firebrand. "I may have some answers for your sachem by then."

"So soon?" He looked skeptical.

"I know where to find purple paint," Halvar said. "Now all I have to do is find out who is using it."

"And then?"

"Then I turn them over to Sultan Petrus. Changing the currency is an offense against the calif, punishable by death," Halvar reminded him. "But first, I will go to the Souk and get a new jacket. The Calif's Hireling can't be seen looking like a ragged beggar."

Chapter 7

THE GUARDSMEN SHUT THE GATE TO CLOSE OFF MANA-tas Town from the dangers of night animals of both the two- and four-legged kind.

"You're Don Álvaro, the Calif's Hireling, the one who shoved Tenente Gomez into the river," one of them commented as he shone the light of his lantern into Halvar's face.

"I am," Halvar admitted. "Now, will you open that gate? Or do I have to spend the night in Green Village?"

"They don't want you there," the other guard said. "Open for him, Flores. He's the Calif's Hireling."

They allowed it open far enough for Halvar to squeeze past. One lone donkey cart remained to pick up the last of the merchants coming from the Feria, and Halvar heaved himself into it with a sigh of relief.

"Where to?" the driver asked.

"I need a tailor. Do you know a good one?"

"I have a cousin in the Souk," the driver said. "He is the best tailor in Manatas. I will take you to him."

"Of course you have a cousin," Halvar muttered as the driver prodded his animal with a stick and the cart moved off, jolting along the Broad Way past the blank walls of the houses of the merchants towards the flickering lights of the mokka-shops, tabernas, or other places where food and drink could be bought.

The Muskat was lit for anyone who wished to come in to revere Ilha. Across the road from the elaborate house of worship, the Madrassa seemed to be equally busy, with men of all ages engaged in vigorous discussion of Mulha Abadul's latest diatribe against Kristos, Yehudit, and those who disputed his own dicta on the Holy Words of the Prophet.

Halvar regarded both Muskat and Madrassa with the skepticism of one who had seen too many men killed in the name of both the Prophet and the Redeemer. He had long ago decided the Redeemer would take a second place to his own protector, Thor, who would be more likely to keep an eye on a soldier than either a Yehudit carpenter's son or the owner of a camel caravan in Araby.

Religion aside, he had to get this coat repaired before he could continue his search for the killer of the girl in the clam bed, the counterfeiter of wumpum, and the sultan's son.

The donkey-driver steered his animal westward into the tangle of alleys behind the Madrassa that formed the Souk, the marketplace of Manatas Town. Unlike the neat squares formed by plaster-covered buildings east of the Broad Way, the houses that lined the twisting lanes west of the avenue were built of wood in the style of the mountain towns of Franchenland, with two stories. The lower rooms would be the shop or workroom of the artisan; the rooms above were living quarters for the shopowner and his family.

Like the Feria the Souk was separated into different sectors, each specializing in a different type of merchandise. Halvar sniffed spices and raw mokka-beans, heard the tink-tink of a hammer on metal as someone worked into the night to finish some object.

"Here we are." The donkey-driver rapped on the wooden shutter that had been put up to cover the front window. "Yussif! I have a customer for you!"

Halvar slid out of the cart and handed the driver half a string of white wumpum. The driver grinned happily; now he could go home with the satisfaction of having made a whole day's pay with one fare.

Yussif turned out to be a scrawny specimen in a long multicolored coat that matched that of his namesake in the Holy

Book. Halvar thought he must have concocted it of scraps left over from garments he'd made for his customers.

"It's almost Shabbat," Yussif complained. "I'm closed."

"But this is someone important!" the driver announced. "It's the Calif's Hireling!! The one who rid us of that pestilence Gomez," he added as a final persuasion.

"Oh?" Yussif opened the door to take a better look. "What's happened to him?"

"I was attacked on the road from Green Village," Halvar declared. "They tore this coat."

"Mmmm?" Yussif sighed and beckoned Halvar in. "Come inside, then, and I'll see what I can do. And a bom Shabbat to you, Avaram, for bringing him here."

The donkey driver tapped his animal, ready to head back to the stables. Halvar stopped him.

"You, Avaram. You can go to your prayer-house, if you want, but I'll need you back here to take me places."

"But...it's Shabbat!" Avaram protested. "It's forbidden to work! And the beast, he needs his rest, too."

"I'll pay a purple wumpum," Halvar offered. "And it's in the name of the calif!"

"Two purple, and you have yourself a driver," Avaram stated. "And may I be forgiven for breaking the Shabbat, for the sake of my wife and children, that they may not starve or freeze this winter."

"Get to the prayer-house, then, and come back in an hour," Halvar ordered. Two beads of purple wumpum was the equivalent of an eight-bit of a silver dinar of Al-Andalus, the price of a taberna meal and a bed at home. If this would feed and house a family in Manatas for the whole winter, there was something amiss, either in Al-Andalus or in Manatas!

Meanwhile, there was the problem of the coat.

He followed Yussif into a small room cluttered with bolts of cloth and garments in various stages of completion. A table held the tailor's meager meal—a round loaf of bread, the leg of a fowl, a dish of cooked vegetables, a cup and a bottle that might have held cider. There was no sign of female niceties, and no sound from the upper rooms of the house. Clearly, this tailor was a bachelor, and not a prosperous one, either. Avaram was being generous when he steered Halvar to his cousin's door.

Halvar let Yussif ease him out of the tight coat. The tailor tut-tutted at the state of the garment, muttering in the Yehudit language. He had had few dealings with Yehudit before the Fates had sent him to Al-Andalus. Their caravans traversed the Dane-March and the plains beyond, trading goods and information, both important to the people they visited, but never settling anywhere for more than a generation at most.

There were legends that Yehudit had been banished from their homeland because they had rejected the Redeemer's message of the Good News. Nevertheless, some of the great lords of Muscovy had allowed Yehudit to make permanent settlements in their lands because they were supposedly cleverer than other peoples, even though the farmers regarded them with suspicion.

Only in Al-Andalus were Yehudit made truly welcome. Those who had settled permanently and built their study-houses there called themselves Sefarat, and held themselves higher than the Askenat, who were forced to wander. In Corduva and Sevilla, where Halvar had found both allies and antagonists among them, they were almost indistinguishable from other Andalusians, living quietly in their own quarters, keeping the calif's laws, working at many occupations, even rising to positions of power as advisers to the calif. They paid the dhimmi tax, they were—for the most part—honest, and they preferred to settle their personal disputes with words, not with knives. As long as they remained that way, Halvar had no particular dislike of Yehudit, even though one particular Yehudit girl had changed his life.

He looked over the stock in the tailor's shop while Yussif fussed over the coat.

"I can put in a patch here and here, under the arms and around the back." Yussif demonstrated the effect it would have. "I have some of the fabric of the coat, or I can use this—it's the woolen stuff the Bretains prefer. They call it after that river where the sheep are…um, Tweed? It's not quite the same color, but It may set a fashion to have a piece in a different color set into a coat."

"Just make it so I don't look as if I've been torn by a lion," Halvar said irritably. He wanted to be out and about, not wasting his time in this tailor's shop. "You don't have anything already made up, do you? I'll pay for it."

"With Andalus silver, I hope," Yussif said.

"Not wumpum?" If that false wumpum had gotten into the Souk, there would really be trouble!

"I prefer silver," Yussif said. "Wumpum is good enough for food and drink, but the Bretains insist on silver for their cloth, and so silver is what I must take for the clothing I make from it."

"You haven't seen anything like this?" Halvar pulled out the string of false wumpum. It was showing some wear, flakes of purple paint now chipping off the white beads.

Yussif peered closely at it then shook his head violently.

"No, no, I have never seen such wumpum. Nor would I pass it if I had."

"Then you don't know where it comes from?"

"I have heard," the tailor said slowly, "that some of the others in this Street of Tailors, the ones who deal with the Bretains of the Feria, and some of the Franchen who stay at the waterfront tabernas, they may have taken some purple wumpum that was not what it was supposed to be. But I, myself, I did not see it."

"You're sure you didn't get fooled by this painted wumpum?" Halvar persisted. "Because if you did, I'd be very interested to know who passed it to you. The calif will not stand for his currency being forged."

"The calif is there, we are here," Yussif pointed out. He looked around the shop. "I have few customers as large as you, Calif's Man." He found one garment, hung on a peg behind his sewing-table. "I made this jacket for Tenente Gomez, may he go to the demons in Sheol, but he was shorter than you, although he was as wide in the chest." He pointed to the black woolen jacket trimmed with bands of heavy silk ribbon at the cuffs and hems.

"And wider in the belly," Halvar commented. He looked the jacket over. The style was close to what he had seen before he left Al-Andalus for Manatas—sleeves padded to make the shoulders look broader, waist belted to look slimmer, and most unusual of all, a high collar turned up around the neck instead of a plain band around the neckline to be covered by a pleated ruff.

"Something new," Yussif explained. "One of the Guards, a man trom Italia, told me about it. He was cut in the wars, but he swears his collar saved him, because it had been made stiff with a paste of flour and fish-glue."

"Could be useful." He slid his arms into the jacket, shrugging to test the fit. "This may work," he declared. He fastened the jacket with the wooden buttons that hooked into loops across the chest. Then he ran a finger around the collar where it rubbed against his neck. "This isn't useful. It's painful."

Yussif produced a long piece of soft kutton trimmed with silk ribbon along each edge and a fringe at either end.

"This goes under the collar," he explained. "They call it for the ones who made the fashion—H'varat."

"Cavarat?" Halvar tried to approximate the sound, somewhere between coughing and spitting. "Whatever it is, I'll take it. Finish the coat, send it to the Rabat, and collect your payment there."

"And who will believe a Yehudit tailor who says that the Calif's Hireling came to him after sundown on the Shabbat and bought a jacket? No, Calif's Man, you will pay me here and now, in silver, or you will go away as you came!" The tailor struck a defiant pose.

Halvar grinned and shook his head.

"I didn't come out prepared for bargaining," he said. "All I have is wumpum, and not enough of that, either. If you want to be paid, you'll have to come with me to the Rabat right now, Shabbat or no Shabbat."

Yussif looked at his meal, then at Halvar, then towards the prayer-house, where Halvar could hear a wailing chant. Piety warred with avarice, and piety won.

"I will be at the Rabat as soon as the Shabbat is over," Yussif stated.

"And I will pay you, in silver—you have the word of the calif on it," Halvar promised.

"I am a fool, but I will trust you. Shalaam, calif's man. You have taken Gomez's coat. I only hope you do not take Gomez's place. He levied a tax on everyone in the Souk, over the usual tax we pay the sultan."

"I don't suppose he paid for the jacket, either," Halvar said.

Yussif snorted, "No, he never did."

"A pity, because you seem to be very good at your craft." Another thought struck him. "Did you ever make anything for Leon di Vicenza?"

151

"That one?" Yussif said with contempt. "Not likely! He got his clothes sent from Al-Andalus, when he didn't concoct his own designs and have them made up by Lady Ayesha's own sewing-women. Very interesting, those designs, but not the sort of thing working folk would wear.

"Now, if you have finished, Don Álvaro, I will have my little Shabbat meal, and you can be on your way to the Rabat, or wherever you wanted Avaram to take you."

"No wife for you, tailor?" Halvar remarked as Yussif fussed over the new jacket, showing him how to adjust the scarf so the edges showed just a bit over the collar and the fringed ends were tucked into the front.

"Not enough Yehudit girls here in Manatas, and I don't want a widow with children I can't support." Yussif sighed.

"Have you heard of a Yehudit girl gone missing?"

"We heard the newscriers. Horrible! All I could think of was that we would be blamed for it. They always blame the Yehudit," the tailor added bitterly. "There was plenty of talk at the study-house, but no young girl is missing among our people."

Halvar nodded gravely. "Yussif the Tailor, you will be paid in good silver if you can find out for me if anyone among the Yehudit knows anything about either the false wumpum or the dead girl."

"But what has one to do with the other?" Yussif looked puzzled.

"I don't know," Halvar admitted as he retrieved his leather-lined hat and stepped into the street, where Avaram waited for him. "But I have a feeling they are connected. I just have to find out how."

Chapter 8

A HUGE HARVEST MOON HAD RISEN, BUT ITS LIGHT didn't penetrate the twisting lanes of the Souk, so Avaram had hung a small lantern on a pole next to his seat on the cart.

"I thought every householder was supposed to put a lantern by the door," Halvar complained, as the cart jogged off.

"Too much risk of fire," Avaran explained. "It's all very well for the fine folk on the east side of the Broad Way—they have plaster walls, but we have to make do with wood, and wood burns. Where to, Don Álvaro?"

Halvar thought for a moment.

"You know the House of the Green Crescent?"

"It's run by those Sisters of Fatima, the women of Islim. I've never been there."

"That's where I have to go. If you don't know where it is, find out."

Avaram sighed deeply.

"I will look like a fool, or worse, asking the way to a place used by women," he complained.

"That doesn't matter to me," Halvar said. "I have business with Eva Hakim, and that's the place to find her."

Avaram grimaced, poked the donkey, and headed towards the Broad Way.

The main street of Manatas was full of men, most in the long robes favored by the elite of Al-Andalus but some in the newer

153

style made popular by young Calif Felipe. He had taken on the mode of the students from Parigi—breeches tied at the knee, padded jacket fastened with straps and toggle-buttons, topped with a tall tarboosh. Here and there were Afrikans in long shirts and loose trousers, but Halvar did not see either the wide-brimmed hats favored by Franchen or the woolen shirts of the Bretains that were so common at Green Village.

Avaram made a few inquiries of passersby then informed Halvar, "The place is on the east side of Manatas, between the Broad Way and the waterfront."

He drove down a side street between the blank walls of two plaster-covered brick houses to another long north-south road. The lanterns at each end of the street did little to illuminate the darkness. The long road clearly marked the boundary of the residential area favored by the richer merchants, who built houses in the style of Al-Andalus—rooms arranged around a central courtyard with a tiled roof and plaster-covered brick walls. There was no sign of life other than the faint smells of cooking coming from the inner courtyards of the houses. The windows were narrow and barred, covered with wooden shutters to keep out the wind that was rising from the Great River.

Avaram turned into a small plaza with a central fountain that Halvar dimly recognized as the place where he had been left three nights before.

"The House of the Green Crescent," Avaram announced. "And if it please you, Don Álvaro, here I will leave you. I must get home. My wife will wonder why I am so late."

"Maybe this will take away some of her sorrow," Halvar said as he slid two purple wumpum off the string.

Avaram took them carefully and peered at them by the light of his lantern.

"They're the good ones," Halvar assured him.

"Not that I thought you'd try to pass off the bad wumpum on a poor donkey driver," Avaram protested.

"And just when did you learn about the bad wumpum?"

"They found it at the Feria," Avaram said. "Not that I get purple wumpum," he added. "Only white! But one of the Franchen was talking about it when I took him from the waterfront to the Wall."

"I didn't see too many Franchen on the Broad Way."

"They usually go to the Mermaid Taberna after dark," Avaram told him. "Ever since that Franchen Jacques came to Manatas, that's where the Franchen go. They like the cooking."

"Do they, now?" Halvar mused. He hadn't been too impressed with Lizette, the slovenly wife of the innkeeper Jacques Tavernier.

They were interrupted by the arrival of a horse-drawn carriage, accompanied by a squad of Town Guard led by Tenente Ruiz. The donkey took exception to the huge vehicle, braying and kicking. The horse, for his part, shied and bucked at the donkey's bray. The men scattered to avoid being trampled by the animals. Lights appeared in the windows of the houses across the square from the House of the Green Crescent. A few doors opened so the neighbors could see what odd visitors had disturbed the dinner hour.

"What's going on?" came a roar from inside the carriage. The owner of the voice emerged, first as a silver-studded wooden leg then a booted flesh-and-blood one. The Afrikan slave perched on the back of the carriage sprang forward to help Sultan Petrus out of the carriage. Ruiz assisted in the tricky task of getting the bulky man out of his vehicle with the dignity befitting his years and status.

"Get on home," Halvar told Avaram gruffly as the donkey driver soothed his animal. "Have yourself a good Shabbat. You've earned it. And give the beast an extra measure of hay," he added as Avaram and his donkey plodded off.

He turned to the new arrival.

"Salaam aleikum, Excellent Sultan," he greeted the ruler of Manatas, "I am surprised to see you out of the Rabat, and so late, too." He raised his eyebrows in an unspoken question at Ruiz, who shrugged expressively.

"I could not stay away," the sultan said. "I had to know, to see for myself," he murmured.

Halvar knocked at the door of the house that was marked with the Green Crescent. One of the Sisters of Fatima, draped in the brown gown and green hijab worn by the nurses, opened it.

"We must see that girl, the one who was brought in today," Sultan Petrus ordered before Halvar could speak.

"That is forbidden," the sister stated, and began to shut the door.

155

Eva Hakim appeared.

"Go back to the ward, Sister," she told the nurse. "The sultan and the Calif's Hireling are here on official business." She regarded Ruiz coolly. "I do not know what the Town Guard is doing here."

"I am here to make sure the sultan is properly escorted," Ruiz answered. "And to make my own observations."

"Such as?" Halvar challenged him.

"I know the tides and the currents along the East Channel," Ruiz retorted. "I was brought up on the waterfront. I can make a good guess as to where and when that girl was killed, and how she came to be in the clam bed."

Eva Hakim nodded and led the men through the house, across the courtyard to a stark room at the back where the body of the girl from the clam bed lay on a wooden table. The rigidity of death had relaxed enough the corpse had been straightened out, her nudity covered with a linen cloth.

Eva Hakim's voice was unemotional as she told the sultan, "I know this girl. I did not recognize her at first, her face was so distorted, but then I realized who it was. I would have told you myself. You did not have to come all this way to look."

"Is it...?" The sultan gripped the edge of the table, unwilling to look at the face of the dead girl.

"You may rest easy, Sultan. I believe this is Sharona, one of Lady Ayesha's attendants, who came with her from Al-Andalus as a companion."

The sultan looked first relieved, then puzzled.

"But what was she doing away from the Rabat?" he asked.

Halvar followed this exchange, looking from one to the other.

"Perhaps the girl was sent off on an errand," he suggested. "But why wasn't she missed when she didn't come back?"

"There has been a certain amount of upset," Eva Hakim reminded him. "Lady Ayesha's labor came on suddenly, and there was the excitement of your arrival, Don Álvaro, and then the business about my brother. It is possible that one small servant might be missed."

"Could be," he admitted. "Have you had time to look her over?"

"I have. As I suspected, she was virgin, and not molested. However, she soiled herself when she died."

156

"It happens when someone's strangled," Halvar said sagely. "I've seen it before. The innards release when the killer's cord cuts the throat. I don't know why, but it does."

"Poor thing," Ruiz said. "I don't even remember her. There are six or seven of those harem attendants, and they stay in the harem. They don't even look at us guards."

"It would hardly be fitting if the harem attendants were distracted from their duties by men," Eva Hakim retorted.

"What about her hand?" Halvar asked impatiently.

"Most interesting," Eva Hakim said. She took a small bowl and held it out. "These were what she held."

In the bowl were three white beads.

Chapter 9

EVA HAKIM WENT ON.

"And as you can see, there is a purple stain on her hand." She pointed to it, careful not to touch the body.

"'That connects her to the false wumpum," Halvar said. "She must have seen it being made. She took these beads to bring back to the Rabat."

"And was herself seen and killed before she could get there," Eva Hakim finished for him. "I suppose your next step, Don Álvaro, will be to trace the girl's whereabouts, from the Rabat to wherever she was sent."

Halvar thought this over.

"It's not just where, it's when. This killing must have happened last night, while I was sleeping off that dose of poppy-juice potion that Kristo frater made me drink."

Ruiz had not been able to look at the dead girl.

"I can tell you when it must have happened," he said. "Last night's full moon tide covered the clam beds until just before dawn. She must have been killed between midnight and dawn, then brought to the clam beds by canoe." He pointed to the dark patches on the girl's arms and legs. "Those are the marks made by the ribs of a canoe. My guess? She had to have been killed on the waterfront, from where the killer could transport her upstream, to the clam bed on the far side of the wall.

"Why transport her all the way there?" Halvar objected. "Why not just throw her into the East Channel?"

"The Great River and the East Channel both flow backwards and forwards. Remember how Gomez went north instead of south? The body would have wound up in the clam beds either way. The killer got her away from his own place and hoped the tide would sweep her out to sea. As it happened the killer was too late—the tide had already turned."

"Not familiar with the tides, then," Halvar concluded.

"Or didn't care."

Halvar turned back to Eva Hakim.

"Do you remember whether the girl was at the Rabat when you attended Lady Ayesha?

She gave a rueful sigh

"Between the fuss over your arrival, and the discovery of the body in the Feria, and the delivery of the new child, there was much coming and going at the Rabat. It is possible she slipped away then on some errand of her own."

Halvar considered this.

"I thought the ladies of the harem are kept close in the Rabat. Are they allowed to roam free in Manatas Town?"

Eva Hakim's frown deepened.

"Lady Ayesha was quite young when she came here with the sultan," she said, choosing her words with caution. "She brought some companions to amuse her until she was of an age to take on her full marital duties. They would go into the Souk, or to the Feria—under proper supervision, of course.

"Once she was with child, Lady Ayesha would send her maids out for certain delicacies that were brought in on the ships from Oropa. Dates and figs, for instance, do not grow well here in Manatas, but they are imported from Al-Andalus and Afrika; when a dhow came in, Lady Ayesha would send one of her maids to the waterfront for them."

"And you think this girl Sharona was sent to get dates and figs?" Halvar thought this over. "I don't remember eating any dates or figs at that banquet. Of course, I don't remember very much about the banquet, After that voyage, just getting my feet steady on dry land was a chore."

"I hope your stomach has settled," Eva Hakim said, as a professional courtesy.

Halvar's thoughts lurched elsewhere.

"What about the boy—Selim? Could he have been sent off with this girl? They must have known each other, if they were thrown together at the Rabat, especially if they were the same age."

Eva Hakim's face reddened under her hijab, and she licked her lips as if they had suddenly gone dry.

"If you are implying that Selim and the girl were, um, involved in some youthful romance…"

"It's been known to happen," Halvar said with a wry grin.

"You may forget that hypothesis," Eva Hakim said firmly. "Sharona was, indeed, known to Selim. Selim was only ten years old when he came here, and she perhaps a year older. She was assigned to accompany him and my brother Leon when they went on excursions into Manatas Town, and beyond, before the Wall was built.

"Leon is a believer in the theory that examination of one's surroundings leads to enlightenment. To this end, he would take Selim into the forest to look at the plants and animals of Nova Mundum. Sharona was there to carry their food baskets and any other small packages they might take with them."

"How long did this go on?" Halvar asked.

"Until last year. After that Sharona attended Lady Ayesha exclusively when the lady assumed her full marital role. Hem!" Eva Hakim coughed delicately. "It was a time of some change. Mullah Abadul came from Afrika to take over the Grand Muskat after the retirement of the former mullah.

"He is stricter in his devotion to the Holy Books and the Word of the Prophet, may his name be blessed, than was common in Manatas until to that time. He insisted that someone with my brother's, um, social life was unfit to continue to teach Selim, and the sultan had to comply with the mullah's strictures or lose the respect of the pious."

"And what happened to Selim?" Halvar was beginning to see a pattern emerging.

"Selim was not happy. Not being of an age to be admitted to the Madrassa, he was left to find his own companions."

"And he found them," Ruiz said with one of his wry smiles. "He'd go off to the Souk, him and those other troublemakers, those Seekers of Truth as they called themselves, students at the Madrassa. They'd meet at Benyamin's bookstall, or go over to the Mermaid Taberna to sit at Leon's feet." He sniffed with disdain.

"Selim was quite upset by Lady Ayesha's pregnancy," Eva Hakim added. "It is possible he may have gone to see Leon when she went into labor."

"At the Mermaid Taberna," Halvar said.

"Except Leon wasn't there," Ruiz pointed out. "He'd left for the Feria and Green Village. He must have been whacking that frater over the head at the time Selim came looking for him."

"In that case, where is Selim?" Halvar asked.

No one had an answer.

Eva Hakim led Halvar and Ruiz to the small parlor, where Sultan Petrus had been seated on a chair beside a table; a tray with a pot of mokka and cups had been set for his refreshment.

Halvar salaamed.

"Excellent Sultan, if this dead girl is one of Lady Ayesha's servants, I must question the ladies of the harem. It's possible that one of them can tell me where she went, and when."

"Impossible!" Sultan Petrus exploded. "Lady Ayesha is not to be disturbed!" He turned to Eva Hakim. "Has a wet-nurse been sent for?"

Halvar fidgeted as the domestic arrangements were made. In his experience, limited as it was to the Dane-March, and then to years of fighting with the Free Company, boys of ten were not usually companions of girls of any age. Boys went with their fathers, brothers, and uncles, farming or learning a craft, or studying for the fratery. Girls were at home with mothers, sisters, and aunts, learning the ways of the household. Why would the sultan's son be accompanied by the girl assigned to keep his father's very young wife amused?

There was something going on here, he was sure of it, and somehow, it was connected with Selim's disappearance. But what did it have to do with the false wumpum? That was another question to which he had no answer, only suppositions.

The sultan finished his mokka and shifted on his chair preparatory to hoisting himself upright.

"We'll see to the burial, of course. Sharona was part of my household, one way or another."

"I'll see you back to your carriage, Excellent Sultan," Ruiz offered.

161

Halvar followed them to the courtyard and wondered where to go next. His stomach rumbled. He remembered he had eaten nothing all day, not since that gruel early this morning.

"Are the food shops on the waterfront open?" he wondered aloud.

"I believe they are," Ruiz answered. "Sailors demand food and drink, especially drink, at all hours. Do you plan to go there now? You could find a meal at the Rabat." He paused, then said, "Of course, what you get at the waterfront will be a little better. Not much, but some."

"I need to see what is happening on the waterfront," Halvar decided.

"I'll walk with you,"Ruiz said. "Tenente Gomez was well known there, and you may not be welcome."

"I'm beginning to think I'm not welcome *anywhere* in Manatas," Halvar complained as they started through the darkened alleys between warehouses that separated the waterfront from the residences of the East Side of Manatas.

Chapter 10

BY THE TIME HALVAR AND RUIZ REACHED THE EAST Channel, the moon was fully up, flooding the plaza with cold light. A few sailboats bobbed alongside the pier that had been built over the sandy shore, their sails neatly furled against the spars, while canoes had been pulled out of the water and left to dry on the shore upside-down. The largest ships were anchored in the bay, beyond the tug of the current that made the East Channel so treacherous for the unwary.

The plaza that had been so busy during the day was now deserted. Lights flickered in the windows of the small sheds and shacks that had been thrown up between the larger buildings containing merchandise to be sold at the Feria or exported back to Oropa and Al-Andalus. Scraps of sound hinted at the presence of sailors and those who lived to serve them. The tang of saltwater mixed with the reek of rancid cooking oil from many pots and fires.

Ruiz looked around then headed for one of the ramshackle taverns, where two of his guards lurked in the shadows.

"Anything I should know about?" he asked.

"All quiet," the taller of the two reported.

"A fight at Gershon's. Two sailors wanted the same girl." The second guard dismissed the incident with a shrug. "No one killed. The sailors are at the frater's getting patched up."

"The girl?" Halvar asked.

Another shrug. "She's with another customer. No problem there."

"Business as usual," Ruiz said with a twist of his lips that could have been a grin or a grimace.

"Anyone open besides food and drink?"

"Only Manolo," the taller guard said, nodding towards the shack behind the tavern. "He's always ready to provide wumpum if someone runs out."

"Manolo's the pawnbroker," Ruiz explained. "He'll buy almost anything if he thinks he can sell it again."

"He's always open," the shorter guard said.

"Is he, indeed? Then it's possible he saw or heard someone taking one of those canoes last night, when all good folk should have been home," Halvar said.

"It's possible," Ruiz agreed. "But whether he'll tell us anything, that's another matter. He's a hard nut, is Manolo. Gomez dealt with him, I didn't."

Halvar knocked on the door of the shack then stepped inside. The tiny space was filled with oddments large and small, ranged on shelves and propped up against the walls. Broadswords from Scania jostled strange Afrikan carvings; a small box was set on a long table, open to display brooches and armbands studded with gems that might or might not be real; boots, jackets and trousers were pegged up on the wall. There was even a stack of books laid flat on a shelf in a far corner, almost out of sight. *Odd*, Halvar, thought. *You'd think here would be little use for books in a place like Manatas.*

Behind the long table stood Manolo himself, a crusty-looking man with a shock of white hair, whose age could be anything from fifty to a hundred. He wore the black coat of the Askenat Yehudit and broad hat of the Franchen.

"What can I do for you, sirs?" His rasp had been honed by years of trying to be heard in the gales of the Storm Sea.

Halvar's eye was caught by a coat spread out to show off its gaudy embroidered pattern of stylized flowers.

"That's a very nice garment," he commented. "Where did you get it?"

Ruiz exclaimed, "I know that coat!"

Manolo's eyes narrowed as he looked from one to the other.

"I found it," he stated.

164

"Did you, now?" Halvar said softly.

"That coat belonged to Selim ibn Petrus, the sultan's son," Ruiz continued. "The lad's missing. So, how is it that his coat is here, in your shop, Manolo Pawnbroker?" He reached out to grab him, but the old man leaped aside and took shelter behind his counter.

"I found it, I tell you. I was using the necessary behind the Mermaid Taberna, and I found it right there, jammed into the space under the outside stairs. It was a little messed up, but I got the dirt off and put it up there. It's yours for a two strings of purple, or a silver dinar."

"It's ours, all right," Ruiz said, pulling the coat from its peg. "It's evidence, that's what it is!"

"Evidence of what?" Manolo blustered. "I know nothing about the sultan's son! I was doing my business, I saw the coat jammed under the stairs, and I took it."

"Stole it, you mean!" Ruiz snapped.

"It was filthy!" Manolo protested.

Halvar sniffed the coat and nodded.

"He's right," he said. "Whoever wore this coat last soiled it. Smell it, Ruiz!"

Ruiz jerked his head away from the stench.

"Phew! I should run you in for selling impure merchandise!"

"A little scrubbing, some sunshine, and that coat's as good as new," Manolo insisted.

"Maybe so, but it's still Selim's coat, and he's still missing," Ruiz countered.

Halvar pulled out his string of purple wumpum. Manolo eyed it then produced a small glass lens from some hidden pocket and examined it carefully.

"So, you know about the false wumpum," Halvar said. He grabbed the pawnbroker by the collar of his coat. "When did it start coming into your shop?"

Manolo squirmed.

"Maybe a week ago? Just at the time the Feria opened."

"Interesting." Halvar let the man go. "No one seems to have had any trouble with wumpum until this year's Feria. Then it gets into the Feria, but not the Souk. Why do you suppose that is?"

Ruiz looked blank. "Maybe whoever is passing it goes to the Feria, but not the Souk?"

"Why not? Don't the same goods get sold in both places?"

Manolo and Ruiz looked at each other, then at Halvar.

"Foreigners go to the Feria," Manolo explained. "No one who lives in Manatas bothers to go there, except maybe once in a season to take the kiddies to see the performers. You want value, you go to the Souk."

"What about all this?" Halvar indicated the oddments around him.

"Mostly from sailors," Manolo said. "They run out of gambling money, and they sell what they picked up here and there."

"Gambling? I'm shocked—shocked!" Ruiz said, his signature grin returning. "Where would anyone gamble here in Manatas? I thought that was the attraction at Green Village."

"Oh, you can find a game of tabouli or chess at the Mermaid," Manolo said with a wink. "But sailors will bet on anything— dice, cartes, even whether one drop of rain will fall faster than another. Anything to break the monotony. And they play each other here in Manatas, in their own taverns. They don't go to Green Village. Too far from the waterfront."

"A small game between friends? I know all about those friendly games." Ruiz winked back at Manolo. "I'm not Gomez. I don't ask that you pay me to look the other way when you buy and sell merchandise without paying the calif for the transaction. But I will take this coat, Manolo, and if anyone comes in with more of that fake wumpum, you send word, you hear me?"

"Always glad to help out the Town Guard," Manolo said with a smile as false as his promise.

Outside the pawnbroker's shack, Halvar held the coat up to the light of the lantern that hung outside the door.

"A very pretty coat," he said. "Just how tall would you say Selim is?"

Ruiz shrugged. "I didn't pay much attention to him. No one really did, except maybe Leon. He wasn't very big when he first arrived, but he's shot up in the last year. Lads do around that age. I'd say he's a little shorter than me, maybe as tall as Gomez?" He held a hand level with his chin.

"What does he look like?"

"A lad, I suppose." Ruiz gave another shrug. "I didn't see much of the sultan or his family after the first year they were here.

Lady Ayesha was kept in the harem, and when she went out, she was veiled, with her ladies around her."

"And Selim?" Halvar strolled across the plaza toward the Mermaid Taberna.

"He had the run of the Rabat, of course, under Leon's eye," Ruiz said. He interrupted Halvar's steady stride. "Before you judge me, Don Álvaro, remember that until this morning, I was a humble second to Tenente Gomez, and he held most of Manatas in his grip. My job was to keep things organized, to keep the records straight, since I can write Arabi, Franchen, and Erse.

"If I'm going to be tenente of the Town Guard, I'm going to have to earn the respect of the men, and that won't be easy even with Gomez gone. This business of the girl being killed, one of the sultan's own household—that's bad, very bad. I want to catch this killer as much as you do, Don Álvaro."

"Quite a speech, Tenente Ruiz," Halvar said. "Now I'll tell you what I think. I think the wumpum, the dead girl, and the missing lad are all connected. I think the wumpum comes from here. And I think I'll have something to eat and drink at the Mermaid Taberna. Do you care to join me, Tenente?"

Ruiz's smile was not at all wry.

"Thank you, Don Álvaro," he said. "A meal at the Mermaid Taberna is usually far beyond the reach of a humble Town Guard. I will be happy to join you for dinner."

Chapter 11

WHEN HALVAR HAS BEEN IN THE MERMAID TABERNA two days before, it seemed a hospitable place, much like the eating-houses and inns he had seen in his travels over Oropa. Now the atmosphere seemed more sinister.

The customers, all men, sat at square tables on sturdy chairs or on benches lined up against the walls, instead of reclining on cushions in the Andalusian fashion. The room was lit by oil lamps hanging from an iron wheel suspended from a rafter by chains so the flames would not start a fire with their sparks. Smaller lamps were set on the tables, adding some light, enhanced by the flickering flames of the fireplace at the far end of the room, next to the kitchen door.

There was none of the raucous gaiety of the Gardens of Paradise. This was a place where conversations were held in undertones; the loudest sounds came from the kitchen where Lizette could be heard berating her staff to the accompaniment of clashing pans. Two scrawny young men, in striped trousers and stained shirts covered with white aprons, rushed back and forth from the kitchens, assisted by a lanky girl in a striped skirt and loose shirt with a ruffle around the neckline, her hair covered by a floppy cap whose frilly edge was adorned by a limp strip of ribbon.

Jacques Tavernier, the proprietor, bustled forward as soon as he saw Halvar in the doorway. He bowed, rubbing his hands together, an ingratiating smile pasted on his face.

"Don Álvaro! And Tenente Ruiz! Welcome to the Calif's Hireling and the new tenente of the Town Guard!" he announced loudly.

All conversation stopped. Halvar felt every eye in the place assessing him then moving past him to Ruiz.

"Word travels fast," he muttered as the buzz of talk picked up again.

He scanned the room as Jacques led them through the tables to an unoccupied one in the center of the room where they could be observed by everyone. Halvar would have preferred someplace less prominent, but for now, he was content to let Jacques take the lead while he assessed the patrons of the Mermaid.

These were Franchen and Danes, more staid than the Bretains and Scanians of Green Village; the striped trousers and wide-brimmed hats of the Franchen traders and the blue-dyed jackets of Danic seamen were prominent.

Halvar smelled tabac, but there was no whiff of hemp here. Mokka there was, but no cider or any other alcohol he could detect. Along one wall were tables set up for chess and tabouli, the game the Bretains called backgammon, but there were no cards or dice in evidence; and the players were not the hardened gamblers Halvar had seen in the backstreets of Corduva. Aside from the gawky servant girl, there were no women in sight.

Whatever vices were being sold on the waterfront, they were not being peddled at the Mermaid Taberna.

Jacques seated them with a flourish and proceeded to recite the bill of fare.

"My good wife Lizette is the best of cooks. She has been at it all day. We have roasted chickens—none of your stringy gobble-birds—and a fine fish stew, with the fish fresh-caught this morning. To start your meal, we have herring from the Dane-March, pickled in a crock with onions and capers."

"I haven't had a pickled herring since I left the Dane-March," Halvar admitted.

Ruiz grimaced at the thought.

"Roast fowl will do for me," he decided. "What about that fish stew? I hear some of your waterfront eating places use clams in it. Not halal," he added in case he hadn't made his point.

"Oh, Tenente Ruiz," Jacques protested with another bow and a rub of his hands, "this establishment is within the borders of Manatas Town. We are under Sharia, and of course, we use no swine's flesh nor any other forbidden ingredients in our cooking."

"No wine, either?" Halvar hinted. "No ale or uskebagh?"

"Certainly not," Jacques said indignantly. "Mokka, of course, and the sweet cider, although few here use it. It is more suited to females, which, as you see, we do not serve."

"Not on the menu, eh?" Ruiz winked.

Jacques reacted with an indignant snort.

"If that is your wish, Tenente Ruiz, I recommend you take your custom back to the Gardens of Paradise and the Yehudit tart who runs it. This is a respectable taberna. We do, occasionally, allow a poet to recite his works, and the students from the Madrassa hold their debates here."

"Sounds interesting," Halvar said dryly. "I know about Leon di Vicenza and his debating society, those Seekers of Truth. According to Tenente Gomez, things got lively when they started arguing."

"Lively?" Ruiz laughed. "I had to break up more than one fight here when that bunch got going. And over what? Whether the earth is flat or round? Whether the stars in the sky are set in crystal or just fly about as they will? Whether the Prophet or the Redeemer can save a soul from eternal torments?" He snorted. "None of that is worth drawing knives over!"

"Yet you say knives were drawn," Halvar said. "So, Jacques Tavernier, what kind of fish *is* in this stew? I hear some of the food places here make a stew of shellfish—clams and oysters that the Local women bring in."

Jacques shrugged. "If that is so, then perhaps you should get some in those places. Here at the Mermaid Taberna, all is halal. The fish in the stew were caught this very morning from the bay—shad, salmon, bluefish. I can bring you the pickled herring to whet your appetite, then the chickens, dressed with onions and carrots, cooked in the pot—none of this esquosh or maiz, none of the Local trash. Just good Oropan cooking in the Franchen style."

There was a crash and a volley of Franchen vituperation from the kitchens. The gawky girl dashed through the door with another platter, and Jacques bowed away to deal with his temperamental chef.

"I'll have the herring!" Halvar called after him.

"What do you think of our fine eating place?" Ruiz asked as the gawky girl scampered in to place a platter of fish covered by onions in front of Halvar. She peered at him from under the frill of her cap then glanced at Ruiz; neither one looked at her. Halvar's attention was on his dinner, and Ruiz was scanning the room to assess the clientele.

There was a shout from the kitchens, and the girl scuttled back to answer the call. Halvar picked up a fish and disposed of it in one bite. He closed his eyes in ecstasy at the taste of home.

"Try it," he urged Ruiz.

Ruiz took one sniff, shook his head.

"I'll wait for the fowls," he said. "Pickle doesn't agree with me." He looked around the room again. "I've spotted at least two captains of ships that aren't Andalusian," he said softly. "These merchants aren't staying at Green Village for the Feria. They're here to transfer cargoes from southern Nova Mundum to the Bretain and Franchen lands without paying the Feria tolls."

"I don't see any Afrikans," Halvar said, scanning the room as well.

"They have their own quarter near the smithy," Ruiz said. "And they're even more rigid about halal food than the mokkahouses and food shops along the Broad Way. They're the ones who brought in Mullah Abadul to replace our old imam, who was too lax, by their way of thinking."

Halvar sighed. "I'll never understand religion," he said. "All the fighting over the Redeemer and the Prophet. The things done in the name of either or both." He gazed bleakly into the distance, seeing battlefields and sacked towns he had thought he'd forgotten.

The rest of their food arrived, along with mugs of mokka, and religious matters took second place to the more serious matter of eating.

"Not bad," was Halvar's judgment. "The chicken's a little dry, and the vegetables are a little soggy, but I've had worse."

"I'm not one to criticize any meal someone else is paying for," Ruiz stated. "And I agree—what you'd get at the Rabat would definitely be worse. But I like a little more taste to the food I eat. This stuff just sits there. No bite to it at all."

"Pepper costs," Halvar noted. "It's got enough salt, though."

The tall girl came out of the kitchen with another platter and headed for the table next to the one where Halvar and Ruiz sat. She tripped, sending a portion of roasted meat into Halvar's lap.

"Oh, I am so sorry!" She scooped bits of lamb off his lap. In a hurried undertone, she whispered, "Don Álvaro, I must speak with you! There is something you should know—"

Jacques descended on the girl, radiating fury.

"Sally! Stupid creature! Who let you out of the kitchens? Get back where you belong!" He bowed and rubbed his hands again. "Don Álvaro, my great apologies! This clumsy girl is very new to her job. We only took her on out of charity. Your meal is complimentary, of course! We will not allow you to pay for such rude service!"

Halvar swiped at the mess on his lap.

"You've got a room upstairs formerly occupied by Leon di Vincenza don't you? What have you done with the clothes used by the last tenant?"

Jacques was aghast.

"Surely, you won't want to wear *his* clothing. Those red trousers, that silk shirt—more suited to a woman than a man!"

"He's as tall as me," Halvar said stubbornly. "What did you do with his belongings? Pack them up, sell them?"

"Well," Jacques said, apologetically, "as I told you, he hasn't paid his rent in two months. Lizette thought we should take a few things over to Manolo the Pawnbroker, just to cover the expenses. Leon could always redeem them. Most of it's still there," he added, cringing.

"Let's have a look." Halvar stood and pushed through the crowd toward the stairs. "Leon may be gone, but his books are still there. You can learn a lot from books, I've heard."

He looked behind him to make sure Ruiz and Jacques were following. He was aware the men below were watching his every move. He hid his inward grin. There were things going on in the Mermaid Taberna, and that girl in the kitchen had a story to tell.

First, though, he'd take a closer look at Leon's belongings, especially those books. He remembered how Leon was always scribbling in leather-bound notebooks back in Al-Andalus. He had been the barely tolerated bodyguard for the teenaged grandson of the calif, and Leon the leader of a band of students who ranged the countryside inspecting the ruins of the Old Roumi and arguing, just as these Seekers of Truth were arguing with the established scholars.

Like the Holy Book says, leopards don't change their spots, Halvar thought. *Leon, you're up to your old tricks. But what this has to do with a dead serving-girl or false wumpum, I don't know...yet.*

Chapter 12

LEON'S APARTMENT CONSISTED OF TWO ROOMS IN what was originally a loft where foodstuffs had been stored. Odors and noise from the kitchens below filtered through the floorboards as Lizette smashed through the evening's chores and berated her hapless staff. There was no landing at the top of the stairs.

The door on its leather hinges opened directly into the sitting room where Leon had held court with the Seekers of Truth and exercised his skills at making images in pen and ink and paint.

"Is this the only way in?" Halvar asked.

"There's a staircase outside," Jacques reminded him. "It overlooks the back alley where the public latrines are. Leon wanted to be able to get in and out without having to go through the main room. We cut a door into the wall, and Leon himself designed the struts of the staircase."

"I suppose he wanted to bring his friends up without disturbing your other guests," Ruiz suggested with a grin.

The first time Halvar had seen the apartment, the room had been flooded with light from the glass-paned window in the wall next to the outside door. Now the only illumination came from the lantern in Jacques's hand. By its flickering light, Halvar could see the small table where Leon had left his jars of paints and bottles of inks, along with his pens and brushes. There was a small oil lamp with a single wick. He used the candle inside the lantern to light it

He carried the lamp as he strolled around the room. Ruiz remained at the table, scanning the pots of paint and ink. Jacques followed Halvar, lifting his lamp so that flickering shadows jumped forward and backward across the floorboards.

"Nothing has been moved except what you sold?" Halvar asked.

"As you can see, Don Álvaro," Jacques affirmed. "Even when Leon was declared dead, my good wife and I kept it so, just in case Leon's sister, Eva Hakim, wished to take some memento of her brother."

"Very kind of you," Halvar said dryly. He beckoned Ruiz over to the shelf where Leon had kept his books. "I remember this shelf as being full of books with fine bindings, in different languages. They're not here now. And there was a picture, an image of the Old Roumi goddess of beauty. That's missing, too."

"That was an obscenity!" Jacques sputtered. "Lizette insisted that I get it out! As for the books, the ones with the fancy bindings, those I sold to Manolo the Pawnbroker. He took the drawing, too. There are some people who like that sort of thing."

He wilted under Halvar's stare.

"Leon owed me two months rent!" he protested. "And the notebooks he wrote in had interesting pictures, images. Manolo said he could cut them out and sell them separately."

Ruiz picked up one if the books left on the shelf, then another.

"I can read Arabi," he said. "But these aren't Arabi. I think this one is in Ivrit, the writing the Yehudit use. And this one is in Rune." He turned to Halvar. "Danic is written in Rune. Do you read it?"

Halvar shook his head.

"I can sign my name in Rune, and I can make out a few words, but I was needed on the farm. My older brother got the learning, I didn't." He picked up one of the books with tooled leather binding. "This is one of Leon's personal books, the ones he used to write in when I saw him in Corduva. He had them specially bound, and he was always scribbling in them, never went out without one."

Ruiz's eyes widened at one of the pictures in the notebook. Halvar looked at it, grinned, and said, "Well, now you know just how well Leon knew Otter Tail."

Ruiz slammed the book shut.

"I just hope there isn't anything like that in the books Manolo got! One look at that, and both the frater of the Kristos and Mullah Abadul would have him in a cell in a minute."

Halvar moved back to the table with the inks and paints

"Bring that light closer," he ordered.

He held each jar up to the light, dipped a brush in one after the other, and dripped paint on the nearest piece of paper. Blue, green, yellow, red...

"No purple," he muttered

"Purple?" Ruiz echoed.

"You mix red ink with blue and get purple," Halvar said. "I've seen it done in Corduva. But if the proportions differ, you get slightly different colors each time. True purple, that's not an easy color to get. From clams, I hear.

"A very difficult color to procure," Jacques agreed. "Blue, of course, one gets from indigo plants. They grow in southern Nova Mundum. It is much asked-for, very valuable. Blue cloth is very popular with the Locals. The Bretains in West Caster have a manufactory where kutton is spun then dyed into threads that make good, hard-wearing trousers. As for the red, there are a number of plants here that give red, and a kind of clay— the Locals use it for their facepaint in times of war."

"You seem to know a lot about the cloth trade, and about the Locals, too," Halva observed casually. "Have you always been an innkeeper?"

"Oh, I've done this and that," Jacques said, abruptly evasive.

"In Franchenland?"

"At one time. And in Kibbick—Lizette thought we would do better there."

"Then you came south, to Manatas," Halvar persisted.

"The weather here is less harsh. My poor Lizette suffers in the winter from the cold."

"I should think she's padded well enough," Ruiz commented.

Halvar said nothing but stepped through the heavy damask curtain, of the kind used by the wealthiest Andalusians, into the inner chamber. There was no window in this room, which had also been used for storage until Leon took residence and made it into his bedroom.

The bed filled most of the space. Four carved posts held the wooden frame, and cords had been strung across the frame to hold two down-filled mattresses instead of the hard planks more commonly found. The coverlet was of the same heavy silk as the curtain and there were four pillows at the head of the bed.

Halvar moved around to the chest where Leon had kept his clothes. Pegs hammered into the walls held Leon's heavier garments—a fur jacket, and a leather wamus of the kind worn by the Mahak, decorated with beads made from quills and shells.

"Otter Tail's?" Halvar asked, pointing to the wamus.

Ruiz shrugged, but Jacques frowned.

"The Mahak was not supposed to stay here permanently," he said.

"But he spent the night here from time to time," Halvar said.

He opened the chest and took out the first garment he found, a pair of lightweight kutton pantaloons. He held them up against his waist then turned to Ruiz.

"How tall would you say Leon is?"

Ruiz thought a moment.

"I'd say at least as tall as me. Maybe a little taller. Not as tall as you, Don Álvaro," he added.

"How wide?"

"Slender, but not as slender as those are."

"Would you say these would fit him?" Halvar held out the trousers.

"A little short for him. And definitely too tight."

"And a little light, too," Halvar decided. "Even as braies, I don't think these were Leon's."

"And not Otter Tail's, either," Ruiz added with a sarcastic laugh. "The Mahak wear a leather strap and a breechclout in all weathers."

"So, tell me, Jacques Tavernier, just whose are these? And this?" Halvar held up a long shirt, embroidered at the collar with a pattern of leaves and flowers. "Leon didn't bring girls up here, did he?"

"Leon? Never!" Jacques let out a crack of laughter. "Definitely not his style at all!"

"In that case," Halvar asked, "how did these womens' clothes get into Leon's chest?"

Ruiz turned on Jacques.

"Running girls, are you, Jacques Tavernier? In the very respectable Mermaid Taberna?

"You know the rules, Tavernier. Whores do business only in the licensed houses behind the warehouses. You and I had better have a little talk. I'm not Gomez. I don't want trouble, but you can't bribe me to look the other way while you and that harridan of a wife of yours bring sailors up here for a little playtime!"

"Whores? Here? Never!" Jacques protested. "I don't know how those things got here! As for Lizette, she's here to cook! There's nothing else going on, I swear by the Redeemer and his Mother Mara! Or by the Prophet, if you don't believe me! You can look anywhere you like, Tenente Ruiz!"

"I will, tomorrow morning, in the daylight. And if I find any evidence that you and that wife of yours are lying to me, I will bring you to the Rabat and let some of Gomez's bullyboys find the truth."

Halvar let them argue while he sat on the bed. The cords creaked alarmingly, but they held firm.

He put aside any thoughts of what Leon and Otter Tail had been up to on that bed and fell back against the pillows. His eyes closed. It had been a very long, very intense day. Before he knew it, he was snoring loudly.

Chapter 13

HALVAR'S EYES POPPED OPEN AS A SUDDEN NOISE jolted him awake. He felt cold air, and the whisper of the heavy silk curtain moving.

Someone had opened the door to the outside stairs, sending a breeze into the apartment, and whoever that someone was, he had no business being there.

Halvar carefully eased out of the bed, wincing .The cords holding the feather-filled mattresses creaked, and he hoped the burglar would discount the sound as being made by the sleeper shifting to a more comfortable position. He let out a sigh and a grunt, as he swung his feet down to the floor in hope of reinforcing that illusion. Slowly he stood and crept to the doorway, treading as lightly as he could.

There was the flicker of a tiny flame. By its light, he could just make out a stout figure bending over Leon's collection of paints.

Halvar took two long steps to the intruder and grabbed his arm, ready to swing him around to see his face. The arm was rounder and plumper than he expected. He squeezed, and felt smooth fabric under his fingers.

The burglar let out a startled yelp and threw the contents of the nearest bottle into Halvar's face. He hissed as the ink blinded him, and the intruder leaped for the door to the outside staircase. Swiping the ink off his face, he stumbled across the room in pursuit.

A chair crashed to the floor when he tripped on it. The thief, if so he was, struggled with the door, which must have blown shut.

Halvar's fingers closed on a loose collar—some kind of jacket or coat, he thought. He tried to swing the wearer around to get in a good blow. His captive slid out of the coat and finally managed to get the door unlatched. Halvar grasped a fistful of shirt and swung.

The punch landed on someone soft, not muscular.

The door opened, and the intruder scrambled outside. Halvar followed.

But someone was waiting there, someone who cast a slender shadow in the sliver of moonlight falling between the wall of the taberna and the warehouse beyond. A cord tightened against his throat.

He tried to shake the attacker off, slamming him against the wall as the garrote was drawn tighter. Halvar gasped for breath. Back and forth they went on the narrow landing, until Halvar gave one mighty spin that threw the killer off his back, over the railing and into the muck below.

He nearly followed, but he managed to cling to the railing around the landing and pulled the garrote off his neck. Only the high, stiff collar of the newfangled jacket had saved him from the same death as the poor girl in the clam beds.

Below, the body of the killer sprawled in the mud of the noisome alley that led to the public latrines. Halvar tottered down the stairs, trying to make out the man's features in the faint light of the early dawn.

"It's Henri."

He spun to the source of the voice, ready for more battle. The girl, Sally, stood, eyes wide, clutching a knitted shawl to her chest in the doorway under the stairs. She stepped back into the darkness, and he followed her into the entrance to what seemed to be a scullery.

"One of the servers," Halvar identified him.

"He's the maitre's chief server," Sally corrected him. "They came from Kibbick—Maitre Jacques, Madame Lizette, Robert and Henri. Is he dead?"

Halvar went back outside and bent over the body, pressing two fingers to the man's throat.

"His neck's broken," he said. "I'll have to send for Ruiz to take him up to the Rabat. He tried to kill me with this." He held out the garrote. "Any idea why?"

Sally regarded the dead server with horror.

"Maybe because you're the Calif's Hireling, and you're here to oversee the Feria. They don't like the calif on the waterfront, especially not when he makes them pay fees at the Feria."

"There are easier ways to evade paying the calif's taxes than by killing his Hireling," Halvar said gravely.

Sally edged closer.

"There's something else going on," she whispered. "They're taking the purple paint and doing something with it."

"Coating white wumpum to make it purple," Halvar said.

Sally nodded. "Sharona and I saw them doing it. I told her to go to the Rabat with the false wumpum."

"She never got there," Halvar said grimly. "She's dead."

Sally gasped, "Oh, no! I've killed her!"

"No, you didnt. More likely, Henri did. But someone gave him the order, and I'll bet anything you like it was our friend Tavernier."

"You'll never prove it." Sally's voice was sharper. "I know Sharia law. You have to have a confession, or a witness."

The first rays of the rising sun found their way into the back alley. Halvar could get a better look at the lanky young woman who stood in front of him, arms crossed over her chest to hold the shawl in place. Not a pretty girl, he decided, not with those heavy eyebrows and a shading of hair on her upper lip, but there was something about her that made him feel he had seen her before.

"What do we do now?" Sally asked.

"You get back to the kitchen and start the fire." Halvar ordered. "I'll find one of those waterfront brats, the halflings, and send him over to the Rabat. Then I'll have another look around this taberna, and another word with Jacques and his good wife. I'm getting tired of being a target for every villain in Manatas. This ends now!"

Chapter 14

AS THE LIGHT PENETRATED THE ALLEY, HALVAR COULD
see why no one had been awakened by the noise of the fight.
The Mermaid was one of a line of buildings that cut the waterfront off from the rest of the town. Behind it was the blank wall
of a warehouse whose entrance was on the street leading down
to the wharves.

The taverns and lodging-houses where sailors could find a
temporary resting place were farther north, tucked in between
the warehouses. At the very end of the paved plaza, where warehouses and tabernas gave way to the huts and shacks of those
who worked in them, was the small chapel used by the Kristos
and the cabin behind it where the frater lived when he was not
performing his daily duties.

An Afrikan in a tattered tunic that had once been dyed in
brilliant colors shambled into the alley, leading a donkey cart
loaded with large jars. The unmistakable aroma proclaimed this
individual's mission was to remove the contents of the latrine
for use or disposal elsewhere. He stopped when he saw Halvar and the body of Henri then backed away, making a sign.

"Go away, bad demon!"

Halvar remembered his face was covered in ink. No wonder this halfwit thought he was some demon.

"I'm human!" he called out to reassure him. "But there's a
dead man in here. Go get the Town Guard!"

"No Guard here," the Afrikan stuttered. "No Guard on the waterfront."

"Yes, there is," Halvar insisted. "If you can't find one at the sailor's tavern next to Manolo's pawn shop, get to the Rabat and give a message to Tenente Ruiz. Tell him he's needed at the Mermaid Taberna."

"I don't go to Rabat," the Afrikan stated flatly. "I clean bog."

"Thor's Hammer!" Halvar swore with frustration. "Then you stay here and guard this man while *I* go to the Rabat

"I don't do that." The Afrikan grabbed for an amulet under his rags. "Bad things happen here. I go to Rabat." Presumably, whatever happened to him at the Rabat would be better than staying in the presence of a corpse.

Halvar was left alone in the alley with the dead man. He sat on the steps and stared at the footprints in the muck. They pointed along the path back to the houses built between the warehouses, one of which was the home of Jacques Tavernier and his ferocious wife.

He frowned. They weren't made by the macassins of the Locals nor the boots favored by the Guards, although there was the shape of a round heel. He measured them against his foot. Almost as large, definitely not dainty. He recalled the heavy tread on the stairs and pulled at his mustache as he tried to put his thoughts together.

The thief had worn a jacket made of some kind of smooth cloth. It was still up in the room. Halvar looked up the stairs then decided it could wait. He re-imagined the fight instead.

Someone was going to be very bruised, that was for sure, but he didn't think he'd hit the burglar in the face. He couldn't very well strip every fat man in Manatas to look for bruises.

He peered out into the plaza to see if anyone else was up at dawn. The wail of the muezzin reminded him of his religious duty. He bowed his head and recited his ritual formula.

Someone was looking after him, he thought. Was it Thor or the Redeemer who had given him the strength to withstand the strangler's attack? Was it Mother Mara who had sent the breeze and the sounds that had awakened him?

Whichever it was, Halvar was grateful he had lived to bring the killer of the harem-girl to justice. He only regretted that Henri's punishment in the next world would not be as nasty as the one reserved for killers of virgins in Al-Andalus.

He could smell the enticing odors of mokka and corn cakes coming from the stands set up on the plaza. He wanted breakfast, but duty kept him in that alley. He could only hope the half-witted Afrikan had done *his* duty as well.

The sun was fully risen by the time Ruiz and his squad arrived. The guardsman had brought a cart to hold the body, along with four of his men and the donkey driver. To Halvar's surprise, Firebrand accompanied the squad.

Ruiz barely suppressed a grin when he saw Halvar.

"What have you done to yourself now?" he asked. "I know the Bretains paint themselves blue when they go into battle. I didn't know the Danes did."

"It's ink," Halvar told him. "It got thrown in my eyes when I interrupted someone raiding Leon's store. What's he doing here?" He nodded at Firebrand.

"My sachem wants to know what progress you've made with the false wumpum," the Mahak said, looking down at the body. "Is this the one who makes it?"

Ruiz rolled the dead man over with one booted toe and surveyed the body with a distinct lack of enthusiasm.

"It's that server at the taberna," he said. "What did he do to deserve this?"

"He tried to strangle me," Halvar stated. He held out the garrote. "With this."

Firebrand took the simple weapon, a cord made of twisted animal sinew attached to two wooden handles.

"You have to get close to use this," he complained. "Not good in a fight."

"It's used by the thieves in Parigi," Halvar explained. "They come up behind you, then do this!" He cast the string over Firebrand's head, crossed the handles, and pulled gently. "Do it fast, and the victim doesn't cry out. The girl never knew what hit her."

"Why didn't it kill you?" Ruiz asked.

"Because I am wearing a jacket with a stiff, high collar," Halvar said. He touched the groove where the garrote had bitten into the fabric. "This saved me."

Or maybe Thor or the Redeemer led me to the tailor's shop where I got it. One thing leads to another, like Old Sergeant Olaf said.

184

"Well, there's no doubt about what killed this fellow," Ruiz announced. "He died from falling off the landing. No other witnesses, I suppose?"

"That girl, Sally, must have heard something," Halvar said. "I think she sleeps in the scullery down below these stairs. No one else in the place at night, though. Didn't that rascal Tavernier say he and his wife live somewhere else nearby?"

"We'll get to them presently," Ruiz said. "Get this fellow to Dr. Moise at the Rabat!" he ordered his men.

The body was carried out of the muck of the alley, to a total lack of consternation from the crowd forming in the plaza.

Bales of kutton were being removed from the warehouse next to the Mermaid Taberna carried by brawny Afrikans to a waiting barge that would be rowed out to the ships anchored in the bay. Another barge was off-loading burlap bags that might hold anything from tabac leaves to the woody stems that yielded the precious blue dye called indigo. No one had more than a glance for the donkey-cart emerging from the alley. Dead men were always being hauled out of the alleys behind the taverns and warehouses of the Waterfront.

"Now what?" Ruiz asked as the donkey cart rounded the corner of the warehouse on its way to the Rabat.

"Go upstairs and find the jacket or coat the one I fought with left behind."

Ruiz grimaced then climbed the stairs, returning with a limp garment.

"Is this it? Strange sort of thing for a robber to wear." He held up a kutton shirt with a torn sleeve.

Halvar ran his hands over it, trying to picture the one who wore it. His rumination was interrupted by a cry from Firebrand.

"Who had this?" He held out the garrote.

"The dead man," Halvar said. "What's wrong with it?"

"This string, the thing that strangles," Firebrand said. "It's a bowstring."

"So?" Ruiz lifted an eyebrow.

"So," Firebrand said, "it is not Mahak. We make bowstrings from fibers of plants the women twist into cords. This is animal sinew. The Huron make their bowstrings from animal sinews."

"So," Halvar concluded, "the cord is Huron. I thought they were up north, near Kibbick."

185

"They should be," Firebrand growled. "But if this bowstring is of Huron make, then either the Huron are here, or this came from Kibbick with Henri and the Taverniers."

"One more black mark against Jacques Tavernier," Halvar said. "I want another word with that Franchen and his wife."

"It looks like you'lll get your wish," Ruiz said. He nodded towards two figures coming from the alley. The slight innkeeper and his bulkier wife materialized out of the morning mist.

They stopped when they saw the uniformed guards,

"What is going on here?" Jacques demanded.

"That's what you're going to tell me," Halvar said. "Get inside, you two. I want some answers, and I want them now!"

Chapter 15

RUIZ AND HIS MEN SHOVED THE INNKEEPER AND HIS wife through the door under the stairs into the kitchen of the Mermaid Taberna. Jacques muttered under his breath in Franchen. Lizette made her displeasure known loudly, in Arabi, with references to the guard's probable ancestry.

The kitchen ran the width of the building, and had a large wooden table in the center, a huge fireplace at one end and a row of shelves holding jars and bags of unknown foodstuffs at the other. A second table was set against the outside wall, under a window opened to let in the morning light.

Here were the cooking tools, the knives and choppers, and the bowls for mixing the various ingredients that would eventually emerge as soups, stews, and sweet cakes. A basket had been left under this table, filled with shellfish packed in seaweed to hold in moisture.

A thin trickle of smoke spiraled up into the chimney of the fireplace. Sally had performed her first task of the day, starting the fire that would eventually be coaxed and blown into a blaze to roast the meat that would be threaded onto the iron spits now propped beside it. Two cauldrons hung on iron hooks that could be swung away from the fire, while a third was already in place, heating the water that would be poured over the roasted mokka-beans to make the fragrant drink imbibed by Andalusians and Afrikans.

Ruiz took up a position next to Halvar, motioning two of his men to guard the outside door and two more to stand by the entrance to the main room of the taberna. Sally huddled next to them, her hair straggling out from under her cap, her arms crossed over her chest, clutching the shawl around her.

Jacques looked from one guard to the other while Lizette stood defiantly beside the fireplace. She had wrapped herself in a green wool cape against the morning chill and put a wide-brimmed hat over her frilled cap. Brassy-looking curls dangled in front of each ear, and her face was smeared with garish rouge, highlighting her already red cheeks.

Once again, Jacques demanded, "What is going on here? What happened to my server? Why was there a dead-wagon in the alley?"

"Last night, someone tried to kill me," Halvar informed him.

Jacques and Lizette made appropriate noises.

"How dreadful!" Lizette cried out. "You can't trust anyone these days. The Town Guards are useless!" She glared at Ruiz, who smiled blandly back at her.

"Why would someone want to kill you?" Jaques asked.

"I do seem to be a target for anyone with a grievance against Al-Andalus," Halvar admitted. "I've only been here five days, and there have already been three tries. Outside Green Village two nights ago someone shot at me with a pistoia. Gomez tried to spit me with his sword yesterday morning, and you know what happened to him. And last night, there was a poor fellow with a garrote. Of course, that was an accident."

"You don't throw this over someone's head by accident," Firebrand objected, shaking the garrote.

Halvar said, "I meant that I *killed* him by accident. He was only there to watch the one who was in Leon's room to take the paint."

"Paint?" Jacques repeated. "Whatever for?"

"To cover white wumpum beads so they'd look like purple ones," Halvar said.

"Why would anyone want to do that?" Jacques asked with a sly smile, rubbing his hands together.

"Why, indeed?" Halvar asked. "Why *would* you, Tavernier?"

"Me?" Jaques became the picture of outraged innocence.

Halvar pulled at his mustache, eyes narrowed.

"It can't be for profit, because you're not selling all that much here. You don't change silver for wumpum here, do you? No, they do that in Green Village, where the Bretains make wagers on cards and dice. Tabouli and chess are the games played here, and you don't bet much on them. So, why would a simple innkeeper play at counterfeiting?"

"An interesting puzzle," Ruiz commented.

"If we *were* painting wumpum beads, how would we do it?" Lisette blustered. "Look about you, Calif's Hireling. There's nothing here but food!"

Halvar nodded slowly.

"Food. Right." He strolled over to the shelves where the ingredients for Lisette's cuisine were stored. "Let's see what's here. I know you have wheat flour." He dipped a finger into one jar, pulled it out, and tasted it. "Hmmm. Salt. You can't cook without salt. And here's a loaf of sugar. Very good, from the Southern Islands. What are these?" He picked up a clump of dried foliage.

"Herbs to be used for flavoring," Lisette snapped, "vegetables."

"Red ones," Halvar noted.

"You ate them last night, with your chicken," Jacques reminded him.

"Did I? I thought those were carrots," Halvar said. He continued his survey of the kitchen, Lizette growing increasingly nervous with each step he took. "I see you keep your knives good and sharp. Nothing worse than a dull knife."

Lisette's round face grew redder.

"What if I do?"

Halvar stopped in his tour to look at the table under the window.

"There's dust here, Dame Tavernier. He drew a finger through it. "Not the usual sort of dust, either. Gritty. Like sand. I thought you didn't cook clams or oysters. Not halal." He kicked at the basket under the table. "Yet here's a whole basket of clams. So, Dame Lizette, why do you have clams in your halal kitchen?"

Lizette only glared at him and edged closer to the fireplace, away from the guards.

"Pots, pans," Halvar went on, taking inventory. He stopped beside one large iron pot and peered inside. "Odd sort of food, Dame Tavernier. Purple?"

"It's just the roots I cook for dinner," Lizette snapped. "What do you know about cooking, Hireling?"

"I know there was no beet-root in last night's mess," Halvar sniffed the pot. "And this stinks of fish. You know," he said, turning to Ruiz, "back in the Dane-march, we make a good strong glue out of fishbones and skins. You boil them down, you see, and while they're hot, you apply the stuff to wood, and it joins the two as tightly as anything I've seen."

Halvar stepped closer to Lizette, who edged towards the stand next to the fireplace that held the poker and shovel.

"It was you, Dame Lizette, who came into Leon's room last night," Halvar said evenly. "You had that server of yours, Henri, stand guard on the landing while you made your way back to your own place. Your footprints are in the muck of the alley."

Lizette lifted her skirt to show her feet.

"No muck on my shoes!" she exclaimed. "And how dare you say that I came into your room! I am a good woman, and I would not go into a man's room other than my husband's!"

"You were in Leon's room last night. You left your shirt there, and I gave you at least one bruise." Halvar grabbed at the cloak, twitching it away to show the woman's plump arms. "Will you pull up those sleeves, Dame Lizette, and show us whether you have the mark of my fingers?"

Jacques glanced at his wife and blurted, "If she shows bruises, then blame me, Don Álvaro. I had to, um, discipline her."

"Beat your wife?" Ruiz jeered. "More likely, she beats you!"

"Look at you all, attacking a helpless woman!" Lizette grabbed the brass poker and shook it at Halvar. "Jacques, you coward, will you let them attack me?"

"Hold him fast," Halvar said, not taking his eyes off Lizette. "As for you, Dame Lizette, I'll see you in the Rabat—for murder!"

"I didn't kill anyone," Lizette said stubbornly.

"It was Henri," Jacques shouted. "He saw the girls outside the kitchen window, and he got the one who was running to the Rabat."

"Don't say another word!" Lizette lunged with the poker.

Halvar didn't even consider using his dagger against such an assault. He grabbed a large pan with a wooden handle to deflect her blows and looked around for a more suitable weapon.

190

The iron spits next to the fireplace caught his eye, one end sharpened to pierce the meat, the other blunt to be notched into the turning-wheel. He cast the pan aside and hefted one. It was heavy, but not much heavier than his old pike. The iron was rough on his hands, but he could maneuver it well enough to defend himself against the furious woman.

He gripped the spit and lunged, jabbing the pointed end at the enraged woman to move her away then aiming the blunt end at her midsection to land a blow that would not kill her.

If I can back her into a corner, Ruiz can take her alive for trial.

Behind him, the Town Guard shouted encouragement, but he wasn't sure who was being encouraged.

He feinted one way then smacked her across the middle with the blunt end of the spit. She cried out in Franchen and clutched her side, but she didn't let go of the poker. They danced around the kitchen, Lizette swiping at Halvar with the sharp end of the poker, Halvar avoiding the wild swings, trying to maneuver her so she could be taken by the Guards. It wasn't easy, in the confines of the kitchen, to avoid hitting her. Her pendulous breasts jiggled as she panted for breath, while he was all too aware of the stabbing pain in his wounded shoulder.

They moved around the table in the middle of the room, Lizette swinging her poker ever more wildly as she became ever more enraged, Halvar fending off the blows with the iron spit,

Lizette saw a chance for escape. She backed into the main room, shoving Firebrand out of her way.

"Stop her!" Halvar yelled.

"Give up, woman!" Ruiz shouted. "You will receive justice!"

Halvar followed her into the main room, Ruiz right behind him. Lizette grabbed one of the spits from the fireplace then turned to confront Halvar once again. He tried to parry her wild swings, but Jacques was now next to him, deflecting his arm.

Lizette rushed headlong, spit aimed at Halvar's chest, just as he yanked his arm free from her husband's interfering grip. The action lowered the sharpened point of his own spit, and Lizette impaled herself on the point. She crumpled to the floor, blood spurting from her mouth and the wound in her chest. She tried to speak then gave one horrible gasp and died.

191

"Lizette! My beautiful Lizette!" Jacques turned fiercely to Halvar. "You killed her! A mere woman!"

"A woman? Yes, and so was Brunnhild," Halvar said, propping the bloody spit against the fireplace. "Your Lizette tried to kill me, in front of witnesses." He motioned to Ruiz and the guards.

"As for you, Tavernier, you are as guilty as she. You knew about the murder of the girl Sharona. You were the one who disposed of the body in the clam bed."

"You can't prove anything!" Jacques protested.

Halvar held up the Franchen's reddened, blistered hands to show Firebrand.

"Mahak, is this the sign of your burnweed?"

Firebrand's smile was nasty.

"It is that," he said. He had picked up the pan Halvar had previously used as a shield. "And there is some kind of sticky stuff in this. I will take it to our shaman, and he will test it. I think it may be the same paint that has been dying white wumpum purple."

"So," Halvar summed up, "you've been caught, Jacques Tavernier. Your wife is dead. Your server accomplice is dead. If you confess, it will mean a quick death for you instead of something much slower and more painful."

The tavern-keeper snarled, "You think you know everything, Hireling? Let me tell you, there is a time coming when your boy calif will beg for mercy from our King Lovis! And this little island, this Manatas, will belong to the Redeemer, as is proper and necessary to save the world from the Evil One!"

"Get him out of here!" Halvar ordered. "Get this woman to the Rabat so Eva Hakim can examine her, and find someone to take charge here."

"And then what?" Ruiz asked.

"And then get me some mokka and some maiz cakes. I'm famished!"

Chapter 16

FOR A LONG MOMENT, THERE WAS SHOCKED SILENCE in the kitchen, broken only by Jacques's sobs over the body of his beloved Lizette.

Then, Sally cried out, "You horrible man! You just killed someone, and all you can think of is breakfast?"

Halvar looked the server over.

"It's what I do," he said, "I don't like killing. I'd prefer not to. But that woman wanted to kill me, and given the choice of me or her, I took me."

He looked around the room. Firebrand gazed impassively at the dead woman. Ruiz took a deep breath then squared his shoulders, as if remembering he was now tenente, in charge of law in Manatas.

"Get another cart," he ordered. "We have to take this…body to the Raba. Don Álvaro claimed she was the one he fought last night. Eva Hakim can check her for bruises. The frater on the waterfront can do the proper things to send her soul to wherever it's supposed to go."

"To the Bad Place," Sally said under her breath. "She was a terrible woman. She was the one who saw Sharona and me looking through the kitchen window. Henri killed Sharona, and then *she* made me stay here and be a serving-maid."

Halvar pulled at his mustache again.

"And you obeyed?"

Sally pulled the shawl closer around her chest.

"I don't have anywhere else to go," she muttered, gaze fixed on the floor.

Halvar looked her over and smiled.

"Oh, I think you do," he said. "Get upstairs, lad, and put on your own shirt and trousers. Your father is waiting for you at the Rabat."

"F–father?" Sally quavered.

"Yes, your father, Selim." Halvar jerked his chin upwards. "Get some decent clothes on and rejoin me, lad. I think you have a story to tell."

Ruiz and Firebrand watched "Sally" climb the stairs to Leon's rooms. Then Ruiz turned on Halvar.

"That's *Selim*?" His eyes narrowed. "How could you tell?"

"It makes sense," Halvar said. "Selim's been missing, and here's this girl who's tall and has a bit of a mustache and only came to the Taverniers a few days ago. No one looks at the servers in a taberna."

"Not unless they're good-looking wenches," Ruiz agreed. "And that clumsy girl was not worth looking at. But why would he come here in the first place?"

"That's for the lad to tell us," Halvar said. "Quite a lot has happened in the few days since I arrived. Doesn't anyone ever sleep on Manatas Island?"

"Oh, a few do," Ruiz said with a yawn. "But you've made things even more lively, Don Álvaro."

Firebrand took all this in with a frown.

"I don't understand Oropans," he said, at last. "And I don't know why the Franchen made the false wumpum. But I am glad you found out who did it, because now I can go to my sachem and tell him that it is done, it is over, and the one who did it is truly punished."

"Not yet," Halvar said. "We've got to question that rascally Tavernier, find out whose bright idea this was, and whether it was done for profit or something else."

"What else could it be?" Ruiz said. "Tavernier would give the false wumpum instead of the true purple when the shipmen came with silver. Then they'd take it with them to the Feria and exchange it back for more silver. It's clear to me that the only reason for changing the white to purple was to exchange it for silver."

"But that wouldn't make enough profit for Tavernier," Halvar objected. "He's not changing money here, not in the amounts that would make the risk worthwhile. No, Tenente Ruiz, there's something else going on here, and I don't like it. Not one bit I don't."

Sally, revealed as Selim, interrupted the discussion, marching defiantly down the stairs. He wore Leon's red silk trousers and a light kutton shirt under a green wool jacket trimmed with beads in the Local style. He still had on his loose macassins, but he had wound a brightly colored scarf around his head in a makeshift turban. His dark brows seemed to meet over his large nose, and the hairs on his upper lip were more visible in the morning light.

"Selim ibn Petrus, salaam aleikum," Halvar greeted him, with a bow.

"Oh, don't be silly," Selim snapped. "And if you insist on eating after all that, there's a stall where I used to go with Leon. We can talk there."

He stalked out of the taberna onto the plaza, where the business of Manatas was being transacted as if there had been no fight, no killing, no tragedy inside the building that loomed over the East Channel side of Manatas.

"What about Tavernier?" Ruiz asked as he followed Selim into the sunlight of the new day.

"Get him to the Rabat," Halvar ordered. "And send some men to that little house he and his wife live in. I think the answers to the questions of why and wherefore are there."

Chapter 17

AS RUIZ AND HIS MEN HAULED THE FRANCHEN IN THE direction of the Rabat, Selim led Halvar to one of the stalls set up beside the wharf. A Local woman manipulated a pot of chicory-infused mokka over a brazier and flipped maiz-cakes on a pan.

She grinned at Selim and automatically piled maiz-cakes on a platter, liberally pouring some sticky brown substance over them.

"As you like them, young sir," she said, waving Selim and Halvar to the stools set up next to the brazier.

Halvar sniffed the cakes.

"What's that on top of them?"

"It's a sweet syrup," Selim explained. "In the spring, the sap rises in the maple trees here in Nova Mundum. The Locals tap it and boil it down and use it for sweetening instead of sugar. It's good!"

He wolfed down the cakes. Halvar took a bite of his, decided that he liked it better than the chickory flavored mokka, and proceeded to finish his portion.

"Alright, lad," he said, sipping gingerly at the mokka. "There's no one here but you and me and these Locals, and they're not interested in us. We can speak Arabi, they won't know what we're saying, so you can tell me the truth. How did you come to be at the Mermaid Taberna?"

Selim fidgeted on his stool.

"I ran away."

"That much I could tell for myself," Halvar said. "Maybe if I tell you what I think, you can tell me if I'm wrong."

"What do you think, Calif's Hireling?" Selim was scornful, as only the young can be of the older.

"I think you were unhappy because of the new arrival and ran away so people would look for you. And I think you saw something you weren't meant to see, and that upset you more. So, Sharona died, and now you're even unhappier. Am I right?"

Selim looked at the boats bobbing on the East Channel—the canoes and the rowboats that towed the barges, and the sail of a dhow that was slipping through the gap between the two islands that guarded the inner bay of Manatas. His lips closed in a pout, as if he was considering just how much he would reveal to this stranger from over the sea.

Finally, he whined, "Everyone was in a pelter, all about how the Calif's Hireling was coming, and the sultan was going to be called to account for his spending money building the Manatas Town Wall instead of sending it all back to the calif for the wars in Al-Andalus."

"Everyone, meaning whom?" Halvar asked sharply.

Selim shrugged. "Just people, talking."

"You don't want to get your friends into trouble," Halvar observed. "That's good, that's loyal, but it's not going to make it any better for you. I can find traitors for myself, I don't need you to betray anyone for what they say. Words are air, and a lot of people say things but don't do anything about them.

"I already know Leon was the one who sent the letter to the calif about the money being spent on the Wall, so you're not betraying a friend. My coming here seems to have sent many people into fits. Tenente Gomez, for instance."

Selim wrinkled his nose in disgust.

"Tenente Gomez was nasty. He took advantage of my father's not being able to go about easily, especially after the second winter here. It gets really cold, and my father's bad leg bothered him. Eva Hakim had some medicines that eased the pain, but not all of it."

"So Gomez took over," Halvar said. "And when I found out about it, he tried to kill me. No surprises there, lad. It still doesn't explain why you had to run away from the Rabat."

"It was Ayesha!" Selim blurted. "All my father could think about was the new baby, and how much he wanted Ayesha to come through the birthing, and how wonderful it was that at his age he had a new child! It was disgusting!"

Halvar took a swill of his mokka, hiding a grin in the clay mug. Selim sounded like any three-year-old being displaced by the next baby in the family, except that Selim was no toddler but a well-grown lad of fifteen.

"Ayesha's only three years older than me," Selim went on. "And everyone in the Rabat was fussing and fretting over her, and then they were fussing and fretting over you."

"And no one paying attention to you," Halvar murmured into his mokka.

"I used to be able to talk to Leon, but he was besotted with Otter Tail," Selim fumed. "And then there was a letter from Lady Maryam, my father's First Wife, and I had to talk to someone about it. And I thought I could talk with Eva Hakim, but she was with Ayesha, and Ayesha was starting to have the new baby. So then I thought I could talk with Leon, at the Mermaid Taberna, and he'd understand, but he wasn't here."

"No, he was on his way to the Feria to see Otter Tail," Halvar said. "And he had his own misadventure. You may as well know, Selim, he's with the Kristos in Green Village. It's not likely you'll ever see him again." He watched Selim carefully to see how the lad took that news.

Selim shook his head and sighed ruefully.

"I suppose it's for the best," he said at last. "But I don't know who will prepare me for Madrassa now that he's gone. I was supposed to enter next year."

"Madrassa, ey?" Halvar shrugged. "Well, why not? What would you study? Are you aiming to be an imam, learned in the Holy Books? Or a physician?"

"Leon thought I might study natural philosophy," Selim said, his sullen face brightening. "We used to take walks, before the Wall was built, and go to the parts of Manatas where the Locals have their lodges and longhouses. And I've learned some of the Local languages. I'm pretty good at Munsi, their tradetalk. I've even tried rendering some of it into a glossary, written in Arabi, that Benyamin ibn Mendel thought was really useful. He even said..." Selim stopped, as if he'd revealed too much.

198

Halvar brought the lad back to the point.

"So, you went to the taberna to find Leon," he summed it up. "But he wasn't there. That was three days ago. Where was the girl, Sharona, all this time?"

"She was with me," Selim confessed. "She insisted! She saw me going out the gate, and she said she had to take care of me. Just like when we were children on the estate in Al-Andalus, or when she had to come with me and Leon when we went outside the Rabat."

Halvar made a disgusted noise.

"As if Leon was going to assault you. Pah!"

Selim ignored the interruption.

"So we came here, and Leon wasn't here, but Lizette was in Leon's room, and we saw her dipping the beads into Leon's purple paint. We were outside, on the landing, and the door was open."

"I thought it was something like that," Halvar said.

"I didn't know why she was doing it, but I saw some of the beads left out to dry, so I took some, and Sharona and I were going down the stairs when Lizette and Henri saw us. I tried to run, but Lizette got me, and Henri went after Sharona..." Selim gulped back tears.

"You saw Henri kill Sharona," Halvar said, flatly.

Selim nodded, unable to speak.

"Why change clothes?" Halvar asked.

"That was my idea," he said. "I remembered a story Leon told, about a holy man who wore a ragged coat to a party and was turned away. Then, when he wore a fine coat, he was welcomed, and he put the food into the coat's pockets and said it was the coat that was invited, not him, so the coat had to eat the food at the party.

"I had told Sharona to wear my coat, so that if I got caught she could get into the Rabat, because they'd see the coat and think it was me. We look a lot alike, you see. Sharona's mother was one of Lady Maryam's sewing women, and I think Sharona may have been my sister, or maybe my cousin, depending on whether her father was mine or my older brother. I think that's why my father brought her to Manatas with us, because Lady Maryam didn't want her around. She was my only real friend here!" Selim began to sob in earnest.

"So, you could wear her clothes, and she wore your coat over her underdrawers and tunic," Halvar said. "Why didn't Lizette kill you?"

Selim's sobs subsided, and he wiped his nose on the edge of his sleeve.

"I'm not sure," he said. "I don't understand Franchen all that well, although I'm not too bad at Erse, because of Padraig coming to the meetings of the Seekers of Truth."

"That circle of youngsters around Leon," Halvar recalled.

Selim nodded. "There weren't any Franchen in it, just me and Benyamin and Padraig and Otter Tail. So I don't really know what Lizette and Henri and Jacques were fighting about after Henri killed Sharona. They put her body into the cold pantry while they argued about what to do with her. I think it was Jacques yelling at Henri for being too hasty, and Lizette calling Jacques bad names for not being more of a man, and Henri insisting that what they were doing had to be kept quiet until something or someone happened."

"Something?" Halvar echoed. "What kind of something?"

"I don't know," Selim said with sniff. "But Lizette took a look at me and said that I had to be kept alive, but she wasn't going to feed me unless I earned my keep. And then Jacques said that I could be a server, and no one would look twice at me because I was so ugly." Another mortified sniff.

"I think you make a fine-looking *lad*," Halvar consoled him.

"Maybe, but I wasn't much of a server," Selim said. "I wasn't good in the kitchen, either. I think Lizette was going to change her mind and kill me anyway, or maybe put me in the cold pantry to starve or freeze to death."

"If they recognized you as the sultan's child, I think they may have decided to keep you alive as a hostage," Halvar assured him. "And now, young sir, I think we'd better get you back to the Rabat. Your father was truly upset when he found you gone."

"He's got another baby to fuss over," Selim said sulkily.

"He set me to find you, didn't he?" Halvar said. "And when they found Sharona, he went all the way to the House of the Green Crescent to make sure it wasn't you." He hauled himself upright. "Let's get you home, Selim."

Selim finished the last of his maiz-cakes.

"I suppose I have to look at the new baby," he said with a sigh.

They were on their way across the plaza when one of Ruiz's squad joined them.

"Salaam aleikum, Don Álvaro. I come from the house where Jacques Tavernier lived. Tenete Ruiz wants you to come there with me right now."

"What about the lad?" Halvar asked.

The guardsman shrugged.

"He might as well come, too," he said. "Maybe he can make sense of what we've found."

Halvar settled his cap more firmly on his head.

"Whatever it is," he stated, "I just hope no one else tries to kill me today. I'm getting really tired of it."

Chapter 18

THE GUARD LED HALVAR AND SELIM AROUND THE TABerna along the path that went up the hill towards the warehouses. Ruiz waited for them.

"Jacques and Lizette made their little home a piece of Franchenland in Nova Mundum," he said. "Take a look for yourself."

The interior of the small cottage was filled with images of holy martyrs, each painful death more gruesomely depicted than the last in glorious colors and with anatomical correctness. Halvar's eyebrows rose as he recognized Leon di Vicenza's distinctive style in an image of Chesu the Redeemer writhing in agony on the crux.

"I'd say the Taverniers were Kristo, following the Roumi Rite," Halvar stated. "That makes sense, since they were Franchen, and the Franchen King Lovis has allied himself with Episcopous Innocente of Rouma."

"Nasty stuff," Ruiz said, sneering at the images. "But that's not what I have to show you. I found this!" He pointed to a stack of folded papers. "Letters, Don Álvaro."

"From whom, to whom?" Halvar asked as he carefully unfolded each paper and frowned at the spiky script. "I don't know this writing."

"It's Franchen," Selim said, reaching for the letters.

"You can read it?" Halvar looked at the lad.

"Of course I can," Selim said with a scornful sniff. "I was educated by a very cultured man. I can read and write Arabi, of course, like everyone in Al-Andalus, but Leon thought I should learn to read Franchen script, too, and the Roumi letters. And Rune, so I could read Danic, and Ogham, so I could read Erse. I am very good at languages."

"I thought you said you couldn't understand what was said the night Sharonna was killed," Halvar said accusingly.

"I can't understand *spoken* Franchen, especially when it's in a kind of thieves' cant," Selim protested. "But I can read some of it, at least, enough to make out what it's about."

"What about these?" Halvar handed him one of the papers.

Selim frowned over it.

"It seems to be some kind of plan," he said at last. "A list of names, and whether they are for or against something."

"For or against what?" Ruiz demanded.

"It doesn't say, only *sic* or *non*—that is, yes or no."

"Jacques made threats," Halvar mused, tugging at his mustache. "Lizette seemed to think that Lovis was going to over-run Al-Andalus and then turn his attention to Manatas."

"If he does, he'll find a cold welcome," Ruiz snarled. "We're not happy about sending our tribute to Al-Andalus, but I can assure you, Don Álvaro, we in Manatas would be even less pleased with Lovis and his Questioners prying into our affairs. Mullah Abadul is bad enough!"

"Where is our friendly tavern-keeper?" Halvar asked.

"Back there, with my men," Ruiz said, casually.

"Why isn't he chained?" Halvar complained. "Slippery, those Franchen! You have to keep a hand on them every minute!" He ducked his head to avoid bumping it on the low doorframe of the cottage.

The muezzin's cry echoed across Manatas, first from the minaret of the Grand Muskat on the Broad Way then picked up by the other muezzins calling from neighborhood muskats. Ruiz knelt, and his men and his men obediently prostrated themselves for the midmorning prayer.

Jacques wasted no time in prayer. He skipped away down the alley towards the plaza and the river, with its promise of freedom. Halvar ran after him, slipping on the muck of the alley, clutching at the sides of the warehouses to steady himself.

Jacques dodged one puddle, leaped another, and zigzagged around the front of the Mermaid Taberna. Halvar splashed through the muck, his boots sliding out from under him. He went down on his rear then scrambled up again, cursing several colorful demons and reminding Thor there was at least one person who depended on his good will.

Behind him, Halvar heard the guards reciting, "Ilha is good, the Prophet is great." Ahead of him, he could see the plaza, where those devoted to Ihla and the Prophet lay flat on the ground and those who revered Kristo the Redeemer knelt on one knee, heads bowed. The Franchen danced between the rows of worshipers, heading for the small Kristo chapel, where a frater rang his bell, calling his people to prayer.

"If he gets there, he'll claim sanctuary!" Halvar gritted out, hoping someone was at his back to hear him. He stretched his long legs to their fullest, trying not to trample on the pious underfoot.

"He won't get there." Ruiz's voice came from somewhere around Halvar's shoulder.

"I can't get to him in time!" Halvar rasped out. He clutched at the stanchion of the nearest stall, his breath coming in ragged gasps.

"I can." Ruiz stated, drawing a pistoia from the pocket of his long green coat.

Halvar heard the snap-hiss of the tinderbox and smelled the reek of burning kutton. There was a loud *bang!* Jacques stopped in mid-stride and fell to the stone pavement of the plaza.

The worshipers leapt to their feet, gabbling in astonishment. Halvar coughed, took another breath, and managed to get over to the fallen Franchen without staggering. He was aware that Firebrand was at his left side, propping him up, and he heard Selim's voice behind him.

Ruiz was already beside the Franchen.

"I got him," he announced. "A lucky shot."

"I wanted him alive," Halvar said grimly.

"He wouldn't have told you anything you didn't already know or have guessed," Ruiz countered blandly. "You saw the pictures in his house. These Franchen, they fancy themselves martyrs for their Redeemer."

"I didn't know you had a pistoia," Halvar commented. "And you're a good shot with it, too."

"I practice," Ruiz said, trying to sound modest. "They are the coming thing, Don Álvaro, firearms. They make pikes and swords old-fashioned."

"Not arrows," Firebrand said scornfully. "Use one of those, and a deer would smell the smoke and run before you could kill it."

"This isn't the time or the place for this kind of argument," Halvar interrupted. He looked around at the crowd. "And we have to get this one back to the Rabat."

The frater had come from the chapel to see what was happening. Now he spoke up, in Arabi with a strong Franchen accent.

"This man was one of my flock," he protested. "He should get proper Kristo burial."

"Him and his wife, and that scum they called a server," Halvar agreed. "They'll be turned over to you when we've finished with them."

"You will not destroy their bodies!"

Both the frater and Ruiz were aghast.

"I want to know exactly what kind of people they were," Halvar said. "Once that's done, we can let you have them, Frater, and you can put them into the ground, where they will no doubt meet their just punishment."

"Or their heavenly home," the frater said.

Halvar grimaced. Ruiz motioned to the nearest donkey cart driver to join the procession that had already formed to take Jacques and Lizette back to the Rabat.

"Let's get this lad back to his father," Halvar said, laying a hand on Selim's shoulder. "Then we can decide what to do next."

Chapter 19

HALVAR STEWED AS HE WALKED BACK TO THE RABAT behind Selim and Ruiz. He had been flummoxed at every turn. He had been forced to kill a woman, something he had never done in all his years of soldiering, and he still didn't know what was going on in Green Village.

Even the discovery of Sharona's killer had been accidental. Worst of all, he still couldn't lay his hands on Leon di Vicenza, and he was stuck here in Manatas while great events were happening across the Storm Sea.

There was something that bothered him about the scene he had just witnessed. Someone had been missing from the plaza at the waterfront, but he couldn't quite put his finger on who it was.

The Rabat loomed ahead of them. Ruiz strutted forward, greeting the guards at the gate to the courtyard with all the aplomb of one who has pulled off a major coup. He mounted the stairs to the sultan's private quarters without waiting to be announced.

Sultan Petrus was waiting eagerly for news. Ruiz gave it to him.

"We've found young Selim," he announced. "And it was that Franchen, Jacques Tavernier, and his wife Lizette who were behind the scheme to dye the wumpum."

"They killed Sharona!" Selim blurted out. "And they didn't kill me, but they made me wear girl's clothes and serve in their rotten taberna."

"I killed one of them in a fight," Halvar said apologetically. "The man Henri—I suspect he was one of the Parigi thieves we chucked out of Corduva just before the Old One went to his heavenly reward. There was a nest of them," he explained further. "We put them on a boat and told them to get themselves gone. They must have gone to Kibbick, where the Franchen dump their refuse."

"And the Huron pick it up," Firebrand added with a sneer.

"Tavernier was probably one of those they call voyagers," Ruiz said. "They work with the Huron, collecting pelts. He could have joined with Lizette and Henri in Kibbick then come here."

"To do what?" Sultan Petrus sounded confused. "I thought they ran a taberna on the waterfront."

"Where merchants and sea captains could meet and bargain and make their deals," Ruiz said. "All under the nose of Tenente Gomez."

"Who probably took a portion of the tolls that should have gone to pay for the wars in Al-Andalus," Halvar finished for him. "But all this is speculation, since all of them are now dead. What I can tell you for certain is that it was Tavernier who took the girl to the clam beds. His hands were covered with sores and blisters."

"Burnweed," Firebrand said with a nasty grin.

"And if we go back to the waterfront, I think Manolo the Pawnbroker can confirm that a canoe was taken out yesterday before daybreak," Halvar went on.

"Back to the waterfront?" Ruiz asked, puzzled.

"There are still some things about this business that I'm not sure of," Halvar said. "As for the counterfeiting, those Franchen used Lizette's fish glue and Leon's paints to coat the wumpum so that the paint would stick to it. Luckily for us, they didn't make very much of it, and it only went to the merchants at the Feria, so it can be collected fairly easily. They didn't have much time to seed it throughout Manatas, and it hasn't reached the Souk. "

The sultan's puzzled frown deepened.

"I don't understand all this. Why would this Franchen inn-keeper distribute false wumpum?"

"Possibly to cause unrest here," Halvar said. "To cause dis-trust of the coin and currency of Al-Andalus, and to disrupt the alliance between Al-Andalus and the Locals."

"We've never had any trouble with the Mahak," Sultan Pe-trus declared. "At least, not while I've been here. Some of my predecessors may have been over-hasty in settling disputes, but I have always respected the sachems of the Mahak and Al-gonkin peoples."

"The sachems are grateful for the protection of Al-Andalus, and the regulation of the Feria," Firebrand responded grace-fully. "But if the Franchen bring the Huron down from the north, you may expect troubles beyond your liking. The Mahak will not allow the Huron to take their hunting-lands."

"We don't know what's happening in Al-Andalus," Halvar complained. "That Tavernier seemed to think the Franchen ar-mies were already taking charge, that Calif Don Felipe was de-feated. We don't know that is true. Until we do, Excellent Sul-tan, you are the ruler of Manatas Town and must be prepared to defend it against whatever comes along to take it from Al-Andalus."

Sultan Petrus harumphed.

"Well, what Ilha, the All-Merciful, may his name be praised, has in store will come, as the Prophet, may his name be blessed, has said. I see you found Selim."

"You could say Selim found me," Halvar admitted. "I pene-trated the disguise, true, but the lad showed great courage in approaching me the way he did. He's a fine youngster. It's a pity he can't study with Leon, but it would be difficult, now that Leon's in the fratery at Green Village."

Selim shifted from one foot to the other, nervous under the scrutiny of many eyes.

"I want to take the examinations for the Madrassah," he mumbled.

"And why not?" the sultan boomed. "Don Álvaro, you must stay in Manatas until the Feria ends, isn't that so?"

"Such is my commission."

"Then you can escort Selim to Green Village for instruction from Leon in preparation for the Madrassah examinations," the sultan decided. "Ruiz, I want you to round up all Franchen and question them. I want to know just how far this conspiracy went."

"I don't know that you can do that," Halvar objected. "There are merchants and sea captains who may have nothing to do with the Taverniers and their conspiracy. They came from Kibbick, after all. I would advise caution."

"There will be no time for caution when the Huron come," Firebrand said

"My commission was to find Leon di Vicenza and bring him back to Al-Andalus," Halvar reminded him. "And that is what I shall do. Finding out who killed who is not my task. Finding Leon was."

They were interrupted by a tap on the door. A guardsman appeared, his tarboosh askew, his face red with exertion and chagrin.

"There is a dhow just come, with messages from Al-Andalus!" he announced between gasps. He thrust a packet of papers at the Sultan.

"What news of the wars?" Halvar demanded.

The messenger took another breath.

"There was a great battle near the fortress at Salamanca. The Franchen had cannons that destroyed the city walls. The calif and his mother were forced to retreat south."

The sultan looked up from the first of the documents in the packet.

"This is an official fatwa from the mullah in Corduva. It seems that Lovis the Franchen has been declared imperator by the Episcopous of Rouma," he said. "He claims all of Al-Andalus and renames it Hispania. The fatwa condemns Lovis to death and his soul to the depths of Sheol."

"What of Don Felipe? What of the calif?" Halvar demanded.

The sultan scanned the paper carefully.

"Calif Don Felipe has not been seen since the battle. His whereabouts are unknown."

"Then he's still alive," Halvar said firmly. "And as long as he is, I am his Hireling, and I will do as I have been ordered. I will get Leon di Vicenza out of his fratery, and I will get him back to Al-Andalus."

"And while you're doing it," the sultan added, "you can find out whether the Franchen at Kibbick are planning to take over Manatas."

As long as it doesn't involve any more killing, Halvar said to himself.

Aloud he said, "Give me a few days, Excellent Sultan. Even a Dane needs a rest."

Chapter 20

HALVAR SPENT THE NEXT THREE DAYS IN MISERY.

He was totally exhausted. In the previous three days he'd been in two furious fights, attacked by bullies with clubs and knives, nearly strangled, and shot. He'd been dosed with poppy-juice, drugged with alcohol and hemp, and poisoned with strange foods. It had all been too much, even for a tough Dane to take.

The last time he had felt so helpless was when he'd been hauled off the battlefield in Italia and stacked with the rest of the wounded onto a cart, to be taken to the ship bound for Al-Andalus. A loud female voice had declared, "Take them all, and let Ilha, the All-Merciful sort them out. Whoever lives, that is the Will of Ilha, may his name be praised!"

Back then, he'd wound up in a hospital run by the Sisters of Fatima, alone in a strange country where he could barely understand what was said to him. It had taken nearly two months for him to recover; he only hoped it wouldn't take that long this time.

His natural resilience served him well as he recuperated in the barracks bed in the Rabat. After all, he'd been on his way to breakfast when everything caught up with him. Surely, he could get over a few blows, a knife-thrust, and a garrote.

At least I can talk to people here. And I've got my wits, and my orders. I can't give up now.

For the first twenty-four hours of recuperation, he lay inert while various medical practitioners talked to each other over him. Frater Iosip had insisted on coming all the way from Green Village to check on his patient's recovery from the bullet wound and argued ferociously with Dr. Moise about the efficacy of moldy bread as opposed to herbal poultices, with references on both sides to arcane medical texts and personal cases. The Mahak medicine woman Nokomis and Sister of Fatima Eva Hakim dosed him with willow-bark teas, each more vile-tasting than the next.

A dour Italian slave also came at odd intervals to administer potions, adjust bandages, spoon soup into his mouth, and attend to his personal needs.

Halvar's mental state was worse than his physical. *Is Calif Don Felipe alive or dead?* he fretted. *Has Imperator Lovis taken all of Al-Andalus and installed his Questioners to make sure everyone follows the Roumi Rite? Will the Islims and Yehudit be banished from Al-Andalus, as they have been from all other Franchen lands?*

To make matters worse, the beautiful blue skies over Manatas turned gray. A howling gale battered the island with gusts of wind that broke trees like reeds and drenched the Feria with sheets of rain. Vendors scurried for shelter in Green Village or Manatas as the fragile tents and shacks of the Feria were destroyed and the fairground reduced to a sea of mud that would take at least another day to dry. Every lost sale was revenue that would not go to support Don Felipe in his war against Imperator Lovis.

So much for my official mission, Halvar groused as he huddled under the blankets and listened to the wind whistle through the unglazed window of his lonely room. *I might as well give up and take the next dhow back to Al-Andalus.*

By his third day of captivity, though, he was ready for any visitors who could find it in their hearts to relieve his boredom. He almost embraced Yussif the Tailor, who arrived with the coat he had left with him for repair.

The tailor pointed out how he had inserted brown tweed gussets into the shoulders, which contrasted nicely with the dark green of the coat, and added cuffs and lengthened the hems with bands of the same material.

"It will start a new fashion in Manatas, Don Álvaro," Yussif assured him as Halvar paid the agreed-upon silver.

212

"Might as well make me another, then." Halvar sighed. "And make it with the turned-up collar. It saved my life." *Considering the way things happen in Manatas, I may need it tomorrow!*

The measuring process was interrupted by Padraig mac-Cormack, bearing a crock of broth and a message of condolence from Dani Glick.

"I was coming into town to see Benyamin, and Fru Glick told me to bring this to you. She wished me to tell you this is her particular recipe, learned from her mother's mother, and that it is considered a sovereign remedy for almost anything,

"I also have a message from Leon di Vicenza. He wants to know when you are going to send him the books he left in his rooms at the Mermaid Taberna. He really wants them."

"Does he now?" Halvar responded. "Tell him I've been a little under the weather lately. And the weather has been a little over the rest of us. I'll get to those books in due time. They're not going anywhere."

Padraig blushed furiously and stepped aside to let the next visitor in. Ruiz had come to report on the progress of the investigation into the deaths of Sharona, Henri, and Jacques.

"Eva Hakim examined Dame Lizette and found bruises on her arms and body," he stated. "The mark on Sharona's neck matches the cord on the garrotte that was used to strangle you. Accordingly, Eva Hakim agrees that Henri most probably was the killer.

"I also had Dr. Moise examine the bodies of Jacques Tarvernier and Henri. According to him, Henri had a broken neck and many bruises, leading to the conclusion his death was due to the fall from the upper landing. Jacques Tavernier was, of course, shot in the back. A mistake—I was aiming for his leg to bring him down. Pistoias are not particularly accurate."

"I suppose I should be grateful for that," Halvar groused. "A little higher, and I would by lying in my grave instead of in this bed. Do you have the bullet?"

"Why do you want it?" Ruiz looked puzzled.

"To compare with the one Frater Iosip took out of me," Halvar expained. "Each pistoia is different, so the bullets are all slightly different. I want to compare the two bullets, to see if they came from the same weapon. There can't be that many in Manatas."

"If you are implying it was I who shot you, Don Álvaro, may I remind you that at the time I was under orders from Tenente Gomez."

"I know." Halvar nodded. "Tenente Ruiz, what's been done about the Mermaid Taberna? The furnishings and books Leon left behind?"

Ruiz shrugged. "I left them where they were. I had the doors to the place barred until the sultan could decide who should take it over."

"Haven't you posted any of your men there?"

"It would be difficult for thieves to break in, especially during the storm," Ruiz assured him. "But if you insist, I will have one of my men stationed there to make sure no one removes anything until you are ready to inspect the place."

He left as Halvar muttered about the inefficiency of provincial police.

His last visitor was the one he most wanted to talk to. Young Selim ibn Petrus edged into the room.

"What's the matter, lad?" Halvar greeted him.

"I didn't think you'd want to talk to me," Selim said. "After all the trouble I caused, running away and getting Sharona killed. If I hadn't —"

Halvar stopped him.

"Don't think of 'ifs,' laddie," he said. "Old Sergeant Olaf used to tell us not to think of what might be, because it does no good. 'If Grandpa had tits, he'd be Grandma, and if Grandma had balls, she'd be Grandpa.' That's how he put it. You can drive yourself mad with 'ifs.' If I hadn't been in a taberna one night, I wouldn't have been able to stop some drunken lout from knifing Don Felipe, and I wouldn't have been made his bodyguard. And if I hadn't been his Hireling, I wouldn't have been sent here at all.

"I remember how Leon used to twit the teachers in the history class at Madrassa in Corduva, where I sat in the back of the room with Don Felipe. He'd point out that if my grandsires hadn't raided Rouma and left it a burning wreck, and if the Roumi hadn't been wasting their time fighting each other instead of banding together to fight Danes, then maybe the Roumi would have been strong enough to fight off the armies of the Prophet when they came along.

214

"And if the Franchen had got to the south side of the mountains and built castles there, maybe we'd all be talking some kind of Old Roumi instead of Arabi. Nothing is fixed in time, he said, and nothing is destined. Of course, the teacher had a fit, and claimed that Ilha had arranged everything, and Leon was mad to think otherwise."

"And is he? Could things have been different?"

"What is, is," Halvar said with a shrug. "That's the way you have to look at it."

Selim sighed. "What are you going to do now, Hireling? If the calif is dead, and the Feria is all blown away by the wind…"

"More ifs. It doesn't matter. Until I know for sure Don Felipe is dead, I am under his orders, and those orders are to get Leon di Vicenza on that boat," Halvar said. "And even though the storm broke up the Feria for a day or two, there's another week of it, and there is still revenue to collect, and I'm under orders to bring that back to Al-Andalus."

"And you obey your orders."

"I do." Halvar frowned. "I just wish there was someone who could keep records for me. I'm no good at that, and I'm not sure who I can trust in Manatas."

"I can keep accounts," Selim reminded him. "I can read and write in many languages, not just Arabi. Can I help? Maybe make up for the trouble I caused?"

Halvar nodded and grinned.

"Get me out of this bed, laddie, and get your pens and paper. We have work to do!"

END

Author's Note

While some characters in this story are based in part on historical figures, all characters in this book are fictional. All religious rituals and practices, while based on historical precedent,
are also fictional.

About the Author

ROBERTA ROGOW always wanted to tell stories from the day she could hold a pencil. At the same time, she could not stop singing. After a brief career as coffeehouse singer and professional chorister, she combined her love of literature with her love of music during a 37-year career as a children's librarian in New Jersey, where she could promote literacy and entertain youngsters.

In her spare time, Roberta wrote stories for fanzines incorporating historical characters into fictional situations. This led to the Dodgson/Doyle mysteries, in which the Reverend Mr. Charles Lutwidge Dodgson (Lewis Carroll) and Dr. Sir Arthur Conan Doyle solve mysteries together, and the Pettigrew and Roth mysteries set in Gilded Age New York City.

Now her love of history has turned in another direction with the Saga of Halvar, set in an alternate universe on what is almost, but not quite, Manhattan Island.

As a longtime fan of science fiction, Roberta made a name for herself as a writer and performer of filk music at conventions and was inducted into the Filk Hall of Fame in 2013.

Roberta is a widow. She has two daughters: Miriam Ann Moore, a travel agent living in San Francisco who has written the Marti Hirsch mysteries, and Louise Katherine Howard, a computer programmer who lives near Washington DC.

About the Artist

Born in Chicago, *WILLIAM NEAGLE* graduated from the University of Tennessee with a BFA. Having done work for the US Department of Energy and other companies, his work has been distributed worldwide. He has done book covers for the writing team of Joreid McFate and for his own novel, *Catching the Ghost*. He lives in North Carolina with his wife and two children.

www.ingramcontent.com/pod-product-compliance
Lightning Source LLC
Chambersburg PA
CBHW020835260626
47169CB00003B/1003